THE DESERTER

MORE WILDSIDE CLASSICS

THE DESERTER

CAPT. CHARLES KING

WILDSIDE PRESS

THE DESERTER

This edition published 2005 by Wildside Press, LLC.
www.wildsidepress.com

PRELUDE.

Far up in the Northwest, along the banks of the broad, winding stream the Sioux call the Elk, a train of white-topped army-wagons is slowly crawling eastward. The October sun is hot at noon-day, and the dust from the loose soil rises like heavy smoke and powders every face and form in the guarding battalion so that features are wellnigh indistinguishable. Four companies of stalwart, sinewy infantry, with their brown rifles slung over the shoulder, are striding along in dispersed order, covering the exposed southern flank from sudden attack, while farther out along the ridgeline, and far to the front and rear, cavalry skirmishers and scouts are riding to and fro, searching every hollow and ravine, peering cautiously over every "divide," and signalling "halt" or "forward" as the indications warrant.

And yet not a hostile Indian has been seen; not one, even as distant vedette, has appeared in range of the binoculars, since the scouts rode in at daybreak to say that big bands were in the immediate neighborhood. It has been a long, hard summer's work for the troops, and the Indians have been, to all commands that boasted strength or swiftness, elusive as the Irishman's flea of tradition. Only to those whose numbers were weak or whose movements were hampered have they appeared in fighting-trim. But combinations have been too much for them, and at last they have been "herded" down to the Elk, have crossed, and are now seeking to make their way, with women, children, tepees, dogs, "travois," and the great pony herds, to the fastnesses of the Big Horn; and now comes the opportunity for which an old Indian-fighter has been anxiously waiting. In a big cantonment he has held the main body under his command, while keeping out constant scouting-parties to the east and north. He knows well that, true to their policy, the Indians will have scattered into small bands capable of reassembling anywhere that signal smokes may call them, and his orders are to watch all the crossings of the Elk and nab them as they come into his district. He watches, despite the fact that it is his profound conviction that the Indians will be no such idiots as to come just where they are wanted, and he is in no wise astonished when a courier comes in on jaded horse to tell him that they have "doubled" on the other column and are now two or three days' march away down stream, "making for the big bend." His own scouting-parties are still out to the eastward: he can pick them up as he goes. He sends the main body of his infantry, a regiment jocularly known as "The Riflers," to push for a landing some fifty miles downstream, scouting the lower valley of the Sweet Root on the way. He sends his wagon-train, guarded by four companies of foot and two of horsemen, by the only practicable road to the bend, while he, with ten seasoned "troops" of his pet regiment, the ___th Cavalry, starts forthwith on a long détour in which he hopes to "round up" such bands as may have slipped away from the general rush. Even as "boots and saddles" is sounding, other couriers come riding in from Lieutenant Crane's party. He has struck the trail of a big band.

When the morning sun dawns on the picturesque valley in which the cantonment nestled but the day before, it illumines an almost deserted village, and brings no joy to the souls of some twoscore of embittered civilians who had arrived only the day previous, and whose unanimous verdict is that the army is a fraud and ought to be abolished. For four months or more some three regiments had been camping, scouting, roughing it thereabouts, with not a cent of pay. Then came the wildly exciting tidings that a boat was on the way up the Missouri with a satrap of the pay department, vast store of shekels, and a strong guard, and as a consequence there would be some two thousand men around the cantonment with pockets full of money and no one to help them spend it, and nothing suitable to spend it on. It was a duty all citizens owed to the Territory to hasten to the scene and gather in for local circulation all that was obtainable of that disbursement; otherwise the curse of the army might get ahead of them and the boys would gamble it away among themselves or spend it for vile whiskey manufactured for their sole benefit. Gallatin Valley was emptied of its prominent practitioners in the game of poker. The stream was black with "Mackinaw" boats and other craft. There was a rush for the cantonment that rivalled the multitudes of the mining days, but all too late. The command was already packing up when the first contingent arrived, and the commanding officer, recognizing the fraternity at a glance, warned them outside the limits of camp that night, declined their services as volunteers on the impending campaign, and treated them with such calmly courteous recognition of their true character that the Eastern press was speedily filled with sneering comment on the hopelessness of ever subduing the savage tribes of the Northwest when the government intrusts the duty to upstart officers of the regular service whose sole conception of their functions is to treat with insult and contempt the hardy frontiersman whose mere presence with the command would be of incalculable benefit. "We have it from indisputable authority," says

The Miner's Light of Brandy Gap, "that when our esteemed fellow citizen Hank Mulligan and twenty gallant shots and riders like himself went in a body to General _____ at the cantonment and offered their services as volunteers against the Sioux now devastating the homesteads and settlements of the Upper Missouri and Yellowstone valleys, they were treated with haughty and contemptuous refusal by that bandbox caricature of a soldier and threatened with arrest if they did not quit the camp. When *will* the United States learn that its frontiers can never be purged of the Indian scourges of our civilization until the conduct of affairs in the field is intrusted to other hands than these martinets of the drill-ground? It is needless to remark in this connection that the expedition led by General _____ has proved a complete failure, and that the Indians easily escaped his clumsily-led forces."

The gamblers, though baffled for the time being, of course "get square," and more too, with the unfortunate general in this sort of warfare, but they are a disgusted lot as they hang about the wagon-train as last of all it is being hitched-in to leave camp. Some victims, of course, they have secured, and there are no devices of commanding officers which can protect their men against those sharks of the prairies when the men themselves are bound to tempt Providence and play. There are two scowling faces in the cavalry escort that has been left back with the train, and Captain Hull, the commanding officer, has reprimanded Sergeants Clancy and Gower in stinging terms for their absence from the command during the night. There is little question where they spent it, and both have been "cleaned out." What makes it worse, both have lost money that belonged to other men in the command, and they are in bad odor accordingly.

The long day's march has tempered the joviality of the entire column. It is near sundown, and still they keep plodding onward, making for a grassy level on the riverbank a good mile farther.

"Old Hull seems bound to leave the sports as far behind as possible, if he has to march us until midnight," growls the battalion adjutant to his immediate commander. "By thunder! one would think he was afraid they would get in a lick at his own pile."

"How much did you say he was carrying?" asks Captain Rayner, checking his horse for a moment to look back over the valley at the long, dust-enveloped column.

"Nearly three thousand dollars in one wad."

"How does he happen to have such a sum?"

"Why, Crane left his pay-accounts with him. He drew all that was due his men who are off with Crane,—twenty of them,—for they had signed the rolls before going, and were expected back today. Then he has some six hundred dollars company fund; and the men of his troop asked him to take care of a good deal besides. The old man has been with them so many years they look upon him as a father and trust him as implicitly as they would a savings-bank."

"That's all very well," answers Rayner; "but I wouldn't want to carry any such sum with me."

"It's different with Hull's men, captain. They are ordered in through the posts and settlements. They have a three weeks' march ahead of them when they get through their scout, and they want their money on the way. It was only after they had drawn it that the news came of the Indians' crossing and of our having to jump for the warpath. Everybody thought yesterday morning that the campaign was about over so far as we are concerned. Halloo! here comes young Hayne. Now, what does *he* want?"

Riding a quick, nervous little bay troop horse, a slim-built officer, with boyish face, laughing blue eyes, and sunny hair, comes loping up the long prairie wave; he shouts cheery greeting to one or two brother subalterns who are plodding along beside their men, and exchanges some merry chaff with Lieutenant Ross, who is prone to growl at the luck which has kept him afoot and given to this favored youngster a "mount" and a temporary staff position. The boy's spirits and fun seem to jar on Rayner's nerves. He regards him blackly as he rides gracefully towards the battalion commander, and with decidedly nonchalant ease of manner and an "off-hand" salute that has an air about it of saying, "I do this sort of thing because one has to, but it doesn't really mean anything, you know," Mr. Hayne accosts his superior:

"Ah, good-evening, captain. I have just come back from the front, and Captain Hull directed me to give you his compliments and say that we would camp in the bend yonder, and he would like you to post strong pickets and have a double guard tonight."

"Have *me* post double guards! How the devil does he expect me to do that after marching all day?"

"I did not inquire, sir: he might have told me 'twas none of my business, don't you know?" And Mr. Hayne has the insufferable hardihood to wink at the battalion adjutant,—a youth of two years' longer service than his own.

"Well, Mr. Hayne, this is no matter for levity," says Rayner, angrily. "What does Captain Hull mean to do with his own men, if I'm to do the guard?"

"That is another point, Captain Rayner, which I had not the

requisite effrontery to inquire into. Now, *you* might ask him, but I couldn't, don't you know?" responds Hayne, smiling amiably the while into the wrathful face of his superior. It serves only to make the indignant captain more wrathful; and no wonder. There has been no love lost between the two since Hayne joined the Riflers early the previous year. He came in from civil life, a city-bred boy, fresh from college, full of spirits, pranks, fun of every kind; a wonderfully keen hand with the billiard-cue; a knowing one at cards and such games of chance as college boys excel at; a musician of no mean pretensions, and an irrepressible leader in all the frolics and frivolities of his comrades. He had leaped to popularity from the start. He was full of courtesy and gentleness to women, and became a pet in social circles. He was frank, free, off-handed with his associates, spending lavishly, "treating" with boyish ostentation on all occasions, living quite *en grand seigneur*, for he seemed to have a little money outside his pay,—"a windfall from a good old duffer of an uncle," as he had explained it. His father, a scholarly man who had been summoned to an important under-office in the State Department during the War of the Rebellion, had lived out his honored life in Washington and died poor, as such men must ever die. It was his wish that his handsome, spirited, brave-hearted boy should enter the army, and long after the sod had hardened over the father's peaceful grave the young fellow donned his first uniform and went out to join "The Riflers." High-spirited, joyous, full of laughing fun, he was "Pet" Hayne before he had been among them six months. But within the year he had made one or two enemies. It could not be said of him that he showed that deference to rank and station which was expected of a junior officer; and among the seniors were several whom he speedily designated "unconscionable old duffers" and treated with as little semblance of respect as a second lieutenant could exhibit and be permitted to live. Rayner prophesied of him that, as he had no balance and was burning his candle at both ends, he would come to grief in short order. Hayne retorted that the only balance that Rayner had any respect for was one at the banker's, and that it was notorious in Washington that the captain's father had made most of his money in government contracts, and that the captain's original commission in the regulars was secured through well-paid Congressional influence. The fact that Rayner had developed into a good officer did not wipe out the recollection of these facts; and he could have throttled Hayne for reviving them. It was "a game of give and take," said the youngster; and he "behaved himself" to those who were at all decent in their manner to him.

It was a thorn in Rayner's flesh, therefore, when Hayne joined from leave of absence, after experiences not every officer would care to encounter in getting back to his regiment, that Captain Hull should have induced the general to detail him in place of the invalided field quartermaster when the command was divided. Hayne would have been a junior subaltern in Rayner's little battalion but for that detail, and it annoyed the captain more seriously than he would confess.

"It is all an outrage and a blunder to pick out a boy like that," he growls between his set teeth as Hayne canters blithely away. "Here he's been away from the regiment all summer long, having a big time and getting head over ears in debt, I hear, and the moment he rejoins they put him in charge of the wagon-train as field quartermaster. It's putting a premium on being young and cheeky,—besides absenteeism," he continues, growing blacker every minute.

"Well, captain," answers his adjutant, injudiciously, "I think you don't give Hayne credit for coming back on the jump the moment we were ordered out. It was no fault of his he could not reach us. He took chances *I* wouldn't take."

"Oh, yes! you kids all swear by Hayne because he's a good fellow and sings a jolly song and plays the piano—and poker. One of these days he'll swamp you all, sure as shooting. He's in debt *now*, and it'll fetch him before you know it. What he needs is to be under a captain who could discipline him a little. By Jove, I'd do it!" And Rayner's teeth emphasize the assertion.

The young adjutant thinks it advisable to say nothing that may provoke further vehemence. All the same, he remembers Rayner's bitterness of manner, and has abundant cause to.

When the next morning breaks, chill and pallid, a change has come in the aspect of affairs. During the earliest hour of the dawn the red light of a light-draught river-boat startled the outlying pickets down-stream, and the Far West, answering the muffled hail from shore, responded, through the medium of a mate's stentorian tones, "News that'll rout you fellows out." The sun is hardly peeping over the jagged outline of the eastern hills when, with Rayner's entire battalion aboard, she is steaming again down-stream, with orders to land at the mouth of the Sweet Root. There the four companies will disembark in readiness to join the rest of the regiment.

All day long again the wagon-train twists and wriggles through an ashen section of Les Mauvaises Terres. It is a tedious, trying march for Hull's little command of troopers,—all that is now left to guard the train. The captain is constantly out on the exposed flank, eagerly scanning the rough country to the south, and expectant any moment of an attack from that direction. He and his men, as well as the horses, mules, and teamsters, are fairly tired out when at nightfall they park the wagons in a big semicircle, with the broad river forming a shining chord to the arc of white canvas. All the live-stock are safely herded within the enclosure; a few reliable soldiers are posted well out to the south and east, to guard against surprise, and the veteran Sergeant Clancy is put in command of the sentries. The captain gives strict injunctions as to the importance of these duties; for he is far from easy in his mind over the situation. The Riflers, he knows, are over in the valley of the Sweet Root. The steamer with Rayner's men is tied up at the bank some five miles below, around the bend. The ___th are far off to the northward across the Elk, as ordered, and must be expecting on the morrow to make for the old Indian "ferry" opposite Battle Butte. The main body of the Sioux are reported farther down stream, but he feels it in his bones that there are numbers of them within signal, and he wishes with all his heart the ___th were here. Still, the general was sure he would stir up war-parties on the other shore. Individually, he has had very little luck in scouting during the summer, and he cannot help wishing he were with the rest of the crowd instead of here, train-guarding.

Presently Mr. Hayne appears, elastic and debonair as though he had not been working like a horse all day. His voice sounds so full of cheer and life that Hull looks up smilingly:

"Well, youngster, you seem to love this frontier life."

"Every bit of it, captain. I was cut out for the army, as father thought."

"We used to talk it over a good deal in the old days when I was stationed around Washington," answers Hull. "Your father was the warmest friend I had in civil circles, and he made it very pleasant for me. How little we thought it would be my luck to have you for quartermaster!"

"The fellows seemed struck all of a heap in the Riflers at the idea of your applying for me, captain. I was ready to swear it was all on father's account, and would have told them so, only Rayner happened to be the first man to tackle me on the subject, and he was so crusty about it I kept the whole thing to myself rather than give him any satisfaction."

"Larry, my boy, I'm no preacher, but I want to be the friend to you your father was to me. You are full of enthusiasm and life and spirits, and you love the army ways and have made yourself very popular with the youngsters, but I'm afraid you are too careless and independent where the seniors are concerned. Rayner is a good soldier; and you show him very scant respect, I'm told."

"Well, he's such an interfering fellow. They will all tell you I'm respectful enough to—to the captains I like—"

"That's just it, Lawrence. So long as you like a man your manner is what it should be. What a young soldier ought to learn is to be courteous and respectful to senior officers whether he likes them or not. It costs an effort sometimes, but it tells. You never know what trouble you are laying up for yourself in the army by bucking against men you don't like. They may not be in position to resent it at the time, but the time is mighty apt to come when they *will* be, and then you are helpless."

"Why, Captain Hull, I don't see it that way at all. It seems to me that so long as an officer attends to his duty, minds his own business, and behaves like a gentleman, no one can harm him; especially when all the good fellows of the regiment are his friends, as they are mine, I think, in the Riflers."

"Ah, Hayne, it is a hard thing to teach a youngster that—that there are men who find it very easy to make their juniors' lives a burden to them, and without overstepping a regulation. It is harder yet to say that friends in the army are a good deal like friends out of it: one only has to get into serious trouble to find how few they are. God grant you may never have to learn it, my boy, as many another has had to, by sharp experience! Now we must get a good night's rest. You sleep like a log, I see, and I can only take cat-naps. Confound this money! How I wish I could get rid of it!"

"Where do you keep it tonight?"

"Right here in my saddlebags under my head. Nobody can touch them that I do not wake; and my revolver is here under the blanket. Hold on! Let's take a look and see if everything is all right." He holds a little camp-lantern over the bags, opens the flap, and peers in. "Yes,—all serene. I got a big hunk of green sealing-wax from the paymaster and sealed it all up in one package with the memorandum-list inside. It's all safe so far,—even to the hunk of sealing-wax.—What is it, sergeant?"

A tall, soldierly, dark-eyed trooper appears at the doorway of the little tent, and raises his gauntleted hand in salute. His language, though couched in the phraseology of the soldier, tells both in choice of words and in the intonation of every phrase that he is a man whose antecedents have been far different from those of the majority of the rank and file:

"Will the captain permit me to take my horse and those of three or four more men outside the corral? Sergeant Clancy says he has no authority to allow it. We have found a patch of excellent grass, sir, and there is hardly any left inside. I will sleep by my picket-pin, and one of us will keep awake all the time, if the captain will permit."

"How far away is it, sergeant?"

"Not seventy-five yards, sir,—close to the riverbank east of us."

"Very well. Send Sergeant Clancy here, and I'll give the necessary orders."

The soldier quietly salutes, and disappears in the gathering darkness.

"That's what I like about that man Gower," says the captain, after a moment's silence. "He is always looking out for his horse. If he were not such a gambler and rake he would make a splendid first-sergeant. Fine-looking fellow, isn't he?"

"Yes, sir. That is a face that one couldn't well forget. Who was the other sergeant you overhauled for getting fleeced by those sharps at the cantonment?"

"Clancy? He's on guard tonight. A very different character."

"I don't know him by sight as yet. Well, good-night, sir. I'll take myself off and go to my own tent."

Daybreak again, and far to the east the sky is all ablaze. The mist is creeping from the silent shallows under the banks, but all is life and vim along the shore. With cracking whip, tugging trace, sonorous blasphemy, and ringing shout, the long train is whirling ahead almost at the run. All is athrill with excitement, and bearded faces have a strange, set look about the jaws, and eyes gleam with eager light and peer searchingly from every rise far over to the southeast, where stands a tumbling heap of hills against the lightening sky. "Off there, are they?" says a burly trooper, dismounting hastily to tighten up the "cinch" of his weather-beaten saddle. "We can make it quick enough, 's soon as we get rid of these blasted wagons." And, swinging into saddle again, he goes cantering down the slope, his charger snorting with exhilaration in the keen morning air.

Before dawn a courier has galloped into camp, bearing a despatch from the commanding officer of the Riflers. It says but few words, but they are full of meaning: "We have found a big party of hostiles. They are in strong position, and have us at disadvantage. Rayner with his four companies is hurrying to us. Leave all wagons with the boat under guard, and come with every horse and man you can bring."

Before seven o'clock the wagons are parked close along the

bank beside the Far West, and Hull, with all the men he can muster,—some fifty,—is trotting ahead on the trail of Rayner's battalion. With him rides Mr. Hayne, eager and enthusiastic. Before ten o'clock, far up along the slopes they see the blue line of skirmishers, and the knots of reserves farther down, all at a stand. In ten minutes they ride with foaming reins in behind a low ridge on which, flat on their faces and cautiously peering over the crest, some hundred infantrymen are disposed. Others, officers and file-closers, are moving to and fro in rear. They are of Rayner's battalion. Farther back, down in a ravine a dozen forms are outstretched upon the turf, and others are bending over them, ministering to the needs of those who are not past help already. Several officers crowd around the leading horsemen, and Hull orders, "Halt, dismount, and loosen girths." The grave faces show that the infantry has had poor luck, and the situation is summarized in few words. The Indians are in force occupying the ravines and ridges opposite them and confronting the six companies farther over to the west. Two attacks have been made, but the Indian fire swept every approach, and both were unsuccessful. Several soldiers were shot dead, others severely wounded. Lieutenant Warren's leg is shattered below the knee; Captain Blount is killed.

"Where's Rayner?" asks Hull, with grave face.

"Just gone off with the chief to look at things over on the other front. The colonel is hopping. He is bound to have those Indians out of there or drop a-trying. They'll be back in a minute. The general had a rousing fight with Dull Knife's people down the river last evening. You missed it again, Hull: all the ___th were there but F and K,—and of course old Firewater wants to make as big a hit here."

"The ___th fighting down the river last night?" asks Hull, in amaze.

"Yes,—swept clean round them and ran 'em into the stream, they say. I wish we had them where we could see 'em at all. You don't get the glimpse of a head, even; but all those rocks are lined with the beggars. Damn them!" says the adjutant, feelingly.

"We'll get our chance *here*, then," replies Hull, reflectively. "I'll creep up and take a look at it. Take my horse, orderly."

He is back in two minutes, graver than before, but his bearing is spirited and firm. Hayne watches him with kindling eye.

"You'll take me in with you when you charge?" he asks.

"It is no place to charge there. The ground is all cut up with ravines and gullies, and they've got a cross-fire that sweeps it clean. We'll probably go in on the other flank; it's more open there. Here comes the chief now."

Two officers come riding hastily around a projecting point of the slope and spur at rapid gait towards the spot where the cavalry have dismounted and are breathing their horses. There is hardly time for salutations. A gray-headed, keen-eyed, florid-faced old soldier is the colonel, and he is snapping with electricity, apparently.

"This way, Hull. Come right here, and I'll show you what you are to do." And, followed by Rayner, Hull, and Hayne, the chief rides sharply over to the extreme left of the position and points to the frowning ridge across the intervening swale.

"There, Hull: there are twenty or thirty of the rascals in there who get a flank fire on us when we attack on our side. What I want you to do is to mount your men, let them draw pistol and be all ready. Rayner, here, will line the ridge to keep them down in front. I'll go back to the right and order the attack at once. The moment we begin and you hear our shots, you give a yell, and charge full tilt across there, so as to drive out those fellows in that ravine. We can do the rest. Do you understand?"

"I understand, colonel; but—is it your order that I attempt to charge mounted across that ground?"

"Why, certainly! It isn't the best in the world, but you can make it. They can't do very much damage to your men before you reach them. It's *got* to be done; it's the only way."

"Very good, sir: that ends it!" is the calm, soldierly reply; and the colonel goes bounding away.

A moment later the troop is in saddle, eager, wiry, bronzed fellows every one, and the revolvers are in hand and being carefully examined. Then Captain Hull signals to Hayne, while Rayner and three or four soldiers sit in silence, watching the man who is to lead the charge. He dismounts at a little knoll a few feet away, tosses his reins to the trumpeter, and steps to his saddlebags. Hayne, too, dismounts.

Taking his watch and chain from the pocket of his hunting-shirt, he opens the saddlebag on the near side and takes therefrom two packets,—one heavily sealed,—which he hands to Hayne.

"In case I—don't come back, you know what to do with these,—as I told you last night."

Hayne only looks imploringly at him: "You are not going to leave me *here*, captain?"

"Yes, Hayne. You can't go with us. Hark! There they go at the right. Are the packages all right?"

Hayne, with stunned faculties, thinking only of the charge he longs to make,—not of the one he has to keep,—replies he knows not what. There is a ringing bugle-call far off among the rocks to the westward; a rousing cheer; a rattling volley. Rayner springs off to his men on the hill-side. Hull spurs in front of his eager troop, holding high his pistol-hand:

"Now, men, follow till I drop; and then keep ahead! Come on!"

There is a furious sputter of hoofs, a rush of excited steeds up the gentle slope, a glad outburst of cheers as they sweep across the ridge and out of sight, then the clamor and yell of frantic battle; and when at last it dies away, the Riflers are panting over the hard-won position and shaking hands with some few silent cavalrymen. They have carried the ridge, captured the migrating village, squaws, ponies, travois, and pappooses; their "long Toms" have sent many a stalwart warrior to the mythical hunting-grounds, and the peppery colonel's triumph is complete.

But Lawrence Hayne, with all the light gone from his brave young face, stands mutely looking down, upon the stiffening frame of his father's old friend, and his, who lies shot through the heart.

I.

In the Pullman car of the westward-bound express, halfway across the continent, two passengers were gazing listlessly out over the wintry landscape. It was a bitter morning in February. North and south the treeless prairie rolled away in successive ridge and depression. The snow lay deep in the dry ravines and streaked the sealike surface with jagged lines of foam between which lay broad spaces clean-swept by the gale. Heavy masses of cloud, dark and forbidding, draped the sky from zenith to horizon, and the air was thick with spiteful gusts and spits of snow, crackling against the window-panes, making fierce dashes every time a car door was hurriedly opened, and driving about the platforms like a myriad swarm of fleecy and aggressive gnats raging for battle. Every now and then, responsive to some wilder blast, a blinding white cloud came whirling from the depths of the nearest gully and breaking like spray over the snow fence along the line. Not a sign of life was visible. The tiny mounds in the villages of the prairie-dogs seemed blocked and frozen; even the trusty sentinel had "deserted post" and huddled with his fellows for warmth and shelter in the bowels of the earth. Fluttering owl and skulking coyote, too, had vanished from the face of nature. Timid antelope—fleetest coursers of the prairie—and stolid horned cattle had gone, none knew whither, nor cared to know until the "blizzard" had subsided. Two heavy engines fought their way, panting, into the very teeth of the gale and slowly wound the long train after them up-grade among the foot-hills of the great plateau of the Rockies. Once in a while, when stopping for a moment at some group of brown-painted sheds and earth-battened shanties, the wind moaned and howled among the iron braces and brake-chains beneath the car and made such mournful noise that it was a relief to start once more and lose sound of its wailing in the general rumble. As for the scenery, only as a picture of shiver-provoking monotony and desolation would one care to take a second look.

And yet, some miles ahead, striving hard to reach the railway in time to intercept this very train, a small battalion of cavalry was struggling through the blasts, officers and men afoot and dragging their own benumbed limbs and half benumbed chargers through the drifts that lay deep at the bottom of every "coulée." Some few soldiers remained in saddle: they were too frozen to walk at all. Some few fell behind, and would have thrown themselves flat upon the prairie in the lethargy that is but premonition of death by freezing. Like men half deadened by morphine, their rescue depended on heroic measures, humane in their seeming brutality. Officers who at other times were all gentleness now fell upon the hapless stragglers with kicks and blows. As the train drew up at the platform of a station in mid-prairie, a horseman enveloped in fur and frost and steam from his panting steed reined up beside the leading engine and shouted to the occupants of the cab,—

"For God's sake hold on a few minutes. We've got a dozen frozen men with us we must send on to Fort Warrener." And the train was held.

Meantime, those far to the rear in the sleeper knew nothing of what was going on ahead. The car was warm and comfortable, and most of its occupants were apparently appreciative of its shelter and coseyness in contrast with the cheerless scene without. A motherly-looking woman had produced her knitting, and was blithely clicking away at her needles, while her enterprising son, a youth of four summers and undaunted confidence in human nature, tacked up and down the aisle and made impetuous incursions on the various sections by turns, receiving such modified welcome as could be accorded features streaked with mingled candy and cinders, and fingers whose propensity to cling to whatsoever they touched was due no more to instincts of a predatory nature than to the adhesive properties of the glucose which formed so large a constituent of the confections he had been industriously consuming since early morning. Four men playing whist in the rearmost section, two or three commercial travellers, whose intimacy with the porter and airs of easy proprietorship told of an apparent controlling interest in the road, a young man of reserved manners, reading in a section all by himself, a baby sleeping quietly upon the seat opposite the two passengers first mentioned, and a Maltese kitten curled up in the lap of one of them, completed the list of occupants.

The proximity of the baby and the kitten furnishes strong presumptive evidence of the sex and general condition of the two passengers referred to, and renders detail superfluous. A baby rarely travels without a woman, or a kitten with a woman already encumbered with a baby. The baby belonged to the elder passenger, the kitten to the younger. The one was a buxom matron, the other a slender maid. In their ages there must have been a difference of fifteen years; in feature there was still wider disparity. The elder was a fine-looking woman, and one who prided herself upon the Junoesque proportions which she occasionally exhibited in a stroll for exercise up and down the aisle. Yet no one would call her a beauty. Her eyes were of a somewhat fishy and uncertain blue; the lids were tinged with an unornamental pink that told of irritation of the adjacent interior surface and of possible irritability of temper. Her complexion was of that mottled type which is so sore a trial to its possessor and yet so inestimable a comfort to social rivals; but her features were handsome, her teeth fine, her dress, bearing, and demeanor those of a woman of birth and breeding, and yet one who might have resented the intimation that she was not strikingly handsome. She looked like a woman with a will of her own; her head was high, her step was firm; it was of just such a walk as hers that Virgil wrote his "*vera incessu patuit dea*," and she made the young man in the section by himself think of that very passage as he glanced at her from under his heavy, bushy eyebrows. She looked, moreover, like a woman with a capacity for influencing people contrary to their will and judgment, and with a decided fondness for the exercise of that unpopular function. There was the air of *grande dame* about her, despite the simplicity of her dress, which, though of rich material, was severely plain. She wore no jewelry. Her hands were snugly gloved, and undisfigured by the distortions of any ring except the marriage circlet. Her manner attested her a person of consequence in her social circle and one who realized the fact. She had repelled, though without rudeness or discourtesy, the garrulous efforts of the motherly knitter to be sociable. She had promptly inspired the small, candy-crusted explorer with such awe that he had refrained from further visits after his first confiding attempt to poke a sticky finger through the baby's velvety cheek. She had spared little scorn in her rejection of the *bourgeois* advances of the commercial traveller with the languishing eyes of Israel: he confided to his comrades, in relating the incident, that she was smart enough to see that it wasn't *her* he was hankering to know, but the pretty sister by her side; and when challenged to prove that they *were* sisters,—a statement which aroused the scepticism of his shrewd associates,—he had replied, substantially,—

"How do I know? 'Cause I saw their pass before you was up this morning, cully. It's for Mrs. Captain Rayner and sister, and they're going out here to Fort Warrener. That's how I know." And the porter of the car had confirmed the statement in the sanctity of the smoking-room.

And yet—such is the uncertainty of feminine temperament—Mrs. Rayner was no more incensed at the commercial "gent" because he had obtruded his attentions than she was at the young man reading in his own section because he had refrained. Nearly twenty-four hours had elapsed since they crossed the Missouri, and in all that time not once had she detected in him a glance that betrayed the faintest interest in her, or—still more remarkable—in the unquestionably lovely girl at her side. Intrusiveness she might resent, but indifference she would and did. Who was this youth, she wondered, who not once had so much as stolen a look at the sweet, bonny face of her maiden sister? Surely 'twas a face any man would love to gaze upon,—so fair, so exquisite in contour and feature, so pearly in complexion, so lovely in the deep, dark brown of its shaded eyes.

The bold glances of the four card-players she had defiantly returned, and vanquished. Those men, like the travelling gents, were creatures of coarser mould; but her experienced eye told her the solitary occupant of the opposite section was a gentleman. The clear cut of his pale features, the white, slender hand and shapely foot, the style and finish of his quiet travelling-dress, the soft modulation and refined tone of his voice on the one occasion when she heard him reply to some importunity of the train-boy with his endless round of equally questionable figs and fiction, the book he was reading,—a volume of Emerson,—all combined to speak of a culture and position equal to her own. She had been over the transcontinental railways often enough to know that it was permissible for gentlemen to render their fellow-passengers some slight attention which would lead to mutual introductions if desirable; and this man refused to see that the opportunity was open to him.

True, when first she took her survey of those who were to be her fellow-travellers at the "transfer" on the Missouri, she decided that here was one against whom it would be necessary to guard the approaches. She had good and sufficient reasons for wanting no young man as attractive in appearance as this one making himself interesting to pretty Nellie on their journey. She had already decided what Nellie's future was to be. Never, indeed, would she have taken her to the gay frontier station whither she was now *en route*, had not that future been already settled to her satisfaction. Nellie Travers, barely out of school, was betrothed, and willingly so, to the man she, her devoted elder sister, had especially chosen. Rare and most unlikely of conditions! she had apparently fallen in love with the man picked out for her by somebody else. She was engaged to Mrs. Rayner's fascinating friend Mr. Steven Van Antwerp, a scion of an old and esteemed and wealthy family; and Mr. Van Antwerp, who had been educated abroad, and had a Heidelberg scar on his left cheek, and dark, lustrous eyes, and wavy hair,—almost raven,—was a devoted lover, though fully fifteen years Miss

Nellie's senior.

Full of bliss and comfort was Mrs. Rayner's soul as she journeyed westward to rejoin her husband at the distant frontier post she had not seen since the early spring. Army woman as she was, born and bred under the shadow of the flag, a soldier's daughter, a soldier's wife, she had other ambitions for her beautiful Nell. Worldly to the core, she herself would never have married in the army but for the unusual circumstance of a wealthy subaltern among the officers of her father's regiment. Tradition had it that Mr. Rayner was not among the number of those who sighed for Kate Travers's guarded smiles. Her earlier victims were kept a-dangling until Rayner, too, succumbed, and then were sent adrift. She meant that no penniless subaltern should carry off her "baby sister,"—they had long been motherless,—and a season at the seashore had done her work well. Steven Van Antwerp, with genuine distress and loneliness, went back to his duties in Wall Street after seeing them safely on their way to the West. "Guard her well for me," he whispered to Mrs. Rayner. "I dread those fellows in buttons." And he shivered unaccountably as he spoke.

Nellie was pledged, therefore, and this youth in the Pullman was not one of "those fellows in buttons," so far as Mrs. Rayner knew, but she was ready to warn him off, and meant to do so, until, to her surprise, she saw that he gave no symptom of a desire to approach. By noon of the second day she was as determined to extract from him some sign of interest as she had been determined to resent it. I can in no wise explain or account for this. The fact is stated without remark.

"What on earth can we be stopping so long here for?" was Mrs. Rayner's somewhat petulant inquiry, addressed to no one in particular. There was no reply. Miss Travers was busily twitching the ears of the kitten at the moment and sparring with upraised finger at the threatening paw.

"Do look out of the window, Nell, and see."

"There is nothing to see, Kate,—nothing but whirling drifts and a big water-tank all covered with ice. Br-r-r-r!? how cold it looks!" she answered, after vainly flattening her face against the inner pane.

"There must be something the matter, though," persisted Mrs. Rayner. "We have been here full five minutes, and we are behind time now. At this rate we'll never get to Warrener tonight. I do wish the porter would stay here where he belongs."

The young man quietly laid down his book and arose. "I will inquire, madame," he said, with grave courtesy. "You shall know in a moment."

"How *very* kind of you!" said the lady. "Indeed I must not trouble you. I'm sure the porter will be here after a while."

And even as she spoke, and as he was pulling on an overcoat, the train rumbled off again. Then came an exclamation, this time from the younger:

"Why, Kate! Look! see all these men,—and horses! Why, they are soldiers,—cavalry! Oh, how I love to see them again! But, oh, how cold they look!—frozen!"

"Who *can* they be?" said Mrs. Rayner, all vehement interest now, and gazing eagerly from the window at the lowered heads of the horses and the muffled figures in blue and fur. "What *can* they be doing in the field in such awful weather? I cannot recognize one of them, or tell officers from men. Surely that must be Captain Wayne,—and Major Stannard. Oh, what can it mean?"

The young man had suddenly leaped to the window behind them, and was gazing out with an eagerness and interest little less apparent than her own, but in a moment the train had whisked them out of sight of the storm-beaten troopers. Then he hurried to the rear window of the car, and Mrs. Rayner as hastily followed.

"*Do* you know them?" she asked.

"Yes. That *was* Major Stannard. It is his battalion of the ___th Cavalry, and they have been out scouting after renegade Cheyennes. Pardon me, madame, I must go forward and see who have boarded the train."

He stopped at his section, and again she followed him, her eyes full of anxiety. He was busy tugging at a flask in his travelling-bag.

"You know them! Do you know—have you heard of any infantry being out? Pardon me for detaining you, but I am very anxious. My husband is Captain Rayner, of Fort Warrener."

"No infantry have been sent, madame, I—have reason to know; at least, none from Warrener."

And with that he hurriedly bowed and left her. The next moment, flask in hand, he was crossing the storm-swept platform and making his way to the head of the train.

"I believe he is an officer," said Mrs. Rayner to her sister. "Who else would be apt to know about the movement of the troops? Did you notice how gentle his manner was?—and he never smiled: he has such a sad face. Yet he can't be an officer, or he would have made himself known to us long ago."

"Is there no name on the satchel?" asked Miss Travers, with pardonable curiosity. "He has an interesting face,—not handsome." And a dreamy look came into her deep eyes. She was thinking, no doubt, of a dark, oval, *distingué* face with raven hair and moustache. The youth in the travelling-suit was not tall, like Steven,—not singularly, romantically handsome, like Steven. Indeed, he was of less interest to her than to her married sister.

Mrs. Rayner could see no name on the satchel,—only two initials; and they revealed very little.

"I have half a mind to peep at the fly-leaf of that book," she said. "He walked just like a soldier: but there isn't anything there to indicate what he is," she continued, with a doubtful glance at the items scattered about the now vacant section. "Why isn't that porter here? He ought to know who people are."

As though to answer her request, in came the porter, dishevelled and breathless. He made straight for the satchel they had been scrutinizing, and opened it without ceremony. Both ladies regarded this proceeding with natural astonishment, and Mrs. Rayner was about to interfere and question his right to search the luggage of passengers, when the man turned hurriedly towards them, exhibiting a little bundle of handkerchiefs, his broad Ethiopian face clouded with anxiety and concern:

"The gentleman told me to take all his handkerchiefs. We'se got a dozen frozen soldiers in the baggage-car,—some of 'em mighty bad,—and they'se tryin' to make 'em comfortable until they get to the fort."

"Soldiers frozen! Why do you take them in the baggage-car?— such a barn of a place! Why weren't they brought here, where we could make them warm and care for them?" exclaimed Mrs. Rayner, in impulsive indignation.

"Laws, ma'am! never do in the world to bring frozen people into a hot car! Sure to make their ears an' noses drop off, that would! Got to keep 'em in the cold and pile snow around 'em. That gentleman sittin' here,—he knows," he continued: "he's an officer, and him and the doctor's workin' with 'em now."

And Mrs. Rayner, vanquished by a statement of facts well known to her yet forgotten in the first impetuosity of her criticism, relapsed into the silence of temporary defeat.

"He *is* an officer, then," said Miss Travers, presently. "I wonder what he belongs to."

"Not to our regiment, I'm sure. Probably to the cavalry. He knew Major Stannard and other officers whom we passed there."

"Did he speak to them?"

"No: there was no time. We were beyond hearing-distance when he ran to the back door of the car; and there was no time before that. But it's very odd!"

"What's very odd?"

"Why, his conduct. It is so strange that he has not made himself known to us, if he's an officer."

"Probably he doesn't know you—or we—are connected with the army, Kate."

"Oh, yes, he does. The porter knows perfectly well, and I told him just before he left."

"Yes, but he didn't know before that time, did he?"

"He ought to have known," said Mrs. Rayner, uncompromisingly. "At least, he should if he had taken the faintest interest. I mentioned Captain Rayner so that he could not help hearing."

This statement being one that Miss Travers could in no wise contradict,—as it was one, indeed, that Mrs. Rayner could have dispensed with as unnecessary,—the younger lady again betook herself to silence and pulling the kitten's ears.

"Even if he didn't know before," continued her sister, after a pause in which she had apparently been brooding over the indifference of the young man in question, "he ought to have made himself known after I told him who I was." Another pause. "That's what I did it for," she wound up, conclusively.

"And that's what I thought," said Miss Travers, with a quiet smile. "However, he had no time then: he was hurrying off to see whether any of the soldiers had come on board. He took his flask with him, and apparently was in haste to offer someone a drink. I'm sure that is what papa used to do," she added, as she saw a frown gathering on her sister's face.

"What papa did just after the war—a time when everybody drank—is not at all the proper thing now. Captain Rayner never touches it; and I don't allow it in the house."

"Still, I should think it a very useful article when a lot of frozen and exhausted men are on one's hands," said Miss Travers. "That was but a small flask he had, and I'm sure they will need more."

There came a rush of cold air from the front, and the swinging door blew open ahead of the porter, who was heard banging shut the outer portal. Then he hurried in.

"Can some of you gentlemen oblige me with some whiskey or brandy?" he asked. "We've got some frozen soldiers aboard. Two of 'em are pretty nearly gone."

Two of the card-players dropped their hands and started for their section at once. Before they could rummage in their bags for the required article, Mrs. Rayner's voice was heard: "Take this, porter." And she held forth a little silver flask. "I have more in my trunk if it is needed," she added, while a blush mounted to her forehead as she saw the quizzical smile on her sister's face. "You know I *always* carry it in travelling, Nellie,—in case of accident or illness; and I'm most thankful I have it now."

"Ever so much obliged, ma'am," said the porter, "but this would be only a thimbleful, and I can get a quart bottle of this gentleman."

"Where are they?" said the person thus referred to, as he came down the aisle with a big brown bottle in his hand. "Come, Jim, let's go and see what we can do. One of you gentlemen take my place in the game," he continued, indicating the commercial gents, two of whom, nothing loath, dropped into the vacated seats, while the others pushed on to the front of the train. The porter hesitated one moment.

"Yes, take my flask: I shouldn't feel satisfied without doing something. And please say to the officer that I'm Mrs. Rayner,— Mrs. Captain Rayner, of the infantry,—and ask if there isn't something I can do to help."

"Yes, ma'am; I will, ma'am. Oh, he knows who you are: I done told him last night. He's goin' to Fort Warrener, too." And, touching his cap, away went the porter.

"There! He *did* know all along," said Mrs. Rayner, triumphantly. "It is most extraordinary!"

"Well, is it the proper thing for people in the army to introduce themselves when travelling? How are they to know it will be agreeable?"

"Agreeable! Why, Nellie, it's *always* done,—especially when ladies are travelling without escort, as we are. The commonest civility should prompt it; and officers always send their cards by the porter the moment they find army ladies are on the train. I don't understand this one at all,—especially—" But here she broke off abruptly.

"Especially what?" asked Miss Nell, with an inspiration of maidenly curiosity.

"Especially nothing. Never mind now." And here the baby began to fidget, and stir about, and stretch forth his chubby hands, and thrust his knuckles in his eyes, and pucker up his face in alarming contortions preparatory to a wail, and, after one or two soothing and tentative sounds of "sh—sh—sh—sh" from the maternal lips, the matron abandoned the attempt to induce a second nap, and picked him up in her arms, where he presently began to take gracious notice of his pretty aunt and the kitten.

Two hours later, just as the porter had notified them that Warrener Station would be in sight in five minutes, the young man of the opposite section returned to the car. He looked tired, very anxious, and his face was paler and the sad expression more pronounced than before. The train-conductor stopped him to speak of some telegrams that had been sent, and both ladies noted the respect which the railway official threw into the tone in which he spoke. The card-players stopped their game and went up to ask after the frozen men. It was not until the whistle was sounding for the station that he stood before them and with a grave and courteous bow held forth Mrs. Rayner's silver flask.

"It was a blessing to one poor fellow at least, and I thank you for him, madame," he said.

"I have been so anxious. I wanted to do something. Did you not get my message, Mr.—?" she asked, with intentional pause that he might supply the missing name.

"Indeed there was nothing we could ask of you," he answered, totally ignoring the evident invitation. "I am greatly obliged to you for your kindness, but we had abundant help, and you really could not have reached the car in the face of this gale. Good-morning, madame." And with that he raised his fur travelling-cap and quickly turned to his section and busied himself strapping up his various belongings.

"The man must be a woman-hater," she whispered to Miss Travers, "He's going to get out here, too. Who *can* he be?"

There was still a moment before the train would stop at the platform, and she was not to be beaten so easily. Bending partly across the aisle, she spoke again:

"You have been so kind to those poor fellows that I feel sure you must be of the army. I think I told you I am Mrs. Rayner, of Fort Warrener. May we not hope to see you there?"

A deep flush rose to his forehead, suffusing his cheeks, and passed as quickly away. His mouth twitched and trembled. Gazing at him in surprise and trouble, Nellie Travers saw that his face was full of pain and was turning white again. He half choked before he could reply: he spoke low, and yet distinctly, and the words were full of sadness:

"It—it is not probable that we shall meet at all."

And with that he turned away.

II.

Even in the excitement attendant upon their reception at the station neither Mrs. Rayner nor her sister could entirely recover from the surprise and pain which the stranger's singular words had caused. So far from feeling in the least rebuffed, Mrs. Rayner well understood from his manner that not the faintest discourtesy was intended. There was not a symptom of rudeness, not a vestige of irritation or haste, in his tone. Deep embarrassment, inexpressible sadness even, she read in the brief glimpse she had of his paling face. It was all a mystery to her and to the girl seated in silence by her side. Both followed him with their eyes as he hurried away to the rear of the car, and then, with joyous shouts, three or four burly, fur-enveloped men came bursting in the front door, and the two ladies, the baby, and the kitten were pounced upon and surrounded by a group that grew larger every minute. Released finally from the welcoming embrace of her stalwart husband, Mrs. Rayner found time to present the other and younger officers to her sister. As many as half a dozen had followed the captain in his wild rush upon the car, and, while he and his baby boy were resuming acquaintanceship after a separation of many long months, Miss Travers found herself the centre of a circle of young officers who had braved the wintry blizzard in their eagerness to do her proper homage. Her cheeks were aflame with excitement and pleasure, her eyes dancing, and despite the fatigue of her long journey she was looking dangerously pretty, as Captain Rayner glanced for a moment from the baby's wondering eyes, took in the picture like an instantaneous photograph, and then looked again into Mrs. Rayner's smiling face.

"You were wise in providing against possibilities as you did, Kate," he said, with a significant nod of the head. "There are as many as a dozen of them,—or at least there will be when the ___th gets back from the field. Stannard is out yet with his battalion."

"Oh, yes: we saw them at a station east of here. They looked frozen to death; and there *are* ever so many of the soldiers frozen. The baggage-car is full of them. Didn't you know it?"

"Not a word of it. We have been here for three mortal hours waiting at the station, and any telegrams must have been sent right out to the fort. The colonel is there, and he would have all arrangements made. Here, Graham! Foster! Mrs. Rayner says there are a lot of frozen cavalrymen forward in the baggage-car. Run ahead and see what is necessary, will you? I'll be there in a minute, as soon as we've got these ladies off the train."

Two of the young gentlemen who had been hovering around Miss Travers took themselves off without a moment's delay. The others remained to help their senior officer. Out into the whirling eddies of snow, bundling them up in the big, warm capes of their regulation overcoats, the officers half led, half carried their precious charges. The captain bore his son and heir; Lieutenant Ross escorted Mrs. Rayner; two others devoted themselves exclusively to Miss Travers; a fourth picked up the Maltese kitten. Two or three smart, trim-looking infantry soldiers cleared the section of bags and bundles of shawls, and the entire party was soon within the doorway of the waiting-room, where a red-hot coal-stove glowed fierce welcome. Here the ladies were left for a moment, while all the officers again bustled out into the storm and fought their way against the northwest gale until they reached the little crowd gathered about the doorway of the freight-sheds. A stout, short, burly man in beaver overcoat and cap pushed through the knot of half numbed spectators and approached their leader:

"We have only two ambulances, captain,—that is all there was at the post when the despatch came,—and there are a dozen of these men, besides Dr. Grimes, all more or less crippled, and Grimes has both hands frozen. We must get them out at once. Can we take your wagon?"

"Certainly, doctor. Take anything we have. If the storm holds, tell the driver not to try to come back for us. We can make the ladies comfortable here at the hotel for the night. Some of the officers have to get back for duties this evening. The rest will have to stay. How did they happen to get caught in such a freeze?"

"They couldn't help it. Stannard had chased the Cheyennes across the range, and was ordered to get back to the railway. It was twenty below when they started, and they made three days' chase in that weather; but no one seemed to care so long as they were on the trail. Then came the change of wind, and a driving snowstorm, in which they lost the trail as a matter of course; and then this blizzard struck them on the back-track. Grimes is so exhausted that he could barely hold out until he got here. He says he never could have brought them through from Bluff Siding but for Mr. Hayne: he did everything."

"Mr. Hayne! Was he with them?"

"He was on the train, and came in at once to offer his services. Grimes says he was invaluable."

"But Mr. Hayne was East on leave: I *know* he was. He was promoted to my company last month,—confound the luck!—and was to have six months' leave before joining. I wish it was six years. Where is he now?" And the captain peered excitedly around from under his shaggy cap. Oddly, too, his face was paling.

"He left as soon as I took charge. I don't know where he's gone; but it's God's mercy he was with these poor fellows. His skill and care have done everything for them. Where did he get his knowledge?"

"I've no idea," said Captain Rayner, gruffly, and in evident ill humor. "He is the last man I expected to see this day or for days to come. Is there anything else I can do, doctor?"

"Nothing, thank you, captain." And the little surgeon hastened back to his charges, followed by some of the younger officers, eager to be of assistance in caring for their disabled comrades. Rayner himself hesitated a moment, then turned about and trudged heavily back along the wind-swept platform. The train had pulled away, and was out of sight in the whirl of snow over the Western prairies. He went to his own substantial wagon, and shouted to the driver, who sat muffled in buffalo fur on the box,—

"Get around there to the freight-house and report to the doctor. There are a lot of frozen cavalrymen to be taken out to the hospital. Don't try to come back for us tonight: we'll stay here in town. Send the quartermaster's team in for the trunks as soon as the storm is over and the road clear. That's all."

Then he rejoined the party at the waiting-room of the station, and Mrs. Rayner noted instantly that all the cheeriness had gone and that a cloud had settled on his face. She was a shrewd observer, and she knew him well. Something more serious than a mishap to a squad of soldiers had brought about the sudden change. He was all gladness, all rejoicing and delight, when he clasped her and his baby boy in his arms but ten minutes before, and now—something had occurred to bring him serious discomfort. She rested her hand on his arm and looked questioningly in his face. He avoided her glance, and quickly began to talk. She saw that he desired to answer no questions just then, and wisely refrained.

Meantime, Miss Travers was chatting blithely with two young gallants who had returned to her side, and who had thrown off their heavy furs and now stood revealed in their becoming undress uniforms. Mr. Ross had gone to look over the rooms which the host of the railway hotel had offered for the use of the party; the baby was yielding to the inevitable and gradually condescending to notice the efforts of Mr. Foster to scrape acquaintance; the kitten, with dainty step, and ears and tail erect, was making a leisurely inspection of the premises, sniffing about the few benches and chairs with which the bare room was burdened, and reconnoitring the door leading to the hall-way with evident desire to extend her researches in that direction. Presently that very door opened, and in came two or three bundles of fur in masculine shape, and with them two shaggy deer-hounds, who darted straight at the kitten. There was a sudden flurry and scatter, a fury of spits and scratching, a yelp of pain from one brute with lacerated nose, a sudden recoil of both hounds, and then a fiery rush through the open door-way in pursuit of puss. After the first gallant instinct of battle her nerve had given out, and she had sought safety in flight.

"Oh, don't let them hurt her!" cried Miss Travers, as she darted into the hall and gazed despairingly up the stairway to the second story, whither the dogs had vanished like a flash. Two of the young officers sped to the rescue and turned the wrong way. Mrs. Rayner and the captain followed her into the hall. A rush of canine feet and an excited chorus of barks and yelps were heard aloft; then a stern voice ordering, "Down, you brutes!" a sudden howl as though in response to a vigorous kick, and an instant later, bearing the kitten, ruffled, terrified, and wildly excited, yet unharmed, there came springing lightly down the steps the young man in civilian dress who was their fellow-traveller on the Pullman. Without a word he gave his prize into the dainty hands outstretched to receive it, and, never stopping an instant, never listening to the eager words of thanks from her pretty lips, he darted back as quickly as he came, leaving Miss Travers suddenly stricken dumb.

Captain Rayner turned sharply on his heel and stepped back into the waiting-room. Mr. Ross nudged a brother lieutenant and whispered, "By gad! that's awkward for Midas!" The two subalterns who had taken the wrong turn at the top of the stairs reappeared there just as the rescuer shot past them on his way back, and stood staring, first after his disappearing form, and then at each other. Miss Travers, with wonder and relief curiously mingled in her sweet face, clung to her restored kitten and gazed vacantly up the stairs.

Mrs. Rayner looked confusedly from one to the other, quickly noting the constraint in the manner of every officer present and the sudden disappearance of her husband. There was an odd silence for a moment: then she spoke:

"Mr. Ross, do you know that gentleman?"

"I know who he is. Yes."

"Who is he, then?"

"He is your husband's new first lieutenant, Mrs. Rayner. That is Mr. Hayne."

"*That!*—Mr. Hayne?" she exclaimed, growing suddenly pale.

"Certainly, madame. Had you never seen him before?"

"Never; and I expected—I didn't expect to see such a—" And she broke short off, confused and plainly distressed, turned abruptly, and left the hall as had her husband.

III.

The officers of Fort Warrener were assembled, as was the daily morning custom, in the presence of the colonel commanding. It had long been the practice of that veteran soldier to require all his commissioned subordinates to put in an appearance at his office immediately after the ceremony of guard-mounting. He might have nothing to say to them, or he might have a good deal; and he was a man capable of saying a good deal in very few words, and meaning exactly what he said. It was his custom to look up from his writing as each officer entered and respond to the respectful salutation tendered him with an equally punctilious "Good-morning, Captain Gregg," or "Good-morning, Mr. Blake,"—never omitting the mention of the name, unless, as was sometimes tried, a squad of them came in together and made their obeisance as a body. In this event the colonel simply looked each man in the face, as though taking mental note of the individual constituents of the group, and contented himself with a "Good-morning, gentlemen."

When in addition to six troops of his own regiment of cavalry there were sent to the post a major and four companies of infantry, some of the junior officers of the latter organization had suggested to their comrades of the yellow stripes that as the colonel had no roll-call it might be a matter of no great risk to "cut the *matinée*" on some of the fiendishly cold mornings that soon set in; but the experiment was never designedly tried, thanks, possibly, to the frank exposition of his personal views as expressed by Lieutenant Blake, of the cavalry, who said, "Try it if you are stagnating for want of a sensation, my genial plodder, but not if you value the advice of one who has been there, so to speak. The chief will spot you quicker than he can a missing shoe,—a missing *horse*shoe, Johnny, let me elaborate for your comprehension,—and the next question will be, 'Mr. Bluestrap, did you intentionally absent yourself?' and *then* how will you get out of it?"

The *matinées*, so called, were by no means unpopular features of the daily routine. The officers were permitted to bring their pipes or cigars and take their after-breakfast smoke in the big, roomy office of the commander, just as they were permitted to enjoy the post-prandial whiff when at evening recitation in the same office they sat around the room, chatting in low tones, for half an hour, while the colonel received the reports of his adjutant, the surgeon, and the old and the new officer of the day. Then any matters affecting the discipline or instruction or general interests of the command were brought up; both sides of the question were presented, if question arose; the decision was rendered then and there, and the officers were dismissed for the day with the customary "That's all, gentlemen." They left the office well knowing that only in the event of some sudden emergency would they be called thither again or disturbed in their daily vocations until the same hour on the following morning. Meantime, they must be about their work: drills, if weather permitted; stable-duty, no matter what the weather; garrison courts, boards of survey, the big general court that was perennially dispensing justice at the post, and the long list of minor but none the less exacting demands on the time and attention of the subalterns and company commanders. The colonel was a strict, even severe, disciplinarian, but he was cool, deliberate, and just. He "worked" his officers, and thereby incurred the criticism of a few, but held the respect of all. He had been a splendid cavalry-commander in the field of all others where his sterling qualities were sure to find responsive appreciation in his officers and men,—on active and stirring campaigns against the Indians,—and among his own regiment he knew that deep in their hearts the ___th respected and believed in him, even when they growled at garrison exactions which seemed uncalled for. The infantry officers knew less of him as a sterling campaigner, and were not so well pleased with his discipline. It was all right for him to "rout out" every mother's son in the cavalry at reveille, because all the cavalry officers had to go to stables soon afterwards,—that was all they were fit for,—but what on earth was the use of getting them—the infantry—out of their warm beds before sunrise on a wintry morning and having no end of roll-calls and such things through the day, "just to keep them busy"? The real objection—the main objection—to the colonel's system was that it kept a large number of officers, most of whom were educated gentlemen, hammering all day long at an endless routine of trivial duties, allowing actually no time in which they could read, study, or improve their minds; but, as ill luck would have it, the three young gentlemen who decided to present to the colonel this view of the case had been devoting what spare time they could find to a lively game of poker down at "the store," and their petition for "more time to themselves" brought down a reply from the oracular lips of the commander that became immortal on the frontier and made the petitioners nearly frantic. For a week the trio was the butt of all the wits at Fort Warrener. And yet the entire commissioned force felt that they were being kept at the grindstone because of the frivolity of these few youngsters, and they did not like it. All the same the cavalrymen stuck up for their colonel, and the infantrymen respected him, and the *matinées* were businesslike and profitable. They were rarely unpleasant in any feature; but this particular morning—two days after the arrival of Mrs. Rayner and her sister—there had been a scene of somewhat dramatic interest, and the groups of officers in breaking up and going away could discuss nothing else. The colonel had requested one of their number to remain, as he wished to speak to him further; and that man was Lieutenant Hayne.

Seven years had that young gentleman been a second lieutenant of the regiment of infantry a detachment of which was now stationed at Warrener. Only this very winter had promotion come to him; and, of all companies in the regiment, he was gazetted to the first-lieutenancy of Captain Rayner's. For a while the regiment when by itself could talk of little else. Mr. Hayne had spent three or four years in the exile of a little "two-company post" far up in the mountains. Except the officers there stationed, none of his comrades had seen him during that time. No one of them would like to admit that he would care to see him. And yet, when once in a while they got to talking among themselves about him, and the question was sometimes confidentially asked of comrades who came down on leave from that isolated station, "How is Hayne doing?" or, "What is Hayne doing?" the language in which he was referred to grew by degrees far less truculent and confident than it had been when he first went thither. Officers of other regiments rarely spoke to the "Riflers" of Mr. Hayne. Unlike one or two others of their arm of the service, this particular regiment of foot held the affairs of its officers as regimental property in which outsiders had no concern. If they had disagreements, they were kept to themselves; and even in a case which in its day had attracted wide-spread attention the Riflers had long since learned to shun all talk outside. It was evident to other commands that the Hayne affair was a sore point and one on which they preferred silence. And yet it was getting to be whispered around that the Riflers were by no means so unanimous as they had been in their opinion of this very officer. They were becoming divided among themselves; and what complicated matters was the fact that those who felt their views undergoing a reconstruction were compelled to admit that just in proportion as the case of Mr. Hayne rose in their estimation the reputation of another officer was bound to suffer; and that officer was Captain Rayner.

Between these two men not a word had been exchanged for five years,—not a single word since the day when, with ashen face and broken accents, but with stern purpose in every syllable, Lieutenant Hayne, standing in the presence of nearly all the officers of his regiment, had hurled this prophecy in his adversary's teeth: "Though it take me years, I will live it down despite you; and you will wish to God you had bitten out your perjured tongue before ever you told the lie that wrecked me."

No wonder there was talk, and lots of it, in the "Riflers" and all through the garrison when Rayner's first lieutenant suddenly threw up his commission and retired to the mines he had located in Montana, and Hayne, the "senior second," was promoted to the vacancy. Speculation as to what would be the result was given a temporary rest by the news that War Department orders had granted the subaltern six months' leave,—the first he had sought in as many years. It was known that he had gone East; but hardly had he been away a fortnight when there came the trouble with the Cheyennes at the reservation,—a leap for liberty by some fifty of the band, and an immediate rush of the cavalry in pursuit. There were some bloody atrocities, as there always are. All the troops in the department were ordered to be in readiness for instant service, while the officials eagerly watched the reports to see which way the desperate band would turn; and the next heard of Mr. Hayne was the news that he had thrown up his leave and had hurried out to join his company the moment the Eastern papers told of the trouble. It was all practically settled by the time he reached the department; but the spirit and intent of his action could not be doubted. And now here he was at Warrener. That very morning during the *matinée* he had entered the office unannounced, walked up to the desk of the commander, and, while every voice but his in the room was stilled, he quietly spoke:

"Permit me to introduce myself, colonel,—Mr. Hayne. I desire to relinquish my leave of absence and report for duty."

The colonel quickly arose and extended his hand:

"Mr. Hayne, I am especially glad to see you and to thank you here for all your care and kindness to our men. The doctor tells me that many of them would have had to suffer the loss of noses and ears, even of hands and feet in some cases, but for your attention. Major Stannard will add his thanks to mine when he returns. Take a seat, sir, for the present. You are acquainted with the officers of your own regiment, doubtless. Mr. Billings, introduce Mr. Hayne to ours."

Whereat the adjutant courteously greeted the new-comer, presented a small party of yellow-strapped shoulders, and then drew him into earnest talk about the adventure of the train. It was noticed that Mr. Hayne neither by word nor glance gave the slightest recognition of the presence of the officers of his own regiment, and that they as studiously avoided him. One or two of their number had, indeed, risen and stepped forward, as though to offer him the civil greeting due to one of their own cloth; but it was with evident doubt of the result. They reddened when he met their tentative—which was that of a gentleman—with a cold look of utter repudiation. He did not choose to see them, and, of course, that ended it.

Nor was his greeting hearty among the cavalrymen. There were only a few present, as most of the ___th were still out in the field and marching slowly homeward. The introductions were courteous and formal, there was even constraint among some two or three, but there was civility and an evident desire to refer to his services in behalf of their men. All such attempts, however, Mr. Hayne waved aside by an immediate change of the subject. It was plain that to them too, he had the manner of a man who was at odds with the world and desired to make no friends.

The colonel quickly noted the general silence and constraint, and resolved to shorten it as much as possible. Dropping his pen, he wheeled around in his chair with determined cheerfulness:

"Mr. Hayne, you will need a day or two to look about before you select quarters and get ready for work, I presume."

"Thank you, colonel. No, sir. I shall move in this afternoon and be on duty tomorrow morning," was the calm reply.

There was an awkward pause for a moment. The officers looked blankly from one to another, and then began craning their necks to search for the post quartermaster, who sat an absorbed listener. Then the colonel spoke again:

"I appreciate your promptness, Mr. Hayne; but have you considered that in choosing quarters according to your rank you will necessarily move somebody out? We are crowded now, and many of your juniors are married, and the ladies will want time to pack."

An anxious silence again. Captain Rayner was gazing at his boot-toes and trying to appear utterly indifferent; others leaned forward, as though eager to hear the answer. A faint smile crossed Mr. Hayne's features: he seemed rather to enjoy the situation:

"I *have* considered, colonel. I shall turn nobody out, and nobody need be incommoded in the least."

"Oh! then you will share quarters with some of the bachelors?" asked the colonel, with evident relief.

"No, sir;" and the answer was stern in tone, though perfectly respectful: "I shall live as I have lived for years,—utterly alone."

One could have heard a pin drop in the office,—even on the matted floor. The colonel half rose:

"Why, Mr. Hayne, there is not a vacant set of quarters in the garrison. You will *have* to move someone out if you decide to live alone."

"There may be no quarters *in* the post, sir, but, if you will permit me, I can live near my company and yet in officers' quarters."

"How so, sir?"

"In the house out there on the edge of the garrison, facing the prairie. It is within stone's-throw of the barracks of Company B, and is exactly like those built for the officers in here along the parade."

"Why, Mr. Hayne, no officers ever lived there. It is utterly out of the way and isolated. I believe it was built for the sutler years ago, but was bought in by the government afterwards.—Who lives there now, Mr. Quartermaster?"

"No one, sir. It is being used as a tailors' shop; half a dozen of the company tailors work there; but I can send them back to their own barracks. The house is in good repair, and, as Mr. Hayne says, exactly like those built for officers' use."

"And you mean you want to live there, alone, Mr. Hayne?"

"I do, sir,—exactly."

The colonel turned sharply to his desk once more. The strained silence continued a moment. Then he faced his officers:

"Mr. Hayne, will you remain a few moments? I wish to speak with you.—Gentlemen, that is all this morning." And so the meeting adjourned.

While many of the cavalry officers strolled into the neighboring club-and reading-room, it was noticed that their comrades of the infantry lost no time at intermediate points, but took the shortest road to the row of brown cottages known as the officers' quarters. The feeling of constraint that had settled upon all was still apparent in the group that entered the club-room, and for a moment no one spoke. There was a general settling into easy-chairs and picking up of newspapers without reference to age or date. No one seemed to want to say anything, and yet everyone felt it necessary to have some apparent excuse for becoming absorbed in other matters. This was so evident to Lieutenant Blake that he speedily burst into a laugh,—the first that had been heard,—and when two or three heads popped out from behind their printed screens to inquire into the cause of his mirth, that light-hearted gentleman was seen sprawling his long legs apart and gazing out of the window after the groups of infantrymen.

"What do you see that's so intensely funny?" growled one of the elders among the dragoons.

"Nothing, old mole,—nothing," said Blake, turning suddenly about. "It looks too much like a funeral procession for fun. What I'm chuckling at is the absurdity of our coming in here like so many mutes in weepers. It's none of *our* funeral."

"Strikes me the situation is damned awkward," growled "the mole" again. "Here's a fellow comes in who's cut by his regiment and has placed ours under lasting obligation before he gets inside the post."

"Well, does any man here know the rights and wrongs of the case, anyhow?" said a tall, bearded captain as he threw aside the paper which he had not been reading, and rose impatiently to his feet. "It seems to me, from the little I've heard of Mr. Hayne and the little I've seen, that there is a broad variation between facts and appearances. He looks like a gentleman."

"No one *does* know anything more of the matter than was known at the time of the court-martial five years ago," answered "the mole." "Of course you have heard all about that; and my experience is that when a body of officers and gentlemen find, after due deliberation on the evidence, that another has been guilty of conduct unbecoming an officer and a gentleman, the chances are a hundred to one he has been doing something disreputable, to say the least."

"Then why wasn't he dismissed?" queried a young lieutenant. "The law says he must be."

"That's right, Dolly: pull your Ives and Benèt on 'em, and show you know all about military law and courts-martial," said the captain, crushingly. "It's one thing for a court to sentence, and another for the President to approve. Hayne *was* dismissed, so far as a court could do it, but the President remitted the whole thing."

"There was more to it than that, though, and you know it, Buxton," said Blake. "Neither the department commander nor General Sherman thought the evidence conclusive, and they said so,—especially old Gray Fox. And you ask any of these fellows here now whether they believe Hayne was really guilty, and I'll bet you that eight out of ten will flunk at the question."

"And yet they all cut him dead. That's *prima facie* evidence of what they think."

"Cut be blowed! By gad, if any man asked me to testify on oath as to where the cut lay, I should say he had cut *them*. Did you see how he ignored Foster and Graham this morning?"

"I did; and I thought it damned ungentlemanly in him. Those fellows did the proper thing, and he ought to have acknowledged it," broke in a third officer.

"I'm not defending *that* point; the Lord knows he has done nothing to encourage civility with his own people; but there are two sides to every story, and I asked their adjutant last fall, when there was some talk of his company's being sent here, what Hayne's status was, and he told me. There isn't a squarer man or sounder soldier in the army than the adjutant of the Riflers; and he said that it was Hayne's stubborn pride that more than anything else stood in the way of his restoration to social standing. He had made it a rule that everyone who was not for him was against him, and refused to admit any man to his society who would not first come to him of his own volition and say he believed him utterly innocent. As that involved the necessity of their looking upon Rayner as either perjured or grossly and persistently mistaken, no one felt called upon to do it. Guilty or innocent, he has lived the life of a Pariah ever since."

"*I* wanted to open out to him, today," said Captain Gregg, "but the moment I began to speak of his great kindness to our men he froze as stiff as Mulligan's ear. What was the use? I simply couldn't thaw an icicle. What made him so effective in getting the frost out of them was his capacity for absorbing it into his own system."

"Well, here, gentlemen," said Buxton, impatiently, "we've got to face this thing sooner or later, and may as well do it now. I know Rayner, and like him, and don't believe he's the kind of man to wilfully wrong another. I *don't* know Mr. Hayne, and Mr. Hayne apparently don't want to know me. *I* think that where a man has been convicted of dishonorable—disgraceful conduct and is cut by his whole regiment it is our business to back the regiment, not the man. Now the question is, where shall we draw the line in this case? It's none of our funeral, as Blake says, but ordinarily it would be our duty to call upon this officer. Shall we do it, now that he is in Coventry, or shall we leave him to his own devices?"

"I'll answer for myself, Buxton," said Blake, "and you can do as, you please. Except that one thing, and the not unusual frivolities of a youngster that occurred previous to his trial, I understand that his character has been above reproach. So far as I can learn, he is a far more reputable character than I am, and a better officer than most of us. Growl all you want to, comrades mine: 'it's a way we have in the army,' and I like it. So long as I include myself in these malodorous comparisons, you needn't swear. It is my conviction that the Riflers wouldn't say he was guilty today if they hadn't said so five years ago. It is my information that he has paid every cent of the damages, whether he caused them or not, and it is my intention to go and call upon Mr. Hayne as soon as he's settled. I don't propose to influence any man in his action; and excuse me, Buxton, I think you *did*."

The captain looked wrathful. Blake was an oddity, of whom he rather stood in awe, for there was no mistaking the popularity and respect in which he was held in his own regiment. The ___th was somewhat remarkable for being emphatically an "outspoken crowd," and for some years, thanks to a leaven of strong and truthful men in whom this trait was pronounced and sustained, it had grown to be the custom of all but a few of the officers to discuss openly and fully all matters of regimental policy and utterly to discountenance covert action of any kind. Blake was thoroughly popular, and generally respected, despite a tendency to rant and rattle on most occasions. Nevertheless, there were signs of dissent as to the line of action he proposed, though it were only for his own guidance.

"And how do you suppose Rayner and the Riflers generally will regard your calling on their black sheep?" asked Buxton, after a pause.

"I don't know," said Blake, more seriously, and with a tone of concern. "I like Rayner, and have found most of those fellows thorough gentlemen and good friends. This will test the question thoroughly. I believe most of them, except of course Rayner, would do the same were they in my place. At all events, I mean to see."

"What are you going to do, Gregg?" asked "the mole," wheeling suddenly on his brother troop-commander.

"I don't know," said Gregg, doubtfully. "I think I'll ask the colonel."

"What do you suppose *he* means to do?"

"I don't know again; but I'll bet we all know as soon as he makes up his mind; and he is making up his mind now,—or he's made it up, for there goes Mr. Hayne, and here comes the orderly. Something's up already."

Every head was turned to the doorway as the orderly's step was heard in the outer hall, and every voice stilled to hear the message, it was so unusual for the commanding officer to send for one of his subordinates after the morning meeting. The soldier tapped at the panel, and at the prompt "Come in" pushed it partly open and stood with one white-gloved hand resting on the knob, the other raised to his cap-visor in salute.

"Lieutenant Blake?" he asked, as he glanced around.

"What is it?" asked Blake, stepping quickly from the window.

"The commanding officer's compliments, sir, and could he see the lieutenant one minute before the court meets?"

"Coming at once," said Blake, as he pushed his way through the chairs, and the orderly faced about and disappeared.

"I'll bet it's about Hayne," was the apparently unanimous sentiment as the cavalry party broke up and scattered for the morning's duties. Some waited purposely to hear.

The adjutant alone stood in the colonel's presence as Blake knocked and entered. All others had gone. There was a moment's hesitation, and the colonel paused and looked his man over before he spoke:

"You will excuse my sending for you, Mr. Blake, when I tell you that it is a matter that has to be decided at once. In this case you will consider, too, that I want you to say yes or no exactly as you would to a comrade of your own grade. If you were asked to meet Mr. Hayne at any other house in the garrison than mine, would you desire to accept? You are aware of all the circumstances, the adjutant tells me."

"I am, sir, and have just announced my intention of calling upon him."

"Then will you dine with us this evening to meet Mr. Hayne?"

"I will do so with pleasure, sir."

It could hardly have been an hour afterwards when Mrs. Rayner entered the library in her cosey home and found Miss Travers entertaining herself with a book.

"Have you written to Mr. Van Antwerp this morning?" she asked. "I thought that was what you came here for."

"I did mean to, but Mrs. Waldron has been here, and I was interrupted."

"It is fully fifteen minutes since she left, Nellie. You might have written two or three pages already; and you know that all manner of visitors will be coming in by noon."

"I was just thinking over something she told me. I'll write presently."

"Mrs. Waldron is a woman who talks about everything and everybody. I advise you to listen to her no more than you can help. What was it she told you?"

Miss Travers smiled roguishly: "Why should you want to know, Kate, if you disapprove of her revelations?"

"Oh," with visible annoyance, "it is to—I wanted to know so as to let you see that it was something unfounded, as usual."

"She said she had just been told that the colonel was going to give a dinner-party this evening to Mr. Hayne."

"What?"

"She—said—she—had—just—been—told—that—the col-onel—was going—to give—a dinner-party—this evening—to Mr.—Hayne."

"Who told her?"

"Kate, I didn't ask."

"Who are invited? None of *ours*?"

"Kate, I don't know."

"Where did she say she had heard it?"

"She didn't say."

Mrs. Rayner paused one moment, irresolute: "Didn't she tell you anything more about it?"

"Nothing, sister mine. Why should you feel such an interest in what Mrs. Waldron says, if she's such a gossip?" And Miss Travers was evidently having hard work to keep from laughing outright.

"*You* had better write your letter," said her big sister, and flounced suddenly out of the room and up the stairs.

A moment later she was at the parlor door with a wrap thrown over her shoulders: "If Captain Rayner comes in, tell him I want particularly to see him before he goes out again."

"Where are you going, Kate?"

"Oh, just over to Mrs. Waldron's a moment."

IV.

Facing the broad, bleak prairie, separated from it only by a rough, unpainted picket fence, and flanked by uncouth structures of pine, one of which was used as a storehouse for quartermaster's property, the other as the post-trader's depository for skins and furs, there stood the frame cottage which Mr. Hayne had chosen as his home. As has been said, it was precisely like those built for the subaltern officers, so far as material, plan, and dimensions were concerned. The locality made the vast difference which really existed. Theirs stood all in a row, fronting the grassy level of the parade, surrounded by verandas, bordering on a well-kept gravel path and an equally well graded drive. Clear, sparkling water rippled in tiny *acequias* through the front yards of each, and so furnished the moisture needed for the life of various little shrubs and flowering plants. The surroundings were at least "sociable," and there was companionship and jollity, with an occasional tiff to keep things lively. The married officers, as a rule, had chosen their quarters farthest from the entrance-gate and nearest those of the colonel commanding. The bachelors, except the two or three who were old in the service and had "rank" in lieu of encumbrances, were all herded together along the eastern end, a situation that had disadvantages as connected with duties which required the frequent presence of the occupants at the court-martial rooms or at headquarters, and that was correspondingly far distant from the barracks of the soldiers. It had its recommendations in being convenient to the card-room and billiard-tables at "the store," and in embracing within its limits one house which possessed mysterious interest in the eyes of every woman and most of the men in the garrison: it was said to be haunted.

A sorely-perplexed man was the post quartermaster when the rumor came out from the railway-station that Mr. Hayne had arrived and was coming to report for duty. As a first lieutenant he would have choice of quarters over every second lieutenant in the garrison: there were ten of these young gentlemen, and four of the ten were married. Every set of quarters had its occupants, and Hayne could move in nowhere, unless as occupant of a room or two in the house of some comrade, without first compelling others to move out. This proceeding would lead to vast discomfort, occurring as it would in the dead of winter, and the youngsters were naturally perturbed in spirit,—their wives especially so. What made the prospects infinitely worse was the fact that the cavalry bachelors were already living three in a house: the only spare rooms were in the quarters of the second lieutenants of the infantry, and they were not on speaking-terms with Mr. Hayne. Everything, therefore, pointed to the probability of his "displacing" a junior, who would in turn displace somebody else, and so they would go tumbling like a row of bricks until the lowest and last was reached. All this would involve no end of worry for the quartermaster, who even under the most favorable circumstances is sure to be the least appreciated and most abused officer under the commandant himself, and that worthy was simply agasp with relief and joy when he heard Mr. Hayne's astonishing announcement that he would take the quarters out on "Prairie Avenue."

It was the talk of the garrison all that day. The ladies, especially, had a good deal to say, because many of the men seemed averse to expressing their views. "Quite the proper thing for Mr. Hayne to do," was the apparent opinion of the majority of the young wives and mothers. As a particularly kind and considerate thing it was not remarked by one of them, though that view of the case went not entirely unrepresented. In choosing to live there Mr. Hayne separated himself from companionship. That, said some of the commentators,—men as well as women,—he simply accepted as the virtue of necessity, and so there was nothing to commend in his action. But Mr. Hayne was said to possess an eye for the picturesque and beautiful. If so, he deliberately condemned himself to the daily contemplation of a treeless barren, streaked in occasional shallows with dingy patches of snow, ornamented only in spots by abandoned old hats, boots, or tin cans blown beyond the jurisdiction of the garrison police-parties. A line of telegraph-poles was all that intervened between his fence and the low-lying hills of the eastern horizon. Southeastward lay the distant roofs and the low, squat buildings of the frontier town; southward the shallow valley of the winding creek in which lay the long line of stables for the cavalry and the great stacks of hay; while the row on which he chose to live—"Prairie Avenue," as it was termed—was far worse at his end of it than at the other. It covered the whole eastern front. The big, brown hospital building stood at the northern end. Then came the quarters of the surgeon and his assistants, then the snug home of the post trader, then the "store" and its scattering appendages, then the entrance-gateway, then a broad vacant space, through which the wind swept like a hurricane, then the little shanty of the trader's fur house and one or two hovellike structures used by the tailors and cobbler of the adjacent infantry companies. Then came the cottage itself: south of it stood the quartermaster's store-room, back of which lay an extension filled with ordnance stores, then other and similar sheds devoted to commissary supplies, the post butcher-shop, the saddler's shop, then big coal-sheds, and then the brow of the bluff, down which at a steep grade plunged the road to the stables. It was as unprepossessing a place for a home as ever was chosen by a man of education or position; and Mr. Hayne was possessed of both.

In garrison, despite the flat parade, there was a grand expanse of country to be seen stretching away towards the snow-covered Rockies. There was life and the sense of neighborliness to one's kind. Out on Prairie Avenue all was wintry desolation, except when twice each day the cavalry officers went plodding by on their way to and from the stables, muffled up in their fur caps and coats, and hardly distinguishable from so many bears, much less from one another.

And yet Mr. Hayne smiled not unhappily as he glanced from his eastern window at this group of burly warriors the afternoon succeeding his dinner at the colonel's. He had been busy all day long unpacking books, book-shelves, some few pictures which he loved, and his simple, soldierly outfit of household goods, and getting them into shape. His sole assistant was a Chinese servant, who worked rapidly and well, and who seemed in no wise dismayed by the bleakness of their surroundings. If anything, he was disposed to grin and indulge in high-pitched commentaries in "pidgin English" upon the unaccustomed amount of room. His master had been restricted to two rooms and a kitchen during the two years he had served him. Now they had a house to themselves, and more rooms than they knew what to do with. The quartermaster had sent a detail of men to put up the stoves and move out the rubbish left by the tailors; "Sam" had worked vigorously with soft soap, hot water, and a big mop in sprucing up the rooms; the adjutant had sent a little note during the morning, saying that the colonel would be glad to order him any men he needed to put the quarters in proper shape, and that Captain Rayner had expressed his readiness to send a detail from the company to unload and unpack his boxes, etc., to which Mr. Hayne replied in person that he thanked the commanding officer for his thoughtfulness, but that he had very little to unpack, and needed no assistance beyond that already afforded by the quartermaster's men. Mr. Billings could not help noting that he made no allusion to that part of the letter which spoke of Captain Rayner's offer. It increased his respect for Mr. Hayne's perceptive powers.

While every officer of the infantry battalion was ready to admit that Mr. Hayne had rendered invaluable service to the men of the cavalry regiment, they were not so unanimous in their opinion as to how it should be acknowledged and requited by its officers. No one was prepared for the announcement that the colonel had asked him to dinner and that Blake and Billings were to meet him. Some few of their number thought it going too far, but no one quite coincided with the vehement declaration of Mrs. Rayner that it was an outrage and an affront aimed at the regiment in general and at Captain Rayner in particular. She was an energetic woman when aroused, and there was no doubt of her being very much aroused as she sped from house to house to see what the other ladies thought of it. Rayner's wealth and Mrs. Rayner's qualities had made her an undoubted though not always popular leader in all social matters in the Riflers. She was an authority, so to speak, and one who knew it. Already there had been some points on which she had differed with the colonel's wife, and it was plain to all that it was a difficult thing for her to come down from being *the* authority—the leader of the social element of a garrison—and from the position of second or third importance which she had been accorded when first assigned to the station. There were many, indeed, who asserted that it was because she found her new position unbearable that she decided on her long visit to the East and departed thither before the Riflers had been at Warrener a month. The colonel's wife had greeted her and her lovely sister with charming grace on their arrival two days previous to the stirring event of the dinner, and everyone was looking forward to a probable series of pleasant entertainments by the two households, even while wondering how long the *entente cordiale* would last,—when the colonel's invitation to Mr. Hayne brought on an immediate crisis. It is safe to say that Mrs. Rayner was madder than the captain her husband, who hardly knew how to take it. He was by no means the best liked officer in his regiment, nor the "deepest" and best informed, but he had a native shrewdness which helped him. He noted even before his wife would speak of it to him the gradual dying out of the bitter feeling that had once existed at Hayne's expense. He felt, though it hurt him seriously to make inquiries, that the man whom he had practically crushed and ruined in the long ago was slowly but surely gaining strength even where he would not make friends. Worse than all, he was beginning to doubt the evidence of his own senses as the years receded, and unknown to any soul on earth, even his wife, there was growing up deep down in his heart a gnawing, insidious, ever-festering fear that after all, after all, he might have been mistaken. And yet on the sacred oath of a soldier and a gentleman, against the most searching cross-examination, again and again had he most confidently and positively declared that he had both seen and heard the fatal interview on which the whole case hinged. And as to the exact language employed, he alone of those within earshot had lived to testify for or against the accused: of the five soldiers who stood in that now celebrated group, three were shot to death within the hour. He was growing nervous, irritable, haggard; he was getting to hate the mere mention of the case. The promotion of Hayne to his own company thrilled him with an almost superstitious dismay. *Were* his words coming true? *Was* it the judgment of an offended God that his hideous pride, obstinacy, and old-time hatred of this officer were now to be revenged by daily, hourly contact with the victim of his criminal persecution? He had grown morbidly sensitive to any remarks as to Hayne's having "lived down" the toils in which he had been encircled. Might he not "live down" the ensnarer? He dreaded to see him,—though Rayner was no coward,—and he feared day by day to hear of his restoration to fellowship in the regiment, and yet would have given half his wealth to bring it about, could it but have been accomplished without the dreadful admission, "I was wrong. I was *utterly* wrong." He had grown lavish in hospitality; he had become almost aggressively open-handed to his comrades, and had sought to press money upon men who in no wise needed it. He was as eager to lend as some are to borrow, and his brother officers dubbed him "Midas" not because everything he touched would turn to gold, but because he would intrude his gold upon them at every turn. There were some who borrowed; and these he struggled not to let repay. He seemed to have an insane idea that if he could but get his regimental friends bound to him pecuniarily he could control their opinions and actions. It was making him sick at heart, and it made him in secret doubly vindictive and bitter against the man he had doomed to years of suffering. This showed out that very morning. Mrs. Rayner had begun to talk, and he turned fiercely upon her:

"Not a word on that subject, Kate, if you love me!—not even the mention of his name! I must have peace in my own house. It is enough to have to talk of it elsewhere."

Talk of it he had to. The major early that morning asked him, as they were going to the *matinée*,—

"Have you seen Hayne yet?"

"Not since he reported on the parade yesterday," was the curt reply.

"Well, I suppose you will send men to help him get those quarters in habitable shape?"

"I will, of course, major, if he ask it. I don't propose sending men to do such work for an officer unless the request come."

"He is entitled to that consideration, Rayner, and I think the men should be sent to him. He is hardly likely to ask."

"Then he is less likely to get them," said the captain, shortly, for, except the post commander, he well knew that no officer could order it to be done. He was angry at the major for interfering. They were old associates, and had entered service almost at the same time, but his friend had the better luck in promotion and was now his battalion commander. Rayner made an excuse of stopping to speak with the officer of the day, and the major went on without him. He was a quiet old soldier: he wanted no disturbance with his troubled friend, and, like a sensible man, he turned the matter over to their common superior, in a very few words, before the arrival of the general audience. It was this that had caused the colonel to turn quietly to Rayner and say, in the most matter-of-fact way,—

"Oh, Captain Rayner, I presume Mr. Hayne will need three or four men to help him get his quarters in shape. I suppose you have already thought to send them?"

And Rayner flushed, and stammered, "They have not gone yet, sir; but I had—thought of it."

Later, when the sergeant sent the required detail he reported to the captain in the company office in five minutes: "The lieutenant's compliments and thanks, but he does not need the men."

The dinner at the colonel's, quiet as it was and with only eight at table, was an affair of almost momentous importance to Mr. Hayne. It was the first thing of the kind he had attended in five years; and though he well knew for knew that it was intended by the cavalry commander more especially as a recognition of the services rendered their suffering men, he could not but rejoice in the courtesy and tact with which he was received and entertained. The colonel's wife, the adjutant's, and those of two captains away with the field battalion, were the four ladies who were there to greet him when, escorted by Mr. Blake, he made his appearance. How long—how very long—it seemed to him since he had sat in the presence of refined and attractive women and listened to their gay and animated chat! They seemed all such good friends, they made him so thoroughly at home, and they showed so much tact and ease, that never once did it seem apparent that they knew of his trouble in his own regiment; and yet there was no actual avoidance of matters in which the Riflers were generally interested. It was mainly of his brief visit to the East, however, that they made him talk,—of the operas and theatres he had attended, the pictures he had seen, the music that was most popular; and when dinner was over their hostess led him to her piano, and he played and sang for them again and again. His voice was soft and sweet, and, though it was uncultivated, he sang with expression and grace, playing with more skill but less feeling and effect than he sang. Music and books had been the solace of lonely years, and he could easily see that he had pleased them with his songs. He went home to the dreary rookery out on Prairie Avenue and laughed at the howling wind. The bare grimy walls and the dim kerosene lamp, even Sam's unmelodious snore in the back room, sent no gloom to his soul. It had been a happy evening. It had cost him a hard struggle to restrain the emotion which he had felt at times; and when he withdrew, soon after the trumpets sounded tattoo, and the ladies fell to discussing him, as women will, there was but one verdict,—his manners were perfect.

But the colonel said more than that. He had found him far better read than any other officer of his age he had ever met; and one and all they expressed the hope that they might see him frequently. No wonder it was of momentous importance to him. It was the opening to a new life. It meant that here at least he had met soldiers and gentlemen and their fair and gracious wives who had welcomed him to their homes, and, though they must have known that a pall of suspicion and crime had overshadowed his past, they believed either that he was innocent of the grievous charge or that his years of exile and suffering had amply atoned. It was a happy evening indeed to him; but there was gloom at Captain Rayner's.

The captain himself had gone out soon after tattoo. He found that the parlor was filled with young visitors of both sexes, and he was in no mood for merriment. Miss Travers was being welcomed to the post in genuine army style, and was evidently enjoying it. Mrs. Rayner was flitting nervously in and out of the parlor with a cloud upon her brow, and for once in her life compelled to preserve temporary silence upon the subject uppermost in her thoughts. She had been forbidden to speak of it to her husband; yet she knew he had gone out again with every probability of needing someone to talk to about the matter. She could not well broach the topic in the parlor, because she was not at all sure how Captain and Mrs. Gregg of the cavalry would take it; and they were still there. She was a loyal wife; her husband's quarrel was hers, and more too; and she was a woman of intuition even keener than that which we so readily accord the sex. She knew, and knew well, that a hideous doubt had been preying for a long time in her husband's heart of hearts, and she knew still better that it would crush him to believe it was even suspected by anyone else. Right or wrong, the one thing for her to do, she doubted not, was to maintain the original guilt against all comers, and to lose no opportunity of feeding the flame that consumed Mr. Hayne's record and reputation. He was guilty,—he must be guilty; and though she was a Christian according to her view of the case,—a pillar of the Church in matters of public charity and picturesque conformity to all the rubric called for in the services, and much that it did not,—she was unrelenting in her condemnation of Mr. Hayne. To those who pointed out that he had made every atonement man could make, she responded with the severity of conscious virtue that there could be no atonement without repentance, and no repentance without humility. Mr. Hayne's whole attitude was that of stubborn pride and resentment; his atonement was that enforced by the unanimous verdict of his comrades; and even if it were so that he had more than made amends for his crime, the rules that held good for ordinary sinners were not applicable to an officer of the army. *He* must be a man above suspicion, incapable of wrong or fraud, and once stained he was forever ineligible as a gentleman. It was a subject on which she waxed declamatory rather too often, and the youngsters of her own regiment wearied of it. As Mr. Foster once expressed it in speaking of this very case, "Mrs. Rayner can talk more charity and show less than any woman I know." So long as her talk was aimed against any lurking tendency of their own to look upon Hayne as a possible martyr, it fell at times on unappreciative ears, and she was quick to see it and to choose her hearers; but here was a new phase,—one that might rouse the latent *esprit de corps* of the Riflers,—and she was bent on striking while the iron was hot. If anything would provoke unanimity of action and sentiment in the regiment, this public recognition by the cavalry, in their very presence, of the man they cut as a criminal, was the thing of all others to do it; and she meant to head the revolt.

Possibly Gregg and his modest helpmeet discovered that there was something she desired to "spring" upon the meeting. The others present were all of the infantry; and when Captain Rayner simply glanced in, spoke hurried good-evenings, and went as hurriedly out again, Gregg was sure of it, and marched his wife away. Then came Mrs. Rayner's opportunity:

"If it were not Captain Rayner's house, I could not have been even civil to Captain Gregg. You heard what he said at the club this morning, I suppose?"

In one form or another, indeed, almost everybody *had* heard.

The officers present maintained an embarrassed silence. Miss Travers looked reproachfully at her flushed sister, but to no purpose. At last one of the ladies remarked,—

"Well, of course I heard of it, but—I've heard so many different versions. It seems to have grown somewhat since morning."

"It sounds just like him, however," said Mrs. Rayner, "and I made inquiry before speaking of it. He said he meant to invite Mr. Hayne to his house tomorrow evening, and if the infantry didn't like it they could stay away."

"Well, now, Mrs. Rayner," protested Mr. Foster, "of course none of us heard what he said exactly, but it is my experience that no conversation was ever repeated without being exaggerated, and I've known old Gregg for ever so long, and never heard him say a sharp thing yet. Why, he's the mildest-mannered fellow in the whole ___th Cavalry. He would never get into such a snarl as that would bring about him in five minutes."

"Well, he said he would do just as the colonel did, anyway,—we have that straight from cavalry authority,—and we all know what the colonel has done. He has chosen to honor Mr. Hayne in the presence of the officers who denounce him, and practically defies the opinion of the Riflers."

"But, Mrs. Rayner, I did not understand Gregg's remarks to be what you say, exactly. Blake told me that when asked by somebody whether he was going to call on Mr. Hayne, Gregg simply replied he didn't know,—he would ask the colonel."

"Very well. That means, he proposes to be guided by the colonel, or nothing at all; and Captain Gregg is simply doing what the others will do. They say to us, in so many words, 'We prefer the society of your *bête noire* to your own.' That's the way I look at it," said Mrs. Rayner, in deep excitement.

It was evident that, though none were prepared to endorse so extreme a view, there was a strong feeling that the colonel had put an affront upon the Riflers by his open welcome to Mr. Hayne. He had been exacting before, and had caused a good deal of growling among the officers and comment among the women. They were ready to find fault, and here was strong provocation. Mr. Foster was a youth of unfortunate and unpopular propensities. He should have held his tongue, instead of striving to stem the tide.

"I don't uphold Hayne any more than you do, Mrs. Rayner, but it seems to me this is a case where the colonel has to make some acknowledgment of Mr. Hayne's conduct—"

"Very good. Let him write him a letter, then, thanking him in the name of the regiment, but don't pick him up like this in the face of ours," interrupted one of the juniors, who was seated near Miss Travers (a wise stroke of policy: Mrs. Rayner invited him to breakfast); and there was a chorus of approbation.

"Well, hold on a moment," said Foster. "Hasn't the colonel had every one of us to dinner more or less frequently?"

"Admitted. But what's that to do with it?"

"Hasn't he invariably invited each officer to dine with him in every case where an officer has arrived?"

"Granted. But what then?"

"If he broke the rule or precedent in Mr. Hayne's case would he not practically be saying that he endorsed the views of the court-martial as opposed to those of the department commander, General Sherman, the Secretary of War, the President of the United—"

"Oh, make out your transfer papers, Foster. You ought to be in the cavalry or some other disputatious branch of the service," burst in Mr. Graham.

"I declare, Mr. Foster, I never thought you would abandon your colors," said Mrs. Rayner.

"I haven't, madame, and you've no right to say so," said Foster, indignantly. "I simply hold that any attempt to work up a regimental row out of this thing will make bad infinitely worse, and I deprecate the whole business."

"I suppose you mean to intimate that Captain Rayner's position and that of the regiment is bad,—all wrong,—that Mr. Hayne has been persecuted," said Mrs. Rayner, with trembling lips and cheeks aflame.

"Mrs. Rayner, you are unjust," said poor Foster. "I ought not to have undertaken to explain or defend the colonel's act, perhaps, but I am not disloyal to my regiment or my colors. What I want is to prevent further trouble; and I know that anything like a concerted resentment of the colonel's invitation will lead to infinite harm."

"*You* may cringe and bow and bear it if you choose; you may humble yourself to such a piece of insolence; but rest assured there are plenty of men and women in the Riflers who won't bear it, Mr. Foster; and for one *I* won't." She had risen to her full height now, and her eyes were blazing. "For his own sake I trust the colonel will omit our names from the next entertainment he gives. Nellie shan't—"

"Oh, think, Mrs. Rayner!" interrupted one of the ladies; "they *must* give her a dinner or a reception."

"Indeed they shall not! I refuse to enter the door of people who have insulted my husband as they have."

"Hush! Listen!" said Mr. Graham, springing towards the door. There was wondering silence an instant.

"It is nothing but the trumpet sounding taps," said Mrs. Rayner, hurriedly.

But even as she spoke they rose to their feet. Muffled cries were heard, borne in on the night wind,—a shot, then another, down in the valley,—the quick peal of the cavalry trumpet.

"It isn't taps. It's fire!" shouted Graham from the doorway. "Come on!"

V.

Down in the valley south of the post a broad glare was already shooting upward and illumining the sky. One among a dozen little shanties and log houses, the homes of the laundresses of the garrison and collectively known as Sudsville, was a mass of flames. There was a rush of officers across the parade, and the men, answering the alarum of the trumpet and the shots and shouts of the sentries, came tearing from their quarters and plunging down the hill. Among the first on the spot came the young men who were of the party at Captain Rayner's, and Mr. Graham was ahead of them all. It was plain to the most inexperienced eye that there was hardly anything left to save in or about the burning shanty. All efforts must be directed towards preventing the spread of the flames to those adjoining. Half clad women and children were rushing about, shrieking with fright and excitement, and a few men were engaged in dragging household goods and furniture from those tenements not yet reached by the flames. Fire-apparatus there seemed to be none, though squads of men speedily appeared with ladders, axes, and buckets, brought from the different company quarters, and the arriving officers quickly formed the bucket-lines and water dipped up from the icy creek began to fly from hand to hand. Before anything like this was fairly under way, a scene of semi-tragic, semi-comic intensity had been enacted in the presence of a rapidly gathering audience. "It was worth more than the price of admission to hear Blake tell it afterwards," said the officers, later.

A tall, angular woman, frantic with excitement and terror, was dancing about in the broad glare of the burning hut, tearing her hair, making wild rushes at the flames from time to time as though intent on dragging out some prized object that was being consumed before her eyes, and all the time keeping up a volley of maledictions and abuse in lavish Hibernian, apparently directed at a cowering object who sat in limp helplessness upon a little heap of firewood, swaying from side to side and moaning stupidly through the scorched and grimy hands in which his face was hidden. His clothing was still smoking in places; his hair and beard were singed to the roots; he was evidently seriously injured, and the sympathizing soldiers who had gathered around him after deluging him with snow and water were striving to get him to arise and go with them to the hospital. A little girl, not ten years old, knelt sobbing and terrified by his side. She, too, was scorched and singed, and the soldiers had thrown rough blankets about her; but it was for her father, not herself, she seemed worried to distraction. Some of the women were striving to reassure and comfort her in their homely fashion, bidding her cheer up,—the father was only stupid from drink, and would be all right as soon as "the liquor was off of him." But the little one was beyond consolation so long as he could not or would not speak in answer to her entreaties.

All this time, never pausing for breath, shrieking anathemas on her drunken spouse, reproaches on her frightened child, and invocations to all the blessed saints in heaven to reward the gintleman who had saved her hoarded money,—a smoking packet that she hugged to her breast,—Mrs. Clancy, "the saynior laundress of Company B," as she had long styled herself, was prancing up and down through the gathering crowd, her shrill voice overmastering all other clamor. The vigorous efforts of the men, directed by cool-headed officers, soon beat back the flames that were threatening the neighboring shanties, and levelled to the ground what remained of Private Clancy's home. The fire was extinguished almost as rapidly as it began, but the torrent of Mrs. Clancy's eloquence was still unstemmed. The adjurations of sympathetic sisters to "Howld yer whist," the authoritative admonition of some old sergeant to "Stop your infernal noise," and the half maudlin yet appealing glances of her suffering lord were all insufficient to check her. It was not until the quiet tones of the colonel were heard that she began to cool down: "We've had enough of this, Mrs. Clancy: be still, now, or we'll have to send you to the hospital in the coal-cart." Mrs. Clancy knew that the colonel was a man of few words, and believed him to be one of less sentiment. She was afraid of him, and concluded it time to cease threats and abuse and come down to the more effective *rôle* of wronged and suffering woman-hood,—a feat which she accomplished with the consummate ease of long practice, for the rows in the Clancy household were matters of garrison notoriety. The surgeon, too, had come, and, after quick examination of Clancy's condition, had directed him to be taken at once to the hospital; and thither his little daughter insisted on following him, despite the efforts of some of the women to detain her and dress her properly.

Before returning to his quarters the colonel desired to know something of the origin of the fire. There was testimony enough and to spare. Every woman in Sudsville had a theory to express, and was eager to be heard at once and to the exclusion of all others. It was not until he had summarily ordered them to go to their homes and not come near him that the colonel managed to get a clear statement from some of the men.

Clancy had been away all the evening, drinking as usual, and Mrs. Clancy was searching about Sudsville as much for sympathy and listeners as for him. Little Kate, who knew her father's haunts, had guided him home, and was striving to get him to his little sleeping-corner before her mother's return, when in his drunken helplessness he fell against the table, overturning the kerosene lamp, and the curtains were all aflame in an instant. It was just after taps—or ten o'clock—when Kate's shrieks aroused the inmates of Sudsville and started the cry of "Fire." The flimsy structure of pine boards burned like so much tinder, and the child and her stupefied father had been dragged forth only in time to save their lives. The little one, after giving the alarm, had rushed again into the house and was tugging at his senseless form when rescue came for both,—none too soon. As for Mrs. Clancy, at the first note of danger she had rushed screaming to the spot, but only in time to see the whole interior ablaze and to howl frantically for some man to save her money,—it was all in the green box under the bed. For husband and child she had for the moment no thought. They were safely out of the fire by the time she got there, and she screamed and fought like a fury against the men who held her back when she would have plunged into the midst of it. It took but a minute for one or two men to burst through the flimsy wall with axes, to rescue the burning box and knock off the lid. It was a sight to see when the contents were handed to her. She knelt, wept, prayed, counted over bill after bill of smoking, steaming greenbacks, until suddenly recalled to her senses by the eager curiosity and the remarks of some of her fellow-women. That she kept money and a good deal of it in her quarters had long been suspected and as fiercely denied; but no one had dreamed of such a sum as was revealed. In her frenzy she had shrieked that the savings of her life-time were burning,—that there was over three thousand dollars in the box; but she hid her treasure and gasped and stammered and swore she was talking "wildlike." "They was nothing but twos and wans," she vowed; yet there were women there who declared that they had seen tens and twenties as she hurried them through her trembling fingers, and Sudsville gossiped and talked for two hours after she was led away, still moaning and shivering, to the bedside of poor Clancy, who was the miserable cause of it all. The colonel listened to the stories with such patience as could be accorded to witnesses who desired to give prominence to their personal ex-ploits in subduing the flames and rescuing life and property. It was not until he and the group of officers with him had been engaged some moments in taking testimony that something was elicited which caused a new sensation.

It was not by the united efforts of Sudsville that Clancy and Kate had been dragged from the flames, but by the individual dash and determination of a single man: there was no discrepancy here, for the ten or a dozen who were wildly rushing about the house made no effort to burst into it until a young soldier leaped through their midst into the blazing doorway, was seen to throw a blanket over some object within, and the next minute appeared again, dragging a body through the flames. Then they had sprung to his aid, and between them Kate and "the ould man" were lifted into the open air. A moment later he had handed Mrs. Clancy her packet of money, and—they hadn't seen him since. He was an officer, said they,—a new one. They thought it must be the new lieutenant of Company B; and the colonel looked quickly around and said a few words to his adjutant, who started up the hill forthwith. A group of officers and ladies were standing at the brow of the plateau east of the guard-house, gazing down upon the scene below, and other ladies, with their escorts, had gathered on a little knoll close by the road that led to Prairie Avenue. It was past these that the adjutant walked rapidly away, swinging his hurricane-lamp in his hand.

"Which way now, Billings?" called one of the cavalry officers in the group.

"Over to Mr. Hayne's quarters," he shouted back, never stopping at all.

A silence fell upon the group at mention of the name. They were the ladies from Captain Rayner's and a few of their immediate friends. All eyes followed the twinkling light as it danced away eastward towards the gloomy coal-sheds. Then there was sudden and intense interest. The lamp had come to a stand-still, was deposited on the ground, and by its dim ray the adjutant could be seen bending over a dark object that was half sitting, half reclining at the platform of the shed. Then came a shout, "Come here, some of you." And most of the men ran to the spot.

For a moment not one word was spoken in the watching group: then Miss Travers's voice was heard:

"What can it be? Why do they stop there?"

She felt a sudden hand upon her wrist, and her sister's lips at her ear:

"Come away, Nellie. I want to go home. Come!"

"But, Kate, I must see what it means."

"No: come! It's—it's only some other drunken man, probably.

Come!" And she strove to lead her.

But the other ladies were curious too, and all, insensibly, were edging over to the east as though eager to get in sight of the group. The recumbent object had been raised, and was seen to be the dark figure of a man whom the others began slowly to lead away. One of the group came running back to them: it was Mr. Foster.

"Come, ladies: I will escort you home, as the others are busy."

"What is the matter, Mr. Foster?" was asked by half a dozen voices.

"It was Mr. Hayne,—badly burned, I fear. He was trying to get home after having saved poor Clancy."

"You don't say so! Oh, isn't there something we can do? Can't we go that way and be of some help?" was the eager petition of more than one of the ladies.

"Not now. They will have the doctor in a minute. He has not inhaled flame; it is all external; but he was partly blinded and could not find his way. He called to Billings when he heard him coming. I will get you all home and then go back to him. Come!" And, offering his arm to Mrs. Rayner, who was foremost in the direction he wanted to go,—the pathway across the parade,—Mr. Foster led them on. Of course there was eager talk and voluble sympathy; but Mrs. Rayner spoke not a word. The others crowded around him with questions, and her silence passed unnoted except by one.

The moment they were inside the door and alone, Miss Travers turned to her sister: "Kate, what was this man's crime?"

VI.

An unusual state of affairs existed at the big hospital for several days: Mrs. Clancy had refused to leave the bedside of her beloved Mike, and was permitted to remain. For a woman who was notorious as a virago and bully, who had beaten little Kate from her babyhood and abused and hammered her Michael until, between her and drink, he was but the wreck of a stalwart manhood, Mrs. Clancy had developed a degree of devotion that was utterly unexpected. In all the dozen years of their marital relations no such trait could be recalled; and yet there had been many an occasion within the past few years when Clancy's condition demanded gentle nursing and close attention,—and never would have got it but for faithful little Kate. The child idolized the broken-down man, and loved him with a tenderness that his weakness seemed but to augment a thousandfold, while it but served to infuriate her mother. In former years, when he was Sergeant Clancy and a fine soldier, many was the time he had intervened to save her from an undeserved thrashing; many a time had he seized her in his strong arms and confronted the furious woman with stern reproof. Between him and the child there had been the tenderest love, for she was all that was left to him of four. In the old days Mrs. Clancy had been the belle of the soldiers' balls, a fine-looking woman, with indomitable powers as a dancer and conversationalist and an envied reputation for outshining all her rivals in dress and adornment. "She would ruin Clancy, that she would," was the unanimous opinion of the soldiers' wives; but he seemed to minister to her extravagance with unfailing good nature for two or three years. He had been prudent, careful of his money, was a war-soldier with big arrears of bounty and, tradition had it, a consummate skill in poker. He was the moneyed man among the sergeants when the dashing relict of a brother non-commissioned officer set her widow's cap for him and won. It did not take many years for her to wheedle most of his money away; but there was no cessation to the demand, no apparent limit to the supply. Both were growing older, and now it became evident that Mrs. Clancy was the elder of the two, and that the artificiality of her charms could not stand the test of frontier life. No longer sought as the belle of the soldiers' ball-rooms, she aspired to leadership among their wives and families, and was accorded that pre-eminence rather than the fierce battle which was sure to follow any revolt. She became avaricious,—some said miserly,—and Clancy miserable. Then began the downward course.

He took to drink soon after his return from a long, hard summer's campaign with the Indians. He lost his sergeant's stripes and went into the ranks. There came a time when the new colonel forbade his re-enlistment in the cavalry regiment in which he had served so many a long year. He had been a brave and devoted soldier. He had a good friend in the infantry, he said, who wouldn't go back on a poor fellow who took a drop too much at times, and, to the surprise of many soldiers,—officers and men,—he was brought to the recruiting officer one day, sober, soldierly, and trimly dressed, and Captain Rayner expressed his desire to have him enlisted for his company; and it was done. Mrs. Clancy was accorded the quarters and rations of a laundress, as was then the custom, and for a time—a very short time—Clancy seemed on the road to promotion to his old grade. The enemy tripped him, aided by the scoldings and abuse of his wife, and he never rallied. Some work was found for him around the quartermaster's shops which saved him from guard-duty or the guard-house. The infantry—officers and men— seemed to feel for the poor, broken-down old fellow and to lay much of his woe to the door of his wife. There was charity for his faults and sympathy for his sorrows, but at last it had come to this. He was lying, sorely injured, in the hospital, and there were times when he was apparently delirious. At such times, said Mrs. Clancy, she alone could manage him; and she urged that no other nurse could do more than excite or irritate him. To the unspeakable grief of little Kate, she, too, was driven from the sufferer's bedside and forbidden to come into the room except when her mother gave permission. Clancy had originally been carried into the general ward with the other patients, but the hospital steward two days afterwards told the surgeon that the patient moaned and cried so at night that the other sick men could not sleep, and offered to give up a little room in his own part of the building. The burly doctor looked surprised at this concession on the part of the steward, who was a man tenacious of every perquisite and one who had made much complaint about the crowded condition of the hospital wards and small rooms ever since the frozen soldiers had come in. All the same the doctor asked for no explanation, but gladly availed himself of the steward's offer. Clancy was moved to this little room adjoining the steward's quarters forthwith, and Mrs. Clancy was satisfied.

Another thing had happened to excite remark and a good deal of it. Nothing short of eternal damnation was Mrs. Clancy's frantic sentence on the head of her unlucky spouse the night of the fire, when she was the central figure of the picture and when hundreds of witnesses to her words were grouped around. Correspondingly had she called down the blessings of the Holy Virgin and all the saints upon the man who rescued and returned to her that precious packet of money. Everybody heard her, and it was out of the question for her to retract. Nevertheless, from within an hour after Clancy's admission to the hospital not another word of the kind escaped her lips. She was all patience and pity with the injured man, and she shunned all allusion to his preserver and her benefactor. The surgeon had been called away, after doing all in his power to make Clancy comfortable,—he was needed elsewhere,—and only two or three soldiers and a hospital nurse still remained by his bedside, where Mrs. Clancy and little Kate were drying their tears and receiving consolation from the steward's wife. The doctor had mentioned a name as he went away, and it was seen that Clancy was striving to ask a question. Sergeant Nolan bent down:

"Lie quiet, Clancy, me boy: you *must* be quiet, or you'll move the bandages."

"Who did he say was burned? who was he going to see?" gasped the sufferer.

"The new lieutenant, Clancy,—him that pulled ye out. He's a good one, and it's Mrs. Clancy that'll tell ye the same."

"Tell him what?" said she, turning about in sudden interest.

"About the lieutenant's pulling him out of the fire and saving your money."

"Indeed yes! The blessings of all the saints be upon his beautiful head, and—"

"But *who* was it? What was his name, I say?" vehemently interrupted Clancy, half raising himself upon his elbow, and groaning with the effort. "What was his name? I didn't see him."

"Lieutenant Hayne, man."

"Oh, my God!" gasped Clancy, and fell back as though struck a sudden blow.

She sprang to his side: "It's faint he is. Don't answer his questions, sergeant! He's beside himself! Oh, will ye never stop talking to him and lave him in pace? Go away, all of ye's,—go away, I say, or ye'll dhrive him crazy wid yer—Be quiet, Mike! don't ye spake agin." And she laid a broad red hand upon his face. He only groaned again, and threw his one unbandaged arm across his darkened eyes, as though to hide from sight of all.

From that time on she made no mention of the name that so strangely excited her stricken husband; but the watchers in the hospital the next night declared that in his ravings Clancy kept calling for Lieutenant Hayne.

Stannard's battalion of the cavalry came marching into the post two days after the fire, and created a diversion in the garrison talk, which for one long day had been all of that dramatic incident and its attendant circumstances. In social circles, among the officers and ladies, the main topic was the conduct of Mr. Hayne and the injuries he had sustained as a consequence of his gallant rescue. Among the enlisted men and the denizens of Sudsville the talk was principally of the revelation of Mrs. Clancy's hoard of greenbacks. But in both circles a singular story was just beginning to creep around, and it was to the effect that Clancy had cried aloud and fainted dead away and that Mrs. Clancy had gone into hysterics when they were told that Lieutenant Hayne was the man to whom the one owed his life and the other her money. Someone met Captain Rayner on the sidewalk the morning Stannard came marching home, and asked him if he had heard the queer story about Clancy. He had not, and it was told him then and there. Rayner did not even attempt to laugh at it or turn it off in any way. He looked dazed, stunned, for a moment, turned very white and old-looking, and, hardly saying good-day to his informant, faced about and went straight to his quarters. He was not among the crowd that gathered to welcome the incoming cavalrymen that bright, crisp, winter day; and that evening Mrs. Rayner went to the hospital to ask what she could do for Clancy and his wife. Captain Rayner always expected her to see that every care and attention was paid to the sick and needy of his company, she explained to the doctor, who could not recall having seen her on a similar errand before, although sick and needy of Company B were not unknown in garrisons where he had served with them. She spent a good while with Mrs. Clancy, whom she had never noticed hitherto, much to the laundress's indignation, and concerning whose conduct she had been known to express herself in terms of extreme disapprobation. But in times of suffering such things are forgotten: Mrs. Rayner was full of sympathy and interest; there was nothing she was not eager to send them, and no thanks were necessary. She could never do too much for the men of her husband's company.

Yet there was a member of her husband's company on whom in his suffering neither she nor the captain saw fit to call. Mr. Hayne's eyes were seriously injured by the flames and heat, and he was now living in darkness. It might be a month, said the doctor, before he could use his eyes again.

"Only think of that poor fellow, all alone out there on that ghastly prairie and unable to read!" was the exclamation of one of the cavalry ladies in Mrs. Rayner's presence; and, as there was an awkward silence and somebody had to break it, Mrs. Rayner responded,—

"If I lived on Prairie Avenue I should consider blindness a blessing."

It was an unfortunate remark. There was strong sympathy developing for Hayne all through the garrison. Mrs. Rayner never meant that it should have any such significance, but inside of twenty-four hours, in course of which her language had been repeated some dozens of times and distorted quite as many, the generally accepted version of the story was that Mrs. Rayner, so far from expressing the faintest sympathy or sorrow for Mr. Hayne's misfortune, so far from expressing the natural gratification which a lady should feel that it was an officer of her regiment who had reached the scene of danger ahead of the cavalry officer of the guard, had said in so many words that Mr. Hayne ought to be thankful that blindness was the worst thing that had come to him.

There was little chance for harmony after that. Many men and some women, of course, refused to believe it, and said they felt confident that she had been misrepresented. Still, all knew by this time that Mrs. Rayner was bitter against Hayne, and had heard of her denunciation of the colonel's action. So, too, had the colonel heard that she openly declared that she would refuse any invitation extended to her or to her sister which might involve her accepting hospitality at his house. These things *do* get around in most astonishing ways.

Then another complication arose: Hayne, too, was mixing matters. The major commanding the battalion, a man in no wise connected with his misfortunes, had gone to him and urged, with the doctor's full consent, that he should be moved over into and become an inmate of his household in garrison. He had a big, roomy house. His wife earnestly added her entreaties to the major's, but all to no purpose: Mr. Hayne firmly declined. He thanked the major; he rose and bent over the lady's hand and thanked her with a voice that was full of gentleness and gratitude; but he said that he had learned to live in solitude. Sam was accustomed to all his ways, and he had every comfort he needed. His wants were few and simple. She would not be content, and urged him further. He loved reading: surely he would miss his books and would need someone to read aloud to him, and there were so many ladies in the garrison who would be glad to meet at her house and read to him by turns. He loved music, she heard, and there was her piano, and she knew several who would be delighted to come and play for him by the hour. He shook his head, and the bandages hid the tears that came to his smarting eyes. He had made arrangements to be read aloud to, he said; and as for music, that must wait awhile. The kind woman retired dismayed,—she could not understand such obduracy,—and her husband felt rebuffed. Stannard of the cavalry, too, came in with his gentle wife. She was loved throughout the regiment for her kindliness and grace of mind, as well as for her devotion to the sick and suffering in the old days of the Indian wars, and Stannard had made a similar proffer and been similarly refused, and he had gone away indignant. He thought Mr. Hayne too bumptious to live; but he bore no malice, and his wrath was soon over. Many of the cavalry officers called in person and tendered their services, and were very civilly received, but all offers were positively declined. Just what the infantry officers should do was a momentous question. That they could no longer hold aloof was a matter that was quickly settled, and three of their number went through the chill gloaming of the wintry eve and sent in their cards by Sam, who ushered them into the cheerless front room, while one of their number followed to the door-way which led to the room in rear, in which, still confined to his bed by the doctor's advice, the injured officer was lying. It was Mr. Ross who went to the door and cleared his throat and stood in the presence of the man to whom, more than five years before, he had refused his hand. The others listened anxiously:

"Mr. Hayne, this is Ross. I come with Foster and Graham to say how deeply we regret your injuries, and to tender our sympathy and our services."

There was a dead silence for a moment. Foster and Graham stood with hearts that beat unaccountably hard, looking at each other in perplexity. Would he never reply?

The answer came at last,—a question:

"To what injuries do you allude, Mr. Ross?"

Even in the twilight they could see the sudden flush of the Scotchman's cheek. He was a blunt fellow, but, as the senior, had been chosen spokesman for the three. The abrupt question staggered him. It was a second or two before he could collect himself.

"I mean the injuries at the fire," he replied.

This time, no answer whatever. It was growing too painful. Ross looked in bewilderment at the bandaged face, and again broke the silence:

"We hope you won't deny us the right to be of service, Mr. Hayne. If there is anything we can do that you need, or would like—" hesitatingly.

"You have nothing further to say?" asked the calm voice from the pillow.

"I—don't know what else we *can* say," faltered Ross, after an instant's pause.

The answer came, firm and prompt, but icily cool:

"Then there is nothing that you can do."

And the three took their departure, sore at heart.

There were others of the infantry who had purposed going to see Hayne that evening, but the story of Ross's experience put an end to it all. It was plain that even now Mr. Hayne made the condition of the faintest advance from his regimental comrades a full confession of error. He would have no less.

That evening the colonel sat by his bedside and had an earnest talk. He ventured to expostulate with the invalid on his refusal to go to the major's or to Stannard's. He could have so many comforts and delicacies there that would be impossible here. He did not refer to edibles and drinkables alone, he said, with a smile; but Hayne's patient face gave no sign of relenting. He heard the colonel through, and then said, slowly and firmly,—

"I have not acted hastily, sir: I appreciate their kindness, and am not ungrateful. Five years ago my whole life was changed. From that time to this I have done without a host of things that used to be indispensable, and have abjured them one and all for a single luxury that I cannot live without,—the luxury of utter independence,—the joy of knowing that I owe no man anything,—the blessing of being beholden to no one on earth for a single service I cannot pay for. It is the one luxury left me."

VII.

It was a clear winter's evening, sharply cold, about a week after the fire, when, as Mrs. Rayner came down the stairway equipped for a walk, and was passing the parlor door without stopping, Miss Travers caught sight of and called to her,—

"Are you going walking, Kate? *Do* wait a moment, and I'll go with you."

Anyone in the hall could have shared the author's privilege and seen the expression of annoyance and confusion that appeared on Mrs. Rayner's face:

"I thought you *were* out. Did not Mr. Graham take you walking?"

"He did; but we wandered into Mrs. Waldron's, and she and the major begged us to stay, and we had some music, and then the first call sounded for retreat, and Mr. Graham had to go, so he brought me home. I've had no walk, and need exercise."

"But I don't like you to be out after sunset. That cough of yours—"

"Disappeared the day after I got here, Kate, and there hasn't been a vestige of it since. This high, dry climate put an end to it. No, I'll be ready in one minute more. Do wait."

Mrs. Rayner's hand was turning the knob while her sister was hurrying to the front door and drawing on her heavy jacket as she did so. The former faced her impatiently:

"I don't think you are at all courteous to your visitors. You know just as well as I do that Mr. Foster or Mr. Royce or some other of those young officers are sure to be in just at this hour. You really are very thoughtless, Nellie."

Miss Travers stopped short in her preparations.

"Kate Rayner," she began, impressively, "it was only night before last that you rebuked me for sitting here with Mr. Blake at this very hour, and asked me how I supposed Mr. Van Antwerp would like it. Now you—"

"Fudge! I cannot stay and listen to such talk. If you *must* go, wait a few minutes until I get back. I—I want to make a short call. Then I'll take you."

"So do I want to make a short call,—over at the doctor's; and you are going right to the hospital, are you not?"

"How do you know I am?" asked Mrs. Rayner, reddening.

"You *do* go there every evening, it seems to me."

"I don't. Who told you I did?"

"Several people mentioned your kindness and attention to the Clancys, Kate. I have heard it from many sources."

"I wish people would mind their own affairs," wailed Mrs. Rayner, peevishly.

"So do I, Kate; but they never have, and never will, especially with an engaged girl. I have more to complain of than you, but it doesn't make me forlorn, whereas you look fearfully worried about nothing."

"Who says I'm worried?" asked Mrs. Rayner, with sudden vehemence.

"You look worried, Kate, and haven't been at all like yourself for several days. Now, *why* shouldn't I go to the hospital with you? Why do you try to hide your going from me? Don't you know that I must have heard the strange stories that are flitting about the garrison? Haven't I asked you to set me right if I have been told a wrong one? Kate, you are fretting yourself to death about something, and the captain looks worried and ill. I cannot but think it has some connection with the case of Mr. Hayne. Why should the Clancys—"

"You have no right to think any such thing," answered her sister, angrily. "We have suffered too much at his hands or on his account already, and I never want to hear such words from your lips. It would outrage Captain Rayner to hear that my sister, to whom he has given a home and a welcome, was linking herself with those who side with that—that thief."

"Kate! Oh, how *can* you use such words? How dare you speak so of an officer? You would not tell me what he was accused of; but I tell you that if it be theft I don't believe it,—and no one else—"

There was a sudden footfall on the porch without, and a quick, sharp, imperative knock at the door. Mrs. Rayner fled back along the hall towards the dining-room. Miss Travers, hesitating but a second, opened the door.

It was the soldier telegraph-operator, with a despatch-envelope in his hand:

"It is for Mrs. Rayner, miss, and an answer is expected. Shall I wait?"

Mrs. Rayner came hastily forward from her place of refuge within the dining-room, took the envelope without a word, and passed into the parlor, where, standing beneath the lamp, she tore it open, glanced anxiously at its contents, then threw it with an exclamation of peevish indignation upon the table:

"You'll have to answer for yourself, Nellie. I cannot straighten your affairs and mine too." And with that she was going; but Miss

Travers called her back.

The message simply read, "No letter in four days. Is anything wrong? Answer paid," and was addressed to Mrs. Rayner and signed S.V.A.

"I think you have been extremely neglectful," said Mrs. Rayner, who had turned and now stood watching the rising color and impatiently tapping foot of her younger sister. Miss Travers bit her lips and compressed them hard. There was an evident struggle in her mind between a desire to make an impulsive and sweeping reply and an effort to control herself.

"Will you answer a quiet question or two?" she finally asked.

"You know perfectly well I will," was the sisterly rejoinder.

"How long does it take a letter to go from here to New York?"

"Five or six days, I suppose."

Miss Travers stepped to the door, briefly told the soldier there was no answer, thanked him for waiting, and returned.

"You are not going to reply?" asked Mrs. Rayner, in amaze.

"*I* am not; and I inferred *you* did not intend to. Now another question. How many days have we been here?"

"Eight or nine,—nine, it is."

"You saw me post a letter to Mr. Van Antwerp as we left the Missouri, did you not?"

"Yes. At least I suppose so."

"I wrote again as soon as we got settled here, three days after that, did I not?"

"You said you did," replied Mrs. Rayner, ungraciously.

"And you, Kate, when you are yourself have been prompt to declare that I say what I mean. Very probably it may have been four days from the time that letter from the transfer reached Wall Street to the time the next one could get to him from here, even had I written the night we arrived. Possibly you forget that you forbade my doing so, and sent me to bed early. Mr. Van Antwerp has simply failed to remember that I had gone several hundred miles farther west; and even had I written on the train twice a day, the letters would not have reached him uninterruptedly. By this time he is beginning to get them fast enough. And as for you, Kate, you are quite as unjust as he. It augurs badly for my future peace; and—I am learning two lessons here, Kate."

"What two, pray?"

"That he can be foolishly unreliable in estimating a woman."

"And the other?"

"That you may be persistently unreliable in your judgment of a man."

Verily, for a young woman with a sweet, girlish face, whom we saw but a week agone twitching a kitten's ears and saying little or nothing, Miss Travers was displaying unexpected fighting qualities. For a moment, Mrs. Rayner glared at her in tremulous indignation and dismay.

"You—you ought to be ashamed of yourself!" was her eventual outbreak.

But to this there was no reply. Miss Travers moved quietly to the doorway, turned and looked her angry sister in the eye, and said,—

"I shall give up the walk, and will go to my room. Excuse me to any visitors this evening."

"You are not going to write to him now, when you are angry, I hope?"

"I shall not write to him until tomorrow, but when I do I shall tell him this, Kate: that if he desire my confidence he will address his complaints and inquiries to me. If I am old enough to be engaged to him, in your opinion, I am equally old enough to attend to such details as these, in my own."

Mrs. Rayner stood one moment as though astounded; then she flew to the door and relieved her surcharged bosom as follows, "Well, I pity the man you marry, whether you are lucky enough to keep this one or not!" and flounced indignantly out of the house.

When Captain Rayner came in, half an hour afterwards, the parlor was deserted. He was looking worn and dispirited. Finding no one on the ground-floor, he went to the foot of the stairs, and called,—

"Kate."

A door opened above: "Kate has gone out, captain."

"Do you know where, Nellie?"

"Over to the hospital, I think; though I cannot say."

She heard him sigh deeply, move irresolutely about the hall for a moment, then turn and go out.

At his gate he found two figures dimly visible in the gathering darkness: they had stopped on hearing his footstep. One was an officer in uniform, wrapped in heavy overcoat, with a fur cap, and a bandage over his eyes. The other was a Chinese servant, and it was the latter who asked,—

"This Maje Waldlon's?"

"No," said he, hastily. "Major Waldron's is the third door beyond."

At the sound of his voice the officer quickly started, but spoke in low, measured tone: "Straight ahead, Sam." And the Chinaman led him on.

Rayner stood a moment watching them, bitter thoughts coursing through his mind. Mr. Hayne was evidently sufficiently recovered to be up and out for air, and now he was being invited again. This time it was his old comrade Waldron who honored him. Probably it was another dinner. Little by little, at this rate, the time would soon come when Mr. Hayne would be asked everywhere and he and his correspondingly dropped. He turned miserably away, and went back to the billiard-rooms at the store. When Mrs. Rayner rang her bell for tea that evening he had not reappeared, and she sent a messenger for him.

It was a brilliant moonlit evening. A strong prairie gale had begun to blow from the northwest, and was banging shutters and whirling pebbles at a furious rate. At the sound of the trumpets wailing tattoo a brace of young officers calling on the ladies took their leave. The captain had retired to his den, or study, where he shut himself up a good deal of late, and thither Mrs. Rayner followed him and closed the door after her. Throwing a cloak over her shoulders, Miss Travers stepped out on the piazza and gazed in delight upon the moonlit panorama,—the snow-covered summits to the south and west, the rolling expanse of upland prairie between, the rough outlines of the foot-hills softened in the silvery light, the dark shadows of the barracks across the parade, the twinkling lights of the sergeants as they took their stations, the soldierly forms of the officers hastening to their companies far across the frozen level. Suddenly she became aware of two forms coming down the walk. They issued from Major Waldron's quarters, and the door closed behind them. One was a young officer; the other, she speedily made out, a Chinese servant, who was guiding his master. She knew the pair in an instant, and her first impulse was to retire. Then she reflected that he could not see, and she wanted to look: so she stayed. They had almost reached her gate, when a wild blast whirled the officer's cape about his ears and sent some sheets of music flying across the road. Leaving his master at the fence, the Chinaman sped in pursuit; and the next thing she noted was that Mr. Hayne's fur cap was blown from his head and that he was groping for it helplessly.

There was no one to call, no one to assist. She hesitated one minute, looked anxiously around, then sprang to the gate, picked up the cap, pulled it well down over the bandaged eyes, seized the young officer firmly by the arm, drew him within the gate, and led him to the shelter of the piazza. Once out of the fury of the gale, she could hear his question, "Did you get it all, Sam?"

"Not yet," she answered. Oh, how she longed for a deep contralto! "He is coming. He will be here in a moment."

"I am so sorry to have been a trouble to you," he began again, vaguely.

"You are no trouble to me. I'm glad I was where I happened to see you and could help."

He spoke no more for a minute. She stood gazing at all that was visible of the pale face below the darkened eyes. It was so clear-cut, so refined in feature, and the lips under the sweeping blonde moustache, though set and compressed, were delicate and pink. He turned his head eagerly towards the parade; but Sam was still far away. The music had scattered, and was leading him a lively dance.

"Isn't my servant coming?" he asked, constrainedly. "I fear I'm keeping you. Please do not wait. He will find me here. You were going somewhere."

"No,—unless it was here." She was trembling now. "Please be patient, Mr.—Mr. Hayne. Sam may be a minute or two yet, and here you are out of the wind."

Again she looked in his face. He was listening eagerly to her words, as though striving to "place" her voice. *Could* she be mistaken? Was he, too, not trembling? Beyond all doubt his lips were quivering now.

"May I not know who it is that led me here?" he asked, gently.

She hesitated, hardly knowing how to tell him.

"Try and guess," she laughed, nervously. "But you couldn't. You do not know my name. It is my good fortune, Mr. Hayne. You—you saved my kitten; I—your cap."

There was no mistaking his start. Beyond doubt he had winced as though stung, and was now striving to grope his way to the railing. She divined his purpose in an instant, and her slender hand was laid pleadingly yet firmly on his arm.

"Mr. Hayne, don't go. Don't think of going. Stay here until Sam comes. He's coming now," she faltered.

"Is this Captain Rayner's house?" he asked, hoarse and low.

"No matter whose it is! I welcome you here. You shall not go," she cried, impulsively, and both little hands were tagging at his arm. He had found the railing, and was pulling himself towards the gate, but her words, her clinging hands, were too persuasive.

"I cannot realize this," he said. "I do not understand—"

"Do not try to understand it, Mr. Hayne. If I am only a girl, I have a right to think for myself. My father was a soldier,—I am Nellie Travers,—and if he were alive I know well he would have had me do just what I have done this night. Now won't you stay?"

And light was beaming in through his darkened eyes and gladdening his soul with a rapture he had not known for years. One instant he seized and clasped her hand. "May God bless you!" was all he whispered, but so softly that even she did not hear him. He bowed low over the slender white hand, and stayed.

VIII.

March had come,—the month of gale and bluster, sleet and storm, in almost every section of our broad domain,—and March at Warrener was to the full as blustering and conscienceless as in New England. There were a few days of sunshine during the first week; then came a fortnight of raging snow-storms. The cavalry troops, officers and men, went about their stable-duties as usual, but, except for roll-call on the porch of the barracks and for guard-mounting over at the guard-house, all military exercise seemed suspended. This meant livelier times for the ladies, however, as the officers were enabled to devote just so many more hours a day to their entertainment. There were two or three hops a week over in the big assembly-room, and there was some talk of getting up a german in honor of Miss Travers, but the strained relations existing between Mrs. Rayner and the ladies of other families at the post made the matter difficult of accomplishment. There were bright little luncheon-, dinner-, and tea-parties, where the young officers and the younger ladies met every day; and, besides all this, despite the fact that Mrs. Rayner had at first shown a fixed determination to discuss the rights and wrongs of "the Hayne affair," as it was now beginning to be termed, with all comers who belonged to the Riflers, it had grown to be a very general thing for the youngsters to drop in at her house at all hours of the day; but that was because there were attractions there which outweighed her combativeness. Then Rayner himself overheard some comments on the mistake she was making, and forbade her discussing the subject with the officers even of her own regiment. She was indignant, and demanded a reason. He would name no names, but told her that he had heard enough to convince him she was doing him more harm than good, and, if anything, contributing to the turn of the tide in Hayne's favor. Then she felt outraged and utterly misjudged. It was a critical time for her, and if deprived of the use of her main weapon of offence and defence the battle was sure to go amiss. Sorely against her inclination, she obeyed her lord, for, as has been said, she was a loyal wife, and for the time being the baby became the recipient of her undivided attention.

True to her declaration, she behaved so coldly and with such marked distance of manner to the colonel and his wife when they met in society immediately after the dinner that the colonel quietly told his wife she need not give either dinner or reception in honor of Mrs. Rayner's return. He would like to have her do something to welcome Miss Travers, for he thought the girl had much of her father in her. He knew him well in the old days before and during the war, and liked him. He liked her looks and her sweet, unaffected, cheery manner. He liked the contrast between her and her sister; for Miss Travers had listened in silence to her sister's exposition of what her manner should be to the colonel and his wife, and when they met she was bright and winsome. The colonel stood and talked with her about her father, whom she could remember only vaguely, but of whom she never tired of hearing; and that night Mrs. Rayner rebuked her severely for her disloyalty to the captain, who had given her a home.

But when Mrs. Rayner heard that Major and Mrs. Waldron had invited Mr. Hayne to dine with them, and had invited to meet him two of the cavalry officers and their wives, she was incensed beyond measure. She and Mrs. Waldron had a brief talk, as a result of which Mrs. Rayner refused to speak to Mrs. Waldron at the evening party given by Mrs. Stannard in honor of her and her sister. It was this that brought on the crisis. Whatever was said between the men was not told. Major Waldron and Captain Rayner had a long consultation, and they took no one into their confidence; but Mrs. Rayner obeyed her husband, went to Mrs. Waldron and apologized for her rudeness, and then went with her sister and returned the call of the colonel's wife; but she chose a bright afternoon, when she knew well the lady was not at home.

She retired from the contest, apparently, as has been said, and took much Christian consolation to herself from the fact that at so great a sacrifice she was obeying her husband and doing the duty she owed to him. In very truth, however, the contest was withdrawn from her by the fact that for a week or more after his evening at the Waldrons' Mr. Hayne did not reappear in garrison, and she had no cause to talk about him. Officers visiting the house avoided mention of his name. Ladies of the cavalry regiment calling upon Mrs. Rayner and Miss Travers occasionally spoke of him and his devotion to the men and his bravery at the fire, but rather as though they meant in a general way to compliment the Riflers, not Mr. Hayne; and so she heard little of the man whose existence was so sore a trial to her. What she would have said, what she would have thought, had she known of the meeting between him and her guarded Nellie, is beyond us to describe; but she never dreamed of such a thing, and Miss Travers never dreamed of telling her,—for the present, at least. Fortunately—or unfortunately—for the latter, it was not so much of her relations with Mr. Hayne as of her relations with half a dozen young bachelors that Mrs. Rayner speedily felt herself compelled to complain. It was a blessed relief to the elder sister. Her surcharged spirit was in sore need of an escape-valve. She was ready to boil over in the mental ebullition consequent upon Mr. Hayne's reception at the post, and with all the pent-up irritability which that episode had generated she could not have contained herself and slept. But here Miss Travers came to her relief. Her beauty, her winsome ways, her unqualified delight in everything that was soldierly, speedily rendered her vastly attractive to all the young officers in garrison. Graham and Foster of the infantry, Merton, Webster, and Royce of the cavalry, haunted the house at all manner of hours, and the captain bade them welcome and urged them to come oftener and stay later, and told Mrs. Rayner he wanted some kind of a supper or collation every night. He set before his guests a good deal of wine, and drank a good deal more himself than he had ever been known to do before, and they were keeping very late hours at Rayner's, for, said the captain, "I don't care if Nellie is engaged: she shall have a good time while she's here; and if the boys know all about it,—goodness knows you've told them often enough, Kate,—and they don't mind it, why, it's nobody's business,—here, at least."

What Mr. Van Antwerp might think or care was another matter. Rayner never saw him, and did not know him. He rather resented it that Van Antwerp had never written to him and asked his consent. As Mrs. Rayner's husband and Nellie's brother-in-law, it seemed to him he stood *in loco parentis*; but Mrs. Rayner managed the whole thing herself, and he was not even consulted. If anything, he rather enjoyed the contemplation of Van Antwerp's fidgety frame of mind as described to him by Mrs. Rayner about the time it became apparent to her that Nellie was enjoying the attentions of which she was so general an object, and that the captain was sitting up later and drinking more wine than was good for him. She was aware that the very number of Nell's admirers would probably prevent her becoming entangled with any one of them, but she needed something to scold about, and eagerly pitched upon this. She knew well that she could not comfort her husband in the anxiety that was gnawing at his heart-strings, but she was jealous of comfort that might come to him from any other source, and the Lethe of wine and jolly companionship she dreaded most of all. Long, long before, she had induced him to promise that he would never offer the young officers spirits in his house. She would not prohibit wine at table, she said; but she never thought of there coming a time when he himself would seek consolation in the glass and make up in quantity what it lacked in alcoholic strength. He was impatient of all reproof now, and would listen to no talk; but Nellie was years her junior,—more years than she would admit except at such times as these, when she meant to admonish; and Nellie had to take it.

Two weeks after their arrival at Warrener the burden of Mrs. Rayner's song—morn, noon, and night—was, "What would Mr. Van Antwerp say if he could but see this or hear that?"

Can any reader recall an instance where the cause of an absent lover was benefited by the ceaseless warning in a woman's ear, "Remember, you're engaged"? The hero of antiquity who caused himself to be attended by a shadowing slave whispering ever and only, "Remember, thou art mortal," is a fine figure to contemplate—at this remote date. He, we are told, admitted the need, submitted to the infliction. But lives there a woman who will admit that she needs any instruction as to what her conduct should be when the lord of her heart is away? Lives there a woman who, submitting, because she cannot escape, to the constant reminder, "Thou art engaged," will not resent it in her heart of hearts and possibly revenge herself on the one alone whom she holds at her mercy? Left to herself,—to her generosity, her conscience, her innate tenderness,—the cause of the absent one will plead for itself, and, if it have even faint foundation, hold its own. "With the best intentions in the world," many an excellent cause has been ruined by the injudicious urgings of a mother; but to talk an engaged girl into mutiny, rely on the infallibility of two women,—a married sister or a maiden aunt.

Just what Mr. Van Antwerp would have said could he have seen the situation at Warrener is perhaps impossible to predict. Just what he did say without seeing was, perhaps, the most unwise thing he could have thought of: he urged Mrs. Rayner to keep reminding Nellie of her promise. His had not been a life of unmixed joy. He was now nearly thirty-five, and desperately in love with a pretty girl who had simply bewitched him during the previous summer. It was not easy to approach her then, he found, for her sister kept vigilant guard; but, once satisfied of his high connections, his wealth, and his social standing, the door was opened, and he was something more than welcomed, said the gossips at the Surf House. What his past history had been, where and how his life had been spent, were matters of less consequence, apparently, than what he was now. He had been wild at college, as other boys had been, she learned; he had tried the cattle-business in the West, she was told; but there had been a quarrel with his father, a reconciliation, a devoted mother, a long sojourn abroad,—Heidelberg,—a sudden summons to return, the death of the father, and then the management of a valuable estate fell to the son. There were other children, brother and sisters, three in all, but Steven was the first-born and the mother's glory. She was with him at the seaside, and the first thing that moved Nellie Travers to like him was his devotion to that white-haired woman who seemed so happy in his care. Between that mother and Mrs. Rayner there had speedily sprung up an acquaintance. She had vastly admired Nellie, and during the first fortnight of their visit to the Surf House had shown her many attentions. The illness of a daughter called her away, and Mrs. Rayner announced that she, too, was going elsewhere, when Mr. Van Antwerp himself returned, and Mrs. Rayner decided it was so late in the season that they had better remain until it was time to go to town. In October they spent a fortnight in the city, staying at the Westminster, and he was assiduous in his attentions, taking them everywhere, and lavishing flowers and bonbons upon Nell. Then Mrs. Van Antwerp invited them to visit her at her own comfortable, old-fashioned house down town, and Mrs. Rayner was eager to accept, but Nellie said no; she would not do it: she could not accept Mr. Van Antwerp; she liked, admired, and was attracted by him, but she felt that love him she did not. He was devoted, but had tact and patience, and Mrs. Rayner at last yielded to her demand and took her off in October to spend some time in the interior of the State with relations of their mother, and there, frequently, came Mr. Van Antwerp to see her and to urge his suit. They were to have gone to Warrener immediately after the holidays, but January came and Nellie had not surrendered. Another week in the city, a long talk with the devoted old mother whose heart was so wrapped up in her son's happiness and whose arms seemed yearning to enfold the lovely girl, and Nellie was conquered. If not fully convinced of her love for Mr. Van Antwerp, she was more than half in love with his mother. Her promise was given, and then she seemed eager to get back to the frontier which she had known and loved as a child. "I want to see the mountains, the snow-peaks, the great rolling prairies, once more," she said; and he had to consent. Man never urged more importunately than he that the wedding should come off that very winter; but Nellie once more said no; she could not and would not listen to an earlier date than the summer to come.

No one on earth knew with what sore foreboding and misery he let her go. It was something that Mrs. Rayner could not help remarking,—his unconquerable aversion to every mention of the army and of his own slight experience on the frontier. He would not talk of it even with Nellie, who was an enthusiast and had spent two years of her girlhood almost under the shadow of Laramie Peak and loved the mere mention of the Wyoming streams and valleys. In her husband's name Mrs. Rayner had urged him to drop his business early in the spring and come to them for a visit. He declared it was utterly impossible. Every moment of his time must be given to the settling of estate affairs, so that he could be a free man in the summer. He meant to take his bride abroad immediately and spend a year or more in Europe. These were details which were industriously circulated by Mrs. Rayner and speedily became garrison property. It seemed to the men that in bringing her sister there engaged she had violated all precedent to begin with, and in this instance, at least, there was general complaint. Mr. Blake said it reminded him of his early boyhood, when they used to take him to the great toy-stores at Christmas: "Look all you like, long for it as much as you please, but don't touch." Merton and Royce, of the cavalry, said it was simply a challenge to any better fellow to cut in and cut out the Knickerbocker; and, to do them justice, they did their best to carry out their theory. Both they and their comrades of the Riflers were assiduous in their attentions to Miss Travers, and other ladies, less favored, made acrimonious comment in consequence. A maiden sister of one of the veteran captains in the ___th, a damsel whose stern asceticism of character was reflected in her features and grimly illustrated in her dress, was moved to censure of her more attractive neighbor. "If I had given my heart to a gentleman," said she, and her manner was indicative of the long struggle which such a bestowal would cost both him and her, "nothing on earth would induce *me* to accept attentions from anyone else, not if *he* were millions of miles away."

But Nellie Travers was "accepting attentions" with laughing grace and enjoying the society of these young fellows immensely. The house would have been gloomy without her and "the boys," Rayner was prompt to admit, for he was ill at ease and sorely worried, while his inflammable Kate was fuming over the situation of her husband's affairs. Under ordinary circumstances she would have seen very little to object to so long as Nellie showed no preference for any one of her admirers at Warrener, and unless peevish or perturbed in spirit would have made little allusion to it. As matters stood, however, she was in a most querulous and excitable mood: she could not rail at the real cause of her misery, and so, womanlike, she was thankful for a pretext for uncorking the vials of her wrath on somebody or something else. If the young matrons in garrison who, with the two or three visiting maidens, were disposed to rebel at Miss Nell's apparent absorption of all the available cavaliers at the post, and call her a too lucky girl, could but have heard Mrs. Rayner's nightly tirades and hourly rebukes, they might have realized that here, as elsewhere, the rose had its stinging thorns. As for Miss Travers, she confounded her sister by taking it all very submissively and attempting no defence. Possibly conscience was telling her that she deserved more than she was getting, or than she would be likely to get until her sister heard of the adventure with Mr. Hayne.

"By the way," said Mr. Royce one evening as they were stamping off the snow and removing their heavy wraps in Rayner's hallway after a series of garrison calls, "Mrs. Waldron says she expects you to play for her tomorrow afternoon, Miss Travers. Of course it will be my luck to be at stables."

"You hear better music every afternoon than I can give you, Mr. Royce."

"Where, pray?" asked Mrs. Rayner, turning quickly upon them.

Mr. Royce hesitated, and—with shame be it said—allowed Miss Travers to meet the question:

"At Mr. Hayne's, Kate."

There was the same awkward silence that always followed the mention of Hayne's name. Mrs. Rayner looked annoyed. It was evident that she wanted more information,—wanted to ask, but was restrained. Royce determined to be outspoken.

"Several of us have got quite in the way of stopping there on our way from afternoon stables," he said, very quietly. "Mr. Hayne has his piano now, and has nearly recovered the full use of his eyes. He plays well."

Mrs. Rayner turned about once more, and, without saying so much as good-night, went heavily up-stairs, leaving her escort to share with Mr. Royce such welcome as the captain was ready to accord them. If forbidden to talk on the subject nearest her heart, she would not speak at all. She would have banged her door, but that would have waked baby. It stung her to the quick to know that the cavalry officers were daily visitors at Mr. Hayne's quarters. It was little comfort to know that the infantry officers did not go, for she and they both knew that, except Major Waldron, no one of their number was welcome under that roof unless he would voluntarily come forward and say, "I believe you innocent." She felt that but for the stand made by Hayne himself most of their number would have received him into comradeship again by this time, and she could hardly sleep that night from thinking over what she had heard.

But could she have seen the figure that was slinking in the snow at the rear door of Hayne's quarters that very evening, peering into the lighted rooms, and at last, after many an irresolute turn, knocking timidly for admission and then hiding behind the corner of the shed until Sam came and poked his pig-tailed head out into the wintry darkness in wondering effort to find the visitor, she would not have slept at all.

It was poor Clancy, once more mooning about the garrison and up to his old tricks. Clancy had been drinking; but he wanted to know, "could he spake with the lieutenant?"

IX.

"**I** have been reading over your letter of Thursday last, dear Steven," wrote Miss Travers, "and there is much that I feel I ought to answer. You and Kate are very much of a mind about the 'temptations' with which I am surrounded; but you are far more imaginative than she is, and far more courteous. There is so much about your letter that touches me deeply that I want to be frank and fair in my reply. I have been dancing all this evening, was out at dinner before that, and have made many calls this afternoon; but, tired as I am, my letter must be written, for tomorrow will be but the repetition of today. Is it that I am cold and utterly heartless that I can sit and write so calmly in reply to your fervent and appealing letter? Ah, Steven, it is what may be said of me; but, if cold and heartless to you, I have certainly given no man at this garrison the faintest reason to think that he has inspired any greater interest in him. They are all kind, all very attentive. I have told you how well Mr. Royce dances and Mr. Merton rides and Mr. Foster reads and talks. They entertain me vastly, and I *do* like it. More than this, Steven, I am pleased with their evident admiration,—not alone pleased and proud that they should admire me who am pledged to you,—not that alone, I frankly confess, but because it in itself is pleasant. It pleases me. Very possibly it is because I am vain.

"And yet, though my hours are constantly occupied, though they are here from morning till night, no one of them is more attentive than another. There are five or six who come daily. There are some who do not come at all. Am I a wretch, Steven? There are two or three that do not call who I wish *would* call. I would like to know them.

"Yet they know—they could not help it, with Kate here, and I never forget—that I am your promised wife. Steven, do you not sometimes forget the conditions of that promise? Even now, again and again do I not repeat to you that you ought to release me and free yourself? Of course your impulse will be to say my heart is changing,—that I have seen others whom I like better. No, I have seen no one I like as well. But *is* 'like' what you deserve,—what you ask? and is it not all I have ever been able to promise you? Steven, bear me witness, for Kate is bitterly unjust to me at times, I told you again and again last summer and fall that I did not love you and ought not to think of being your wife. Yet, poor, homeless, dependent as I am, how strong was the temptation to say yes to your plea! You know that I did not and would not until time and again your sweet mother, whom I *do* love, and Kate, who had been a mother to me, both declared that *that* should make no difference: the love would come: the happiest marriages the world over were those in which the girl respected the man of her choice: love would come, and come speedily, when once she was his wife. You yourself declared you could wait in patience,—you would woo and win by and by. Only promise to be your wife before returning to the frontier, and you would be content. Steven, *are* you content? You know you are not: you know you are unhappy; and it is all, not because I am growing to love someone else, but because I am not growing to love you. Heaven knows I want to love you; for so long as you hold me to it my promise is sacred and shall be kept. More than that, if you say that it is your will that I seclude myself from these attentions, give up dancing, give up rides, drives, walks, and even receiving visits, here, so be it. I will obey. But write this to me, Steven,—not to Kate. I am too proud to ask her to show me the letters I know she has received from you,—and there are some she has not shown me,—but I cannot understand a man's complaining to other persons of the conduct of the woman who is, or is to be, his wife. Forgive me if I pain you: sometimes even to myself I seem old and strange. I have lived so much alone, have had to think and do for myself so many years while Kate has been away, that perhaps I'm not 'like other girls;' but the respect I feel for you would be injured if I thought you strove to guide or govern me through others; and of one thing be sure, Steven, *I must honor and respect and look up to the man I marry,* love or no love.

"Once you said it would kill you if you believed I could be false to you. If by that you meant that, having given my promise to you to be your wife at some future time, I must school myself to love you, and will be considered false if love do not come at my bidding or yours, I say to you solemnly, release me now. I may not love, but I cannot and will not deceive you, even by simulating love that does not exist. Suppose that love were to be kindled in my heart. Suppose I were to learn to care for someone here. You would be the first one to know it; for I would tell you as soon as I knew it myself. *Then* what could I hope for,—or you? Surely you would not want to marry a girl who loved another man. But is it much better to marry one who feels that she does not love you? Think of it, Steven: I am very lonely, very far from happy, very wretched over Kate's evident trouble and all the sorrow I am bringing you and yours; but have I misled or deceived you in any one thing? Once only has a word been spoken or a scene occurred that you could perhaps have objected to. I told you the whole thing in my letter of Sunday last, and why I had not told Kate. We have not met since that night, Mr. Hayne and I, and may not; but he is a man whose story excites my profound pity and sorrow, and he is one of the two or three I feel that I would like to see more of. Is this being false to you or to my promise? If so, Steven, you cannot say that I have not given you the whole truth.

"It is very late at night,—one o'clock,—and Kate is not yet asleep, and the captain is still down-stairs, reading. He is not looking well at all, and Kate is sorely anxious about him. It was his evidence that brought years of ostracism and misery upon Lieutenant Hayne, and there are vague indications that in his own regiment the officers are beginning to believe that possibly he was not the guilty man. The cavalry officers, of course, say nothing to us on the subject, and I have never heard the full story. If he has been, as is suggested, the victim of a scoundrel, and Captain Rayner was at fault in his evidence, no punishment on earth could be too great for the villain who planned his ruin, and no remorse could atone for Captain Rayner's share. I never saw so sad a face on mortal man as Mr. Hayne's. Steven Van Antwerp, I wish I *were* a man! I would trace that mystery to the bitter end.

"This is a strange letter to send to—to you; but I am a strange girl. Already I am more than expecting you to write and release me unconditionally; and you *ought* to do it. I do not say I want it.

"Faithfully, at least, yours,
    "Nellie.

"P.S.—Should you write to Kate, you are not to tell her, remember, of my meeting with Mr. Hayne. Of course I am anxious to have your reply to that letter; but it will be five days yet."

An odd letter, indeed, for a girl not yet twenty, and not of a hope-inspiring character; but when it reached Mr. Van Antwerp he did not pale in reading it: his face was ghastly before he began. If anything, he seemed relieved by some passages, though rejoiced by none. Then he took from an inner pocket the letter that had reached him a few days previous, and all alone in his room, late at night, he read it over again, threw it upon the table at which he was sitting, then, with passionate abandonment, buried his face in his arms and groaned aloud in anguish.

Two days after writing this letter Miss Travers was so unfortunate as to hear a conversation in the dining-room which was not intended for her ears. She had gone to her room immediately after breakfast, and, glancing from her window, saw that the officers were just going to headquarters for the daily *matinée*. For half or three-quarters of an hour, therefore, there could be no probable interruption; and she decided to write an answer to the letter which came from Mr. Van Antwerp the previous afternoon. A bright fire was burning in the old-fashioned stove with which frontier quarters are warmed if not ornamented, and she perched her little, slippered feet upon the hearth, took her portfolio in her lap, and began. Mrs. Rayner was in the nursery, absorbed with the baby and the nurse, when a servant came and announced that "a lady was in the kitchen" and wanted to speak with the lady of the house. Mrs. Rayner promptly responded that she was busy and couldn't be disturbed, and wondered who it could be that came to her kitchen to see her.

"Can I be of service, Kate?" called Miss Travers. "I will run down, if you say so."

"I wish you would," was the reply; and Miss Travers put aside her writing. "Didn't she give any name?" asked Mrs. Rayner of the Abigail, who was standing with her head just visible at the stairway, it being one of the unconquerable tenets of frontier domestics to go no farther than is absolutely necessary in conveying messages of any kind; and this damsel, though new to the neighborhood, was native and to the manner born in all the tricks of the trade.

"She said you knew her name, ma'am. She's the lady from the hospital."

"Here, Jane, take the baby! Never mind, Nellie: I must go!" And Mrs. Rayner started with surprising alacrity; but as she passed her door Miss Travers saw the look of deep anxiety on her face.

A moment later she heard voices at the front door,—a party of ladies who were going to spend the morning with the colonel's wife at some "Dorcas society" work which many of them had embraced with enthusiasm. "I want to see Miss Travers, just a minute," she heard a voice say, and recognized the pleasant tones of Mrs. Curtis, the young wife of one of the infantry officers: so a second time she put aside her writing, and then ran down to the front door. Mrs. Curtis merely wanted to remind her that she must be sure to come and spend the afternoon with her and bring her music, and was dismayed to find that Miss Travers could not come before stable-call: she had an engagement. "Of course: I might have known it: you are besieged every hour. Well, can you come tomorrow? Do." And, tomorrow being settled upon, and despite the fact that several of the party waiting on the sidewalk looked cold and impatient, Mrs. Curtis found it impossible to tear herself away until certain utterly irrelevant matters had been lightly touched upon and lingeringly abandoned. The officers were just beginning to pour forth from headquarters when the group of ladies finally got under way again and Miss Travers closed the door. It was now useless to return to her letter: so she strolled into the parlor just as she heard her sister's voice at the kitchen door:

"Come right in here, Mrs. Clancy. Now, quick, what is it?"

And from the dining-room came the answer, hurried, half whispered, and mysterious,—

"He's been drinkin' ever since he got out of hospital, ma'am, an' he's worse than ever about Loot'nant Hayne. It's mischief he'll be doin', ma'am: he's crazy-like—"

"Mrs. Clancy, you *must* watch him. You—Hush!"

And here she stopped short, for, in astonishment at what she had already heard, and in her instant effort to hear no more of what was so evidently not intended for her, Miss Travers hurried from the parlor, the swish of her skirts telling loudly of her presence there. She went again to her room. What could it mean? Why was her proud, imperious Kate holding secret interviews with this coarse and vulgar woman? What concern was it of hers that Clancy should be "worse" about Mr. Hayne? It could not mean that the mischief he would do was mischief *to* the man who had saved his life and his property. That was out of the question. It could not mean that the poor, broken-down, drunken fellow had the means in his power of further harming a man who had already been made to suffer so much. Indeed, Kate's very exclamation, the very tone in which she spoke, showed a distress of mind that arose from no fear for one whom she hated as she hated Hayne. Her anxiety was personal. It was for her husband and for herself she feared, or woman's tone and tongue never yet revealed a secret. Nellie Travers stood in her room stunned and bewildered, yet trying hard to recall and put together all the scattered stories and rumors that had reached her about the strange conduct of Clancy after he was taken to the hospital,—especially about his heart-broken wail when told that it was Lieutenant Hayne who had rescued him and little Kate from hideous death. Somewhere, somehow, this man was connected with the mystery which encircled the long-hidden truth in Hayne's trouble. Could it be possible that he did not realize it, and that her sister had discovered it? Could it be—oh, heaven! *no!*—could it be that Kate was standing between that lonely and friendless man and the revelation that would set him right? She could not believe it of her! She would not believe it of her sister! And yet what did Kate mean by charging Mrs. Clancy to watch him,—that drunken husband? What could it mean but that she was striving to prevent Mr. Hayne's ever hearing the truth? She longed to learn more and solve the riddle once and for all. They were still earnestly talking together down in the dining-room; but she could not listen. Kate knew her so well that she had not closed the door leading into the hall, though both she and the laundress of Company B had lowered their voices. It was disgraceful at best, thought Miss Travers, it was beneath her sister, that she should hold any private conversation with a woman of that class. Confidences with such were contamination. She half determined to rush down-stairs and put an end to it, but was saved the scene: fresh young voices, hearty ringing tones, and the stamp of heavy boot-heels were heard at the door; and as Rayner entered, ushering in Royce and Graham, Mrs. Rayner and the laundress fled once more to the kitchen.

When the sisters found themselves alone again, it was late in the evening. Mrs. Rayner came to Nellie's room and talked on various topics for some little time, watching narrowly her sister's face. The young girl hardly spoke at all. It was evident to the elder what her thoughts must be.

"I suppose you think I should explain Mrs. Clancy's agitation and mysterious conduct, Nellie," she finally and suddenly said.

"I do not want you to tell me anything, Kate, that you yourself do not wish to tell me. You understand, of course, how I happened to be there?"

"Oh, certainly. I wasn't thinking of that. You couldn't help hearing; but you must have thought it queer,—her being so agitated, I mean."

No answer.

"Didn't you?"

"I wasn't thinking of her at all."

"What did you think, then?" half defiantly, yet trembling and growing white.

"I thought it strange that *you* should be talking with her in such a way."

"She was worried about her husband,—his drinking so much,—and came to consult me."

"Why should she—and you—show such consternation at his connection with the name of Mr. Hayne?"

"Nellie, *that* matter is one you know I cannot bear to talk of." ("Very recently only," thought the younger.) "You once asked me to tell you what Mr. Hayne's crime had been, and I answered that until you could hear the whole story you could not understand the matter at all. We are both worried about Clancy. He is not himself; he is wild and imaginative when he's drinking. He has some strange fancies since the fire, and he thinks he ought to do something to help the officer because he helped him, and his head is full of Police Gazette stories, utterly without foundation, and he thinks he can tell who the real culprits were,—or something of that kind. It is utter nonsense. I have investigated the whole thing,—heard the whole story. It is the trashiest, most impossible thing you ever dreamed of, and would only make fearful trouble if Mr. Hayne got hold of it."

"Why?"

"*Why?* Because he is naturally vengeful and embittered, and he would seize on any pretext to make it unpleasant for the officers who brought about his trial."

"Do you mean that what Clancy says in any way affects them?" asked Nell, with quickening pulse and color.

"It might, if there were a word of truth in it; but it is the maudlin dream of a liquor-maddened brain. Mrs. Clancy and I both know that what he says is utterly impossible. Indeed, he tells no two stories alike."

"Has he told you anything?"

"No; but she tells me everything."

"How do you know she tells the truth?"

"Nellie! Why should she deceive me? I have done everything for them."

"I distrust her all the same; and you had better be warned in time. If he has any theory, no matter how crack-brained, or if he knows anything about the case and wants to tell it to Mr. Hayne, you are the last woman on earth who should stand in the way."

"Upon my word, Nellie Travers, this is going too far! One would think you believed I wish to stand in the way of that young man's restoration."

"Kate, if you lift a hand or speak one word to prevent Clancy's seeing Mr. Hayne and telling him everything he knows, you will make me believe—precisely that."

Captain Rayner heard sobbing and lamentation on the bed-room floor when he came in a few moments after. Going aloft, he found Miss Travers's door closed as usual, and his wife in voluble distress of mind. He could only learn that she and Nellie had had a falling out, and that Nell had behaved in a most unjust, disrespectful, and outrageous way. She declined to give further particulars.

X.

Miss Travers had other reasons for wanting to be alone. That very afternoon, just after stable-call, she found herself unoccupied for the time being, and decided to go over and see Mrs. Waldron a few moments. The servant admitted her to the little army parlor, and informed her that Mrs. Waldron had stepped out, but would be home directly. A bright wood fire was blazing on the hearth and throwing flickering lights and shadows about the cosey room. The piano stood invitingly open, and on the rack were some waltzes of Strauss she remembered having heard the cavalry band play a night or two previous. Seating herself, she began to try them, and speedily became interested. Her back being to the door, she did not notice that another visitor was soon ushered in,—a man. She continued slowly "picking out" the melody, for the light was growing dim and it was with difficulty that she could distinguish the notes. Twice she essayed a somewhat complicated passage, became entangled, bent down and closely scanned the music, began again, once more became involved, exclaimed impatiently, "How absurd!" and whirled about on the piano-stool, to find herself facing Mr. Hayne.

Now that the bandage was removed from his eyes it was no such easy matter to meet him. Her sweet face flushed instantly as he bent low and spoke her name.

"I had no idea anyone was here. It quite startled me," she said, as she withdrew from his the hand she had mechanically extended to him.

"It was my hope not to interrupt you," he answered, in the low, gentle voice she had marked before. "You helped me when my music was all adrift the other night: may I not help you find some of this?"

"I wish you *would* play, Mr. Hayne."

"I will play for you gladly, Miss Travers, but waltz-music is not my forte. Let me see what else there is here." And he began turning over the sheets on the stand.

"Are your eyes well enough to read music,—especially in such a dim light?" she asked, with evident sympathy.

"My eyes are doing very well,—better than my fingers, in fact,—and, as I rarely play by note after I once learn a piece, the eyes make no difference. What music do you like? I merely looked at this collection thinking you might see something that pleased you."

"Mrs. Ray told me you played Rubinstein so well,—that melody in F, for one."

"Did Mrs. Ray speak of that?"—his face brightening. "I'm glad they found anything to enjoy in my music."

"'They' found a great deal, Mr. Hayne, and there are a number who are envious of their good fortune,—I, for one," she answered, blithely. "Now play for me. Mrs. Waldron will be here in a minute."

And when Mrs. Waldron came in, a little later, Miss Travers, seated in an easy-chair and looking intently into the blaze, was listening as intently to the soft, rich melodies that Mr. Hayne was playing. The firelight was flickering on her shining hair; one slender white hand was toying with the locket that hung at her throat, the other gently tapping on the arm of the chair in unison with the music. And Mr. Hayne, seated in the shadow, bent slightly over the key-board, absorbed in his pleasant task, and playing as though all his soul were thrilling in his finger-tips. Mrs. Waldron stood in silence at the doorway, watching the unconscious pair with an odd yet comforted expression in her eyes. At last, in one long, sweet, sighing chord, the melody softly died away, and Mr. Hayne slowly turned and looked upon the girl. She seemed to have wandered off into dream-land. For a moment there was no sound; then, with a little shivering sigh, she roused herself.

"It is simply exquisite," she said. "You have given me such a treat!"

"I'm glad. I owe you a great deal more pleasure, Miss Travers."

Mrs. Waldron hereat elevated her eyebrows. She would have slipped away if she could, but she was a woman of substance, and as solid in flesh as she was warm of heart. She did the only thing left to her,—came cordially forward to welcome her two visitors and express her delight that Miss Travers could have an opportunity of hearing Mr. Hayne play. She soon succeeded in starting him again, and shortly thereafter managed to slip out unnoticed. When he turned around a few minutes afterwards, she had vanished.

"Why, I had no idea she was gone!" exclaimed Miss Travers; and then the color mounted to her brow. He must think her extremely absorbed in his playing; and so indeed she was.

"You are very fond of music, I see," he said, at a venture.

"Yes, very; but I play very little and very badly. Pardon me, Mr. Hayne, but you have played many years, have you not?"

"Not so very many; but—there have been many in which I had little else to do but practise."

She reddened again. It was so unlike him, she thought, to refer to that matter in speaking to her. He seemed to read her:

"I speak of it only that I may say to you again what I began just before Mrs. Waldron came. You gave me no opportunity to thank you the other night, and I may not have another. You do not know what an event in my life that meeting with you was; and you cannot know how I have gone over your words again and again. Forgive me the embarrassment I see I cause you, Miss Travers. We are so unlikely to meet at all that you can afford to indulge me this once." He was smiling so gravely, sadly, now, and had risen and was standing by her as she sat there in the big easy-chair, still gazing into the fire, but listening for his every word. "In five long years I have heard no words from a woman's lips that gave me such joy and comfort as those you spoke so hurriedly and without premeditation. Only those who know anything of what my past has been could form any idea of the emotion with which I heard you. If I could not have seen you to say how—how I thanked you, I would have had to write. This explains what I said awhile ago: I owe you more pleasure than I can ever give. But one thing was certain: I could not bear the idea that you should not be told, and by me, how grateful your words were to me,—how grateful I was to you. Again, may God bless you!"

And now he turned abruptly away, awaiting no answer, re-seated himself at the piano and retouched the keys. But, though she sat motionless and speechless, she knew that he had been trembling so violently and that his hands were still so tremulous he could play no more. It was some minutes that they sat thus, neither speaking; and as he regained his self-control and began to attempt some simple little melodies, Mrs. Waldron returned:

"How very domestic you look, young people! Shall we light the lamps?"

"I've stayed too long already," said Miss Travers, springing to her feet. "Kate does not know I'm out, and will be wondering what has become of her sister." She laughed nervously. "Thank you so much for the music, Mr. Hayne!—Forgive my running off so suddenly; won't you, Mrs. Waldron?" she asked, pleadingly, as she put her hand in hers; and as her hostess reassured her she bent and kissed the girl's flushed cheek. Mr. Hayne was still standing patiently by the centre-table. Once more she turned, and caught his eye, flushed, half hesitated, then held out her hand with quick impulse:

"Good-evening, Mr. Hayne. I *shall* hope to hear you play again."

And, with pulses throbbing, and cheeks that still burned, she ran quickly down the line to Captain Rayner's quarters, and was up-stairs and in her room in another minute.

This was an interview she would find it hard to tell to Kate. But told it was, partially, and she was sitting now, late at night, hearing through her closed door her sister's unmusical lamentations,—hearing still ringing in her ears the reproaches heaped upon her when that sister was quietly told that she and Mr. Hayne had met twice. And now she was sitting there, true to herself and her resolution, telling Mr. Van Antwerp all about it. Can one conjecture the sensations with which he received and read that letter?

Mr. Hayne, too, was having a wakeful night. He had gone to Mrs. Waldron's to pay a dinner-call, with the result just told. He had one or two other visits to make among the cavalry households in garrison, but, after a few moments' chat with Mrs. Waldron, he decided that he preferred going home. Sam had to call three times before Mr. Hayne obeyed the summons to dinner that evening. The sun was going down behind the great range to the southwest, and the trumpets were pealing "retreat" on the frosty air, but Hayne's curtains were drawn, and he was sitting before his fire, deep in thought, hearing nothing. The doctor came in soon after he finished his solitary dinner, chatted with him awhile, and smoked away at his pipe. He wanted to talk with Hayne about some especial matter, and he found it hard work to begin. The more he saw of his patient the better he liked him: he was interested in him, and had been making inquiries. Without his pipe he found himself uninspired.

"Mr. Hayne, if you will permit, I'll fill up and blow another cloud. Didn't you ever smoke?"

"Yes. I was very fond of my cigar six or seven years ago."

"And you gave it up?" asked the doctor, tugging away at the strings of his little tobacco-pouch.

"I gave up everything that was not an absolute necessity," said Hayne, calmly. "Until I could get free of a big load there was no comfort in anything. After that was gone I had no more use for such old friends than certain other old friends seemed to have for me. It was a mutual cut."

"To the best of my belief, you were the gainer in both cases," said the doctor, gruffly. "The longer I live the more I agree with Carlyle: the men we live and move with are mostly fools."

Hayne's face was as grave and quiet as ever:

"These are hard lessons to learn, doctor. I presume few young fellows thought more of human friendship than I did the first two years I was in service."

"Hayne," said the doctor, "sometimes I have thought you did

not want to talk about this matter to any soul on earth; but I am speaking from no empty curiosity now. If you forbid it, I shall not intrude; but there are some questions that, since knowing you, and believing in you as I unquestionably do, I would like to ask. You seem bent on returning to duty here tomorrow, though you might stay on sick report ten days yet; and I want to stand between you and the possibility of annoyance and trouble if I can."

"You are kind, and I appreciate it, doctor; but do you think that the colonel is a man who will be apt to let me suffer injustice at the hands of anyone here?"

"I don't, indeed. He is full of sympathy for you, and I know he means you shall have fair play; but a company commander has as many and as intangible ways of making a man suffer as has a woman. How do you stand with Rayner?"

"Precisely where I stood five years ago. He is the most determined enemy I have in the service, and will down me if he can; but I have learned a good deal in my time. There is a grim sort of comfort now in knowing that while he would gladly trip me I can make him miserable by being too strong for him."

"You still hold the same theory as to his evidence you did at the time of the court? of course I have heard what you said to and of him."

"I have never changed in that respect."

"But supposing that—mind you, *I* believe he was utterly mistaken in what he thought he heard and saw,—supposing that all that was testified to by him actually occurred, have you any theory that would point out the real criminal?"

"Only one. If that money was ever handed me that day at Battle Butte, only one man could have made away with it; and it is useless to charge it to him."

"You mean Rayner?"

"I *have* to mean Rayner."

"But you claim it never reached you?"

"Certainly."

"Yet every other package—memoranda and all—was handed you?"

"Not only that, but Captain Hull handed me the money-packet with the others,—took them all from his saddlebags just before the charge. The packet was sealed when he gave it to me, and when I broke the seal it was stuffed with worthless blanks."

"And you have never suspected a soldier,—a single messenger or servant?"

"Not one. Whom could I?"

"Hayne, had you any knowledge of this man Clancy before?"

"Clancy! The drunken fellow we pulled out of the fire?"

"The same."

"No; never to my knowledge saw or heard of him, except when he appeared as witness at the court."

"Yet he was with the ___th Cavalry at that very fight at Battle Butte. He was a sergeant then, though not in Hull's troop."

"Does he say he knew me? or does he talk of that affair?" asked the lieutenant, with sudden interest.

"Not that. He cannot be said to say anything; but he was wonderfully affected over your rescuing him,—strangely so, one of the nurses persists in telling me, though the steward and Mrs. Clancy declare it was just drink and excitement. Still, I have drawn from him that he knew you well by sight during that campaign; but he says he was not by when Hull was killed."

"Does he act as though he knew anything that could throw any light on the matter?"

"I cannot say. His wife declares he has been queer all winter,—hard drinking,—and of course that is possible."

"Sam told me there was a soldier here two nights ago who wanted to talk with me, but the man was drunk, and he would not let him in or tell me. He thought he wanted to borrow money."

"I declare, I believe it was Clancy!" said the doctor. "If he wants to see you and talk, let him. There's no telling but what even a drink-racked brain may bring the matter to light."

And long that night Mr. Hayne sat there thinking, partly of what the doctor had said, but more of what had occurred during the late afternoon. Midnight was called by the sentries. He went to his door and looked out on the broad, bleak prairie, the moonlight glinting on the tin roofing of the patch of buildings over at the station far across the dreary level and glistening on the patches of snow that here and there streaked the surface. It was all so cold and calm and still. His blood was hot and fevered. Something invited him into the peace and purity of the night. He threw on his overcoat and furs, and strolled up to the gateway, past the silent and deserted store, whose lighted bar and billiard-room was generally the last thing to close along Prairie Avenue. There was not a glimmer of light about the quarters of the trader or the surgeon's beyond. One or two faint gleams stole through the blinds at the big hospital, and told of the night-watch by some fevered bedside. He passed on around the fence and took a path that led to the target-ranges north of the post and back of officers' row, thinking deeply all the while; and finally, re-entering the garrison by the west gate, he came down along the hard gravelled walk that passed in circular sweeps the offices and the big house of the colonel commanding and then bore straight away in front of the entire line. All was darkness and quiet. He passed in succession the houses of the field-officers of the cavalry, looked longingly at the darkened front of Major Waldron's cottage, where he had lived so sweet an hour before the setting of the last sun, then went on again and paused surprised in front of Captain Rayner's. A bright light was still burning in the front room on the second floor. Was she, too, awake and thinking of that interview? He looked wistfully at the lace curtains that shrouded the interior, and then the clank of a cavalry sabre sounded in his ears, and a tall officer came springily across the road.

"Who the devil's that?" was the blunt military greeting.

"Mr. Hayne," was the quiet reply.

"What? Mr. Hayne? Oh! Beg your pardon, man,—couldn't imagine who it was mooning around out here after midnight."

"I don't wonder," answered Hayne. "I am rather given to late hours, and after reading a long time I often take a stroll before turning in."

"Ah, yes: I see. Well, won't you drop in and chat awhile? I'm officer of the day, and have to owl tonight."

"Thanks, no, not this time; I must go to bed. Good-night, Mr. Blake."

"Good-night to you, Mr. Hayne," said Blake, then stood gazing perplexedly after him. "Now, my fine fellow," was his dissatisfied query, "what on earth do you mean by prowling around Rayner's at this hour of the night?"

XI.

It was very generally known throughout Fort Warrener by ten o'clock on the following morning that Mr. Hayne had returned to duty and was one of the first officers to appear at the *matinée*. Once more the colonel had risen from his chair, taken him by the hand, and welcomed him. This time he expressed the hope that nothing would now occur to prevent their seeing him daily.

"Won't you come in to the club-room?" asked Captain Gregg, afterwards. "We will be pleased to have you."

"Excuse me, captain, I shall be engaged all morning," answered Mr. Hayne, and walked on down the row. Nearly all the officers were strolling away in groups of three or four. Hayne walked past them all with quick, soldierly step and almost aggressive manner, and was soon far ahead, all by himself. Finding it an unprofitable subject, there had been little talk between the two regiments as to what Mr. Hayne's status should be on his reappearance. Everybody heard that he had somewhat rudely spurned the advances of Ross and his companions. Indeed, Ross had told the story with strong coloring to more than half the denizens of officers' row. Evidently he desired no further friendship or intercourse with his brother blue-straps; and only a few of the cavalry officers found his society attractive. He played delightfully; he was well read; but in general talk he was not entertaining. "Altogether too sepulchral,—or at least funereal," explained the cavalry. "He never laughs, and rarely smiles, and he's as glum as a Quaker meeting," was another complaint. So a social success was hardly to be predicted for Mr. Hayne.

While he could not be invited where just a few infantry people were the other guests, from a big general gathering or party he, of course, could not be omitted; but there he would have his cavalry and medical friends to talk to, and then there was Major Waldron. It was a grievous pity that there should be such an element of embarrassment, but it couldn't be helped. As the regimental adjutant had said, Hayne himself was the main obstacle to his restoration to regimental friendship. No man who piques himself on the belief that he is about to do a virtuous and praiseworthy act will be apt to persevere when the object of his benevolence treats him with cold contempt. If Mr. Hayne saw fit to repudiate the civilities a few officers essayed to extend to him, no others would subject themselves to similar rebuffs; and if he could stand the *status quo*, why, the regiment could; and that, said the Riflers, was the end of the matter.

But it was not the end, by a good deal. Some few of the ladies of the infantry, actuated by Mrs. Rayner's vehement exposition of the case, had aligned themselves on her side as against the post commander, and by their general conduct sought to convey to the colonel and to the ladies who were present at the first dinner given Mr. Hayne thorough disapproval of their course. This put the cavalry people on their mettle and led to a division in the garrison; and as Major Waldron was, in Mrs. Rayner's eyes, equally culpable with the colonel, it so resulted that two or three infantry households, together with some unmarried subalterns, were arrayed socially against their own battalion commander as well as against the grand panjandrum at post headquarters. If it had not been for the determined attitude of Mr. Hayne himself, the garrison might speedily have been resolved into two parties,—Hayne and anti-Hayne sympathizers; but the whole bearing of that young man was fiercely repellent of sympathy; he would have none of it. "Hayne's position," said Major Waldron, "is practically this: he holds that no man who has borne himself as he has during these five years— denied himself everything that he might make up every cent that was lost, though he was in no wise responsible for the loss—could by any possibility have been guilty of the charges on which he was tried. From this he will not abate one jot or tittle; and he refuses now to restore to his friendship the men who repudiated him in his years of trouble, except on their profession of faith in his entire innocence." Now, this was something the cavalry could not do without some impeachment of the evidence which was heaped up against the poor fellow at the time of the trial; and it was something the infantry would not do, because thereby they would virtually pronounce one at least of their own officers to have repeatedly and persistently given false testimony. In the case of Waldron and the cavalry, however, it was possible for Hayne to return their calls of courtesy, because they, having never "sent him to Coventry," received him precisely as they would receive any other officer. With the Riflers it was different: having once "cut" him as though by unanimous accord, and having taught the young officers joining year after year to regard him as a criminal, *they* could be restored to Mr. Hayne's friendship, as has been said before, only "on confession of error." Buxton and two or three of his stamp called or left their cards on Mr. Hayne because their colonel had so done; but precisely as the ceremony was performed, just so was it returned. Buxton was red with wrath over what he termed Hayne's conceited and supercilious manner when returning his call: "I called upon him like a gentleman, by thunder, just to let him understand I wanted to help him out of the mire, and told him if there was anything I could do for him that a gentleman *could* do, not to hesitate about letting me know; and when he came to my house today, damned if he didn't patronize *me*!—talked to me about the Plevna siege, and wanted to discuss Gourko and the Balkans or some other fool thing: what in thunder have I to do with campaigns in Turkey?—and I thought he meant those nigger soldiers the British have in India,—Goorkhas, I know now,—and I *did* tell him it was an awful blunder, that only a Russian would make, to take those Sepoy fellows and put 'em into a winter campaign. Of course I hadn't been booking up the subject, and he had, and sprung it on me; and then, by gad, as he was going, he said he had books and maps he would lend me, and if there was anything he could do for me that a gentleman *could* do, not to hesitate about asking. Damn his impudence!"

Poor Buxton! One of his idiosyncrasies was to talk wisely to the juniors on the subject of European campaigns and to criticise the moves of generals whose very names and centuries were entangling snares. His own subalterns were, unfortunately for him, at the house when Hayne called, and when he, as was his wont, began to expound on current military topics. "A little learning," even, he had not, and the dangerous thing that that would have been was supplanted by something quite as bad, if not worse. He was trapped and thrown by the quiet-mannered infantry subaltern, and it was all Messrs. Freeman and Royce could do to restrain their impulse to rush after Hayne and embrace him. Buxton was cordially detested by his "subs" and well knew they would tell the story of his defeat, so he made a virtue of necessity and came out with his own version. Theirs was far more ludicrous, and, while it made Mr. Hayne famous, he gained another enemy. The ___th could not fail to notice how soon after that all social recognition ceased between their bulky captain and the pale, slender subaltern; and Mrs. Buxton and Mrs. Rayner became suddenly infatuated with each other, while their lords were seldom seen except together.

All this time, however, Miss Travers was making friends throughout the garrison. No one ever presumed to discuss the Hayne affair in her presence, because of her relationship to the Rayners; and yet Mrs. Waldron had told several people how delightfully she and Mr. Hayne had spent an afternoon together. Did not Mrs. Rayner declare that Mrs. Waldron was a woman who told everything she knew, or words to that effect? It is safe to say that the garrison was greatly interested in the story. How strange it was that he should have had a *tête-à-tête* with the sister of his bitterest foe! *When* did they meet? Had they met since? Would they meet again? All these were questions eagerly discussed, yet never asked of the parties themselves, Mr. Hayne's reputation for snubbing people standing him in excellent stead, and Miss Travers's quiet dignity and reserve of manner being too much for those who would have given a good deal to gain her confidence. But there was Mrs. Rayner. She, at least, with all her high and mighty ways, was no unapproachable creature when it came to finding out what she thought of other people's conduct. So half a dozen, at least, had more or less confidentially asked if she knew of Mr. Hayne and Miss Travers's meeting. Indeed she did! and she had given Nellie her opinion of her conduct very decidedly. It was Captain Rayner himself who interposed, she said, and forbade her upbraiding Nellie any further. Nellie being either in an adjoining room or up in her own on several occasions when these queries were propounded to her sister, it goes without saying that that estimable woman, after the manner of her sex, had elevated her voice in responding, so that there was no possibility of the wicked girl's failing to get the full benefit of the scourging she deserved. Rayner had, indeed, positively forbidden her further rebuking Nellie; but the man does not live who can prevent one woman's punishing another so long as she can get within earshot, and Miss Travers was paying dearly for her independence.

It cannot be estimated just how great a disappointment her visit to the frontier was proving to that young lady, simply because she kept her own counsel. There were women in the garrison who longed to take her to their hearts and homes, she was so fresh and pure and sweet and winning, they said; but how could they, when her sister would recognize them only by the coldest possible nod? Nellie was not happy, that was certain, though she made no complaint, and though the young officers who were daily her devotees declared she was bright and attractive as she could be. There were still frequent dances and parties in the garrison, but March was nearly spent, and the weather had been so vile and blustering that they could not move beyond the limits of the post. April might bring a change for the better in the weather, but Miss Travers wondered how it could better her position.

It is hard for a woman of spirit to be materially dependent on anyone, and Miss Travers was virtually dependent on her brother-in-law. The little share of her father's hard savings was spent on her education. Once free from school, she was bound to another apprenticeship, and sister Kate, though indulgent, fond, and proud, lost no opportunity of telling her how much she owed to Captain Rayner. It got to be a fearful weight before the first summer was well over. It was the main secret of her acceptance of Mr. Van Antwerp. And now, until she would consent to name the day that should bind her for life to him, she had no home but such as Kate Rayner could offer her; and Kate was bitterly offended at her. There was just one chance to end it now and forever, and to relieve her sister and the captain of the burden of her support. *Could* she make up her mind to do it? And Mr. Van Antwerp offered the opportunity.

So far from breaking with her, as she half expected,—so far from being even angry and reproachful on receiving the letter she had written telling him all about her meetings with Mr. Hayne,—he had written again and again, reproaching himself for his doubts and fears, begging her forgiveness for having written and telegraphed to Kate, humbling himself before her in the most abject way, and imploring her to reconsider her determination and to let him write to Captain and Mrs. Rayner to return to their Eastern home at once, that the marriage might take place forthwith and he could bear her away to Europe in May. Letter after letter came, eager, imploring, full of tenderest love and devotion, full of the saddest apprehension, never reproaching, never doubting, never commanding or restraining. The man had found the way to touch a woman of her generous nature: he had left all to her; he was at her mercy; and she knew well that he loved her fervently and that to lose her would wellnigh break his heart. Could she say the word and be free? Surely, as this man's wife there would be no serfdom; and, yet, could she wed a man for whom she felt no spark of love?

They went down to the creek one fine morning early in April. There had been a sudden thaw of the snows up the gorges of the Rockies, and the stream had overleaped its banks, spread over the lowlands, and flooded some broad depressions in the prairie. Then, capricious as a woman's moods, the wind whistled around from the north one night and bound the lakelets in a band of ice. The skating was gorgeous, and all the pretty ankles on the post were rejoicing in the opportunity before the setting of another sun. Coming homeward at luncheon-time, Mrs. Rayner, Mrs. Buxton, Miss Travers, and one or two others, escorted by a squad of bachelors, strolled somewhat slowly along Prairie Avenue towards the gate. It so happened that the married ladies were foremost in the little party, when who should meet them but Mr. Hayne, coming from the east gate! Mrs. Rayner and Mrs. Buxton, though passing him almost elbow to elbow, looked straight ahead or otherwise avoided his eye. He raised his forage-cap in general acknowledgment of the presence of ladies with the officers, but glanced coldly from one to the other until his blue eyes lighted on Miss Travers. No woman in that group could fail to note the leap of sunshine and gladness to his face, the instant flush that rose to his cheek. Miss Travers, herself, saw it quickly, as did the maiden walking just behind her, and her heart bounded at the sight. She bowed as their eyes met, spoke his name in low tone, and strove to hide her face from Mr. Blake, who turned completely around and stole a sudden glance at her. She could no more account for than she could control it, but her face was burning. Mrs. Rayner, too, looked around and stared at her, but this she met firmly, her dark eyes never quailing before the angry glare in her sister's. Blake was beginning to like Hayne and to dislike Mrs. Rayner, and he always *did* like mischief.

"You owe me a grudge, Miss Travers, if you did but know it," he said, so that all could hear.

"You, Mr. Blake! How can that be possible?"

"I spoiled a serenade for you a few nights ago. I was officer of the day, and caught sight of a man gazing up at your window after midnight. I felt sure he was going to sing: so, like a good fellow, I ran over to play an accompaniment, and then—would you believe it?—he wouldn't sing, after all."

She was white now. Her eyes were gazing almost imploringly at him. Something warned him to hold his peace, and he broke off short.

"*Who* was it? Oh, *do* tell us, Mr. Blake!" were the exclamations, Mrs. Rayner being most impetuous in her demands. Again Blake caught the appeal in Miss Travers's eyes.

"That's what I want to know," he responded, mendaciously. "When I woke up next morning, the whole thing was a dream, and I couldn't fix the fellow at all."

There was a chorus of disappointment and indignation. The idea of spoiling such a gem of a sensation! But Blake took it all complacently, until he got home. Then it began to worry him.

Was it possible that she knew he was there?

That night there was a disturbance in the garrison. Just after ten o'clock, and while the sentries were calling off the hour, a woman's shrieks and cries were heard over behind the quarters of Company B and close to the cottage occupied by Lieutenant Hayne. The officers of the guard ran to the spot with several men, and found Private Clancy struggling and swearing in the grasp of two or three soldiers, while Mrs. Clancy was imploring them not to let him go, he was wild-like again; it was drink; he had the horrors, and was batin' her while she was tryin' to get him home. And Clancy's appearance bore out her words. He was wild and drunken; but he swore he meant no harm; he struggled hard for freedom; he vowed he only wanted to see the lieutenant at his quarters; and Mr. Hayne, lamp in hand, had come upon the scene, and was striving to quiet the woman, who only screamed and protested the louder. At his quiet order the soldiers released Clancy, and the man stood patient and subordinate.

"Did you want to see me, Clancy?" asked Mr. Hayne.

"Askin' yer pardon, sir, I did," began the man, unsteadily, and evidently struggling with the fumes of the liquor he had been drinking; but before he could speak again, Mrs. Clancy's shrieks rang out on the still air:

"Oh, for the love of God, howld him, some o' ye's! He'll kill him! He's mad, I say! Shure 'tis I that know him best. Oh, blessed Vargin, save us! *Don't* let him loose, Misther Foster!" she screamed to the officer of the guard, who at that moment appeared on the full run.

"What's the trouble?" he asked, breathlessly.

"Clancy seems to have been drinking, and wants to talk with me about something, Mr. Foster," said Hayne, quietly. "He belongs to my company, and I will be responsible that he goes home. It is really Mrs. Clancy that is making all the trouble."

"Oh, for the love of God, hear him, now, whin the man was tearin' the hair o' me this minute! Oh, howld him, men! Shure 'tis Captain Rayner wud niver let him go."

"What's the matter, Mrs. Clancy?" spoke a quick, stern voice, and Rayner, with face white as a sheet, suddenly stood in their midst.

"Oh, God be praised, it's here ye are, captin! Shure it's Clancy, sir, dhrunk, sir, and runnin' round the garrison, and batin' me, sir."

"Take him to the guard-house, Mr. Foster," was the stern, sudden order. "Not a word, Clancy," as the man strove to speak. "Off with him; and if he gives you any trouble, send for me."

And as the poor fellow was led away, silence fell upon the group. Mrs. Clancy began a wail of mingled relief and misery, which the captain ordered her to cease and go home. More men came hurrying to the spot, and presently the officer of the day. "It is all right now," said Rayner to the latter. "One of my men—Clancy—was out here drunk and raising a row. I have sent him to the guard-house. Go back to your quarters, men. Come, captain, will you walk over home with me?"

"Was Mr. Hayne here when the row occurred?" asked the cavalryman, looking as though he wanted to hear something from the young officer who stood a silent witness.

"I don't know," replied Rayner. "It makes no difference, captain. It is not a case of witnesses. I shan't prefer charges against the man. Come!" And he drew him hastily away.

Hayne stood watching them as they disappeared beyond the glimmer of his lamp. Then a hand was placed on his arm:

"Did you notice Captain Rayner's face,—his lips? He was ashen as death."

"Come in here with me," was the reply; and, turning, Hayne led the post surgeon into the house.

XII.

There was an unusual scene at the *matinée* the following morning. When Captain Ray relieved Captain Gregg as officer of the day, and the two were visiting the guard-house and turning over prisoners, they came upon the last name on the list,—Clancy,—and Gregg turned to his regimental comrade and said,—

"No charges are preferred against Clancy, at least none as yet, Captain Ray; but his company commander requests that he be held here until he can talk over his case with the colonel."

"What's he in for?" demanded Captain Ray.

"Getting drunk and raising a row and beating his wife," answered Gregg; whereat there was a titter among the soldiers.

"I never shtruck a woman in me life, sir," said poor Clancy.

"Silence, Clancy!" ordered the sergeant of the guard.

"No, I'm blessed if I believe that part of it, Clancy, drunk or no drunk," said the new officer of the day.—"Take charge of him for the present, sergeant." And away they went to the office.

Captain Rayner was in conversation with the commanding officer as they entered, and the colonel was saying,—

"It is not the proper way to handle the case, captain. If he has been guilty of drunkenness and disorderly conduct he should be brought to trial at once."

"I admit that, sir; but the case is peculiar. It was Mrs. Clancy that made all the noise. I feel sure that after he is perfectly sober I can give him such a talking-to as will put a stop to this trouble."

"Very well, sir. I am willing to let company commanders experiment at least once or twice on their theories, so you can try the scheme; but we of the ___th have had some years of experience with the Clancys, and were not a little amused when they turned up again in our midst as accredited members of your company."

"Then, as I understand you, colonel, Clancy is not to be brought to trial for this affair," suddenly spoke the post surgeon.

Everybody looked up in surprise. "Pills" was the last man, ordinarily, to take a hand in the "shop talk" at the morning meetings.

"No, doctor. His captain thinks it unnecessary to prefer charges."

"So do I, sir; and, as I saw the man both before and after his confinement last night, I do not think it was necessary to confine him."

"The officer of the day says there was great disorder," said the colonel, in surprise.

"Ay, sir, so there was; and the thing reminds me of the stories they used to tell on the New York police. It looked to me as though all the row was raised by Mrs. Clancy, as Captain Rayner says; but the man was arrested. That being the case, I would ask the captain for what specific offence he ordered Clancy to the guard-house."

Rayner again was pale as death. He glared at the doctor in amaze and incredulity, while all the officers noted his agitation and were silent in surprise. It was the colonel that came to the rescue:

"Captain Rayner had abundant reason, doctor. It was after taps, though only just after, and, whether causing the trouble or not, the man is the responsible party, not the woman. The captain was right in causing his arrest."

Rayner looked up gratefully.

"I submit to your decision, sir," said the surgeon, "and I apologize for anything I may have asked that was beyond my province. Now I wish to ask a question for my own guidance."

"Go on, doctor."

"In case an enlisted man of this command desire to see an officer of his company,—or any other officer, for that matter,—is it a violation of any military regulation for him to go to his quarters for that purpose?"

Again was Rayner fearfully white and aged-looking. His lips moved as though he would interrupt; but discipline prevailed.

"No, doctor; and yet we have certain customs of service to prevent the men going at all manner of hours and on frivolous errands: a soldier asks his first sergeant's permission first, and if denied by him, and he have what he considers good reason, he can report the whole case."

"But suppose a man is not on company duty: must he hunt up his first sergeant and ask permission to go and see some officer with whom he has business?"

"Well, hardly, in that case."

"That's all, sir." And the doctor subsided.

Among all the officers, as the meeting adjourned, the question was, "What do you suppose 'Pills' was driving at?"

There were two or three who knew. Captain Rayner went first to his quarters, where he had a few moments' hurried consultation with his wife; then they left the house together,—he to have a low-toned and very stern talk to rather than with the abashed Clancy, who listened cap in hand and with hanging head; she to visit the sick child of Mrs. Flanigan, of Company K, whose quarters adjoined those to which the Clancys had recently been assigned.

When that Hibernian culprit returned to his roof-tree, released from durance vile, he was surprised to receive a kindly and sympathetic welcome from his captain's wife, who with her own hand had mixed him some comforting drink and was planning with Mrs. Clancy for their greater comfort. "If Clancy will only promise to quit entirely!" interjected the partner of his joys and sorrows.

Later that day, when the doctor had a little talk with Clancy, the ex-dragoon declared he was going to reform for all he was worth. He was only a distress to everybody when he drank.

"All right, Clancy. And when you are perfectly yourself you can come and see Lieutenant Hayne as soon as you like."

"Loot'nant Hayne is it, sir? Shure I'd be beggin' his pardon for the vexation I gave him last night."

"But you have something you wanted to speak with him about. You said so last night, Clancy," said the doctor, looking him squarely in the eye.

"Shure I was dhrunk, sir. I didn't mane it," he answered; but he shrank and cowered.

The doctor turned and left him.

"If it's only when he's drunk that conscience pricks him and the truth will out, then we must have him drunk again," quoth this unprincipled practitioner.

That same afternoon Miss Travers found that a headache was the result of confinement to an atmosphere somewhat heavily charged with electricity. Mrs. Rayner seemed to bristle every time she approached her sister. Possibly it was the heart, more than the head, that ached, but in either case she needed relief from the exposed position she had occupied ever since Kate's return from the Clancys' in the morning. She had been too long under fire, and was wearied. Even the cheery visits of the garrison gallants had proved of little avail, for Mrs. Rayner was in very ill temper, and made snappish remarks to them which two of them resented and speedily took themselves off. Later Miss Travers went to her room and wrote a letter, and then the sunset gun shook the window, and twilight settled down upon the still frozen earth. She bathed her heated forehead and flushed cheeks, threw a warm cloak over her shoulders, and came slowly down the stairs. Mrs. Rayner met her at the parlor door.

"Kate, I am going for a walk, and shall stop and see Mrs. Waldron."

"Quite an unnecessary piece of information. I saw him as well as you. He has just gone there."

Miss Travers flushed hot with indignation:

"I have seen no one; and if you mean that Mr. Hayne has gone to Major Waldron's, I shall not."

"No: I'd meet him on the walk: it would only be a trifle more public."

"You have no right to accuse me of the faintest expectation of meeting him anywhere. I repeat, I had not thought of such a thing."

"You might just as well do it. You cannot make your antagonism to my husband much more pointed than you have already. And as for meeting Mr. Hayne, the only advice I presume to give now is that for your own sake you keep your blushes under better control than you did the last time you met—that I know of." And, with this triumphant insult as a parting shot, Mrs. Rayner wheeled and marched off through the parlor.

What was a girl to do? Nellie Travers was not of the crying kind, and was denied a vast amount of comfort in consequence. She stood a few moments quivering under the lash of injustice and insult to which she had been subjected. She longed for a breath of pure, fresh air; but there would be no enjoyment even in that now. She needed sympathy and help, if ever girl did, but where was she to find it? The women who most attracted her and who would have warmly welcomed her at any time—the women whom she would eagerly have gone to in her trouble—were practically denied to her. Mrs. Rayner in her quarrel had declared war against the cavalry, and Mrs. Stannard and Mrs. Ray, who had shown a disposition to welcome Nellie warmly, were no longer callers at the house. Mrs. Waldron, who was kind and motherly to the girl and loved to have her with her, was so embarrassed by Mrs. Rayner's determined snubs that she hardly knew how to treat the matter. She would no longer visit Mrs. Rayner informally, as had been her custom, yet she wanted the girl to come to her. If she went, Miss Travers well knew that on her return to the house she would be received by a volley of sarcasms about her preference for the society of people who were the avowed enemies of her benefactors. If she remained in the house, it was to become in person the target for her sister's undeserved sneers and censure. The situation was becoming simply unbearable. Twice she began and twice she tore to fragments the letter for which Mr. Van Antwerp was daily imploring, and this evening she once more turned and slowly sought her room, threw off her wraps, and took up her writing-desk. It was not yet dark. There was still light enough for her purpose, if she went close to the window. Every nerve was tingling with the sense of wrong and ignominy, every throb of her heart but intensified the longing for relief from the thraldom of her position. She saw only one path to lead her from such crushing dependence. There was his last letter, received only that day, urging, imploring her to leave Warrener forthwith. Mrs. Rayner had declared to him her readiness to bring her East provided she would fix an early date for the wedding. Was it not a future many a girl might envy? Was he not tender, faithful, patient, devoted as man could be? Had he not social position and competence? Was he not high-bred, courteous, refined,—a gentleman in all his acts and words? Why could she not love him, and be content? There on the desk lay a little scrap of note-paper; there lay her pen; a dozen words only were necessary. One moment she gazed longingly, wistfully, at the far-away, darkening heights of the Rockies, watching the last rose-tinted gleams on the snowy peaks; then with sudden impulse she seized her pen and drew the portfolio to the window-seat. As she did so, a soldierly figure came briskly down the walk; a pale, clear-cut face glanced up at her casement; a quick light of recognition and pleasure flashed in his eyes; the little forage-cap was raised with courteous grace, though the step never slackened, and Miss Travers felt that her cheek, too, was flushing again, as Mr. Hayne strode rapidly by. She stood there another moment, and then—it had grown too dark to write.

When Mrs. Rayner, after calling twice from the bottom of the stairs, finally went up into her room and impatiently pushed open the door, all was darkness except the glimmer from the hearth:

"Nellie, where are you?"

"Here," answered Miss Travers, starting up from the sofa. "I think I must have been asleep."

"Your head is hot as fire," said her sister, laying her firm white hand upon the burning forehead. "I suppose you are going to be downright ill, by way of diversion. Just understand one thing, Nellie: that doctor does not come into my house."

"What doctor?—not that I want one," asked Miss Travers, wearily.

"Dr. Pease, the post surgeon, I mean. Of course you have heard how he is mixing himself in my husband's affairs and making trouble with various people."

"I have heard nothing, Kate."

"I don't wonder your friends are ashamed to tell you. Things have come to a pretty pass, when officers are going around holding private meetings with enlisted men!"

"I hardly know the doctor at all, Kate, and cannot imagine what affairs of your husband's he can interfere with."

"It was he that put up Clancy to making the disturbance at Mr.

Hayne's last night and getting into the guard-house, and tried to prove that he had a right to go there and that the captain had no right to arrest him."

"Was Clancy trying to see Mr. Hayne?" asked Miss Travers, quickly.

"How should I know?" said her sister, pettishly. "He was drunk, and probably didn't know what he was doing."

"And Captain Rayner arrested him for—for trying to see Mr. Hayne?"

"Captain Rayner arrested him for being drunk and creating a disturbance, as it was his duty to arrest any soldier under such circumstances," replied her sister, with majestic wrath, "and I will not tolerate it that you should criticise his conduct."

"I have made no criticism, Kate. I have simply made inquiry; but I have learned what no one else could have made me believe."

"Nellie Travers, be careful what you say, or what you insinuate. What do you mean?"

"I mean, Kate, that it is my belief that there is something at the bottom of those stories of Clancy's strange talk when in the hospital. I believe he thinks he knows something which would turn all suspicion from Mr. Hayne to a totally different man. I believe that, for reasons which I cannot fathom, you are determined Mr. Hayne shall not see him or hear of it. It was you that sent Captain Rayner over there last night. Mrs. Clancy came here at tattoo, and, from the time she left, you were at the front door or window. You were the first to hear her cries, and came running in to tell the captain to go at once. Kate, *why* did you stand there listening from the time she left the kitchen, unless you expected to hear just what happened over there behind the company barracks?"

Mrs. Rayner would give no answer. Anger, rage, retaliation, all in turn were pictured on her furious face, but died away before the calm and unconquerable gaze in her sister's eyes. For the first time in her life Kate Rayner realized that her "baby Nell" had the stronger will of the two. For one instant she contemplated vengeance. A torrent of invective leaped readily to her lips. "Outrage," "ingrate," "insult," were the first three distinguishable epithets applied to her sister or her sister's words; then, "See if Mr. Van Antwerp will tolerate such conduct. I'll write this very day," was the impotent threat that followed; and finally, utterly defeated, thoroughly convinced that she was powerless against her sister's reckless love of "fair play at any price," she felt that her wrath was giving way to dismay, and turned and fled, lest Nellie should see the flag of surrender on her paling cheeks.

XIII.

Two nights after this, as Captain Buxton was sulkily going the rounds of the sentries he made a discovery which greatly enlivened an otherwise uneventful tour as officer of the day. It had been his general custom on such occasions to take the shortest way across the parade to the guard-house, make brief and perfunctory inspection there, then go on down the hill to the creek valley and successively visit the sentries around the stables. If the night were wet or cold, he went back the same way, ignoring the sentries at the coal-and store-sheds along Prairie Avenue. This was a sharply cold night, and very dark, but equally still. It was between twelve and one o'clock—nearer one than twelve—as he climbed the hill on his homeward way, and, instead of taking the short cut, turned northward and struck for the gloomy mass of sheds dimly discernible some forty yards from the crest. He had heard other officers speak of the fact that Mr. Hayne's lights were burning until long after midnight, and that, dropping in there, they had found him seated at his desk with a green shade over his eyes, studying by the aid of two student-lamps; "boning to be a general, probably," was the comment of captains of Buxton's calibre, who, having grown old in the service and in their own ignorance, were fiercely intolerant of lieutenants who strove to improve in professional reading instead of spending their time making out the company muster-rolls and clothing-accounts, as they should do. Buxton wanted to see for himself what the night-lights meant, and was plunging heavily ahead through the darkness, when suddenly brought to a stand by the sharp challenge of the sentry at the coal-shed. He whispered the mystic countersign over the levelled bayonet of the infantryman, swearing to himself at the regulation which puts an officer in such a "stand-and-deliver" attitude for the time being, and then, by way of getting square with the soldier for the sharply military way in which his duty as sentry had been performed, the captain proceeded to catechise him as to his orders. The soldier had been well taught, and knew all his "responses" by rote,—far better than Buxton, for that matter, as the latter was anything but an exemplar of perfection in tactics or sentry duty; but this did not prevent Buxton's snappishly telling him he was wrong in several points and contemptuously inquiring where he had learned such trash. The soldier promptly but respectfully responded that those were the exact instructions he had received at the adjutant's school, and Buxton knew from experience that he was getting on dangerous ground. He would have stuck to his point, however, in default of something else to find fault with, but that the crack of a whip, the crunching of hoofs, and a rattle of wheels out in the darkness quickly diverted his attention.

"What's that, sentry?" he sharply inquired.

"A carriage, sir. Leastwise, I think it must be."

"Why don't you know, sir? It must have been on your post."

"No, sir; it was 'way off my post. It drove up to Lieutenant Hayne's about half an hour ago."

"Where'd it come from?" asked the captain, eagerly.

"From town, sir, I suppose." And, leaving the sentry to his own reflections, which, on the whole, were not complimentary to his superior officer, Captain Buxton strode rapidly through the darkness to Lieutenant Hayne's quarters. Bright lights were still burning within, both on the ground-floor and in a room above. The sentries were just beginning the call of one o'clock when he reached the gate and halted, gazing inquisitively at the house front. Then he turned and listened to the rattle of wheels growing faint in the distance as the team drove away towards the prairie town. If Hayne had gone to town at that hour of the night it was a most unusual proceeding, and he had not the colonel's permission to absent himself from the post: of that the officer of the day was certain. Then, again, he would not have gone and left all his lights burning. No: that vehicle, whatever it was, had brought somebody out to see him,—somebody who proposed to remain several hours; otherwise the carriage would not have driven away. In confirmation of this theory, he heard voices, cheery voices, in laughing talk, and one of them made him prick up his ears. He heard the piano crisply trilling a response to light, skilful fingers. He longed for a peep within, and regretted that he had dropped Mr. Hayne from the list of his acquaintance. He recognized Hayne's shadow, presently, thrown by the lamp upon the curtained window, and wished that his visitor would come similarly into view. He heard the clink of glasses, and saw the shadow raise a wineglass to the lips, and Sam's Mongolian shape flitted across the screen, bearing a tray with similar suggestive objects. What meant this unheard-of conviviality on the part of the ascetic, the hermit, the midnight-oil-burner, the scholarly recluse of the garrison? Buxton stared with all his eyes and listened with all his ears, starting guiltily when he heard a martial footstep coming quickly up the path, and faced the intruder rather unsteadily. It was only the corporal of the guard, and he glanced at his superior, brought his fur-gauntleted hand in salute to the rifle on his shoulder, and passed on. The next moment

Buxton fairly gasped with amaze: he stared an instant at the window as though transfixed, then ran after the corporal, called to him in low, stealthy tone to come back noiselessly, drew him by the sleeve to the front of Hayne's quarters, and pointed to the parlor window. Two shadows were there now,—one easily recognizable as that of the young officer in his snugly-fitting undress uniform, the other slender, graceful, feminine.

"What do you make that other shadow to be, corporal?" he whispered, hoarsely and hurriedly. "*Look!*" And with that exclamation a shadowed arm seemed to encircle the slender form, the moustached image to bend low and mingle with the outlined luxuriance of tress that decked the other's head, and then, together, with clasping arms, the shadows moved from view.

"What was the other, corporal?" he repeated.

"Well, sir, I should say it was a young woman."

Buxton could hardly wait until morning to see Rayner. When he passed the latter's quarters half an hour later, all was darkness; though, had he but known it, Rayner was not asleep. He was at the house before guard-mounting, and had a confidential and evidently exciting talk with the captain; and when he went, just as the trumpets were sounding, these words were heard at the front door:

"She never left until after daylight, when the same rig drove her back to town. There was a stranger with her then."

That morning both Rayner and Buxton looked hard at Mr. Hayne when he came in to the *matinée*; but he was just as calm and quiet as ever, and, having saluted the commanding officer, took a seat by Captain Gregg and was soon occupied in conversation with him. Not a word was said by the officer of the day about the mysterious visitor to the garrison the previous night. With Captain Rayner, however, he was again in conversation much of the day, and to him, not to his successor as officer of the day, did he communicate all the details of the previous night's adventure and his theories thereanent.

Late that night, having occasion to step to his front door, convinced that he heard stealthy footsteps on his piazza, Mr. Hayne could see nobody in the darkness, but found his front gate open. He walked around his little house; but not a man was visible. His heart was full of a new and strange excitement that night, and, as before, he threw on his overcoat and furs and took a rapid walk around the garrison, gazing up into the starry heavens and drinking in great draughts of the pure, bracing air. Returning, he came down along the front of officers' row, and as he approached Rayner's quarters his eyes rested longingly upon the window he knew to be hers now; but all was darkness. As he rapidly neared the house, however, he became aware of two bulky figures at the gate, and, as he walked briskly past, recognized the overcoats as those of officers. One man was doubtless Rayner, the other he could not tell; for both, the instant they recognized his step, seemed to avert their heads. Once home again, he soon sought his room and pillow; but, long before he could sleep, again and again a sweet vision seemed to come to him: he *could not* shut out the thought of Nellie Travers,—of how she looked and what she said that very afternoon.

He had gone to call at Mrs. Waldron's soon after dark. He was at the piano, playing for her, when he became conscious that another lady had entered the room, and, turning, saw Nellie Travers. He rose and bowed to her, extending his hand as he did so, and knowing that his heart was thumping and his color rising as he felt the soft, warm touch of her slender fingers in his grasp. She, too, had flushed,—anyone could see it, though the lamps were not turned high, nor was the firelight strong.

"Miss Travers has come to take tea very quietly with me, Mr. Hayne,—she is so soon to return to the East,—and now I want you to stay and join us. No one will be here but the major; and we will have a lovely time with our music. You will, won't you?"

"So soon to return to the East!" How harsh, how strange and unwelcome, the words sounded! How they seemed to oppress him and prevent his reply! He stood a moment dazed and vaguely worried: he could not explain it. He looked from Mrs. Waldron's kind face to the sweet, flushed, lovely features there so near him, and something told him that he could never let them go and find even hope or content in life again. How, why had she so strangely come into his lonely life, radiant, beautiful, bewildering as some suddenly blazing star in the darkest corner of the heavens? Whence had come this strange power that enthralled him? He gazed into her sweet face, with its downcast, troubled eyes, and then, in bewilderment, turned to Mrs. Waldron:

"I—I had no idea Miss Travers was going East again just now. It seems only a few days since she came."

"It is over a month; but all the same this is a sudden decision. I knew nothing of it until yesterday.—You said Mrs. Rayner was better today, Nellie?"

"Yes, a little; but she is far from well. I think the captain will go, too, just as soon as he can arrange for leave of absence," was the low-toned answer. He had released, or rather she had withdrawn, her hand, and he still stood there, fascinated. His eyes could not quit their gaze. She going away?—She? Oh, it *could* not be! What—what would life become without the sight of that radiant face, that slender, graceful, girlish form?

"Is not this very unexpected?" he struggled to say. "I thought—I heard you were to spend several months here."

"It *was* so intended, Mr. Hayne; but my sister's health requires speedy change. She has been growing worse ever since we came, and she will not get well here."

"And when do you go?" he asked, blankly.

"Just as soon as we can pack; though we may wait two or three days for a—for a telegram."

There was a complete break in the conversation for a full quarter of a minute,—not such a long time in itself, but unconventionally long under such circumstances. Then Mrs. Waldron suddenly and remarkably arose:

"I'll leave you to entertain Mr. Hayne a few moments, Nellie. I am the slave of my cook, and she knows nothing of Mr. Hayne's being here to tea with us: so I must tell her and avert disaster."

And with this barefaced—statement on her lips and conscience, where it rested with equal lightness, that exemplary lady quitted the room. In the sanctity of the connubial chamber that evening, some hours later, she thus explained her action to her silent spouse:

"Right or wrong, I meant that those two young people should have a chance to know each other. I have been convinced for three weeks that she is being forced into this New York match, and for the last week that she is wretchedly unhappy. You say you believe him a wronged and injured man, only you can't prove it, and you have said that nothing could be too good for him in this life as a reward for all his bravery and fortitude under fearful trials. Then Nellie Travers isn't too good for him, sweet as she is, and I don't care who calls me a matchmaker."

But with Mrs. Waldron away the two appeared to have made but halting progress towards friendship. With all her outspoken pluck at school and at home, Miss Travers was strangely ill at ease and embarrassed now. Mr. Hayne was the first to gain self-control and to endeavor to bring the conversation back to a natural channel. It was a struggle; but he had grown accustomed to struggles. He could not imagine that a girl whom he had met only once or twice should have for him anything more than the vaguest and most casual interest. He well knew by this time how deep and vehement was the interest she had aroused in his heart; but it would never do to betray himself so soon. He strove to interest her in reference to the music she would hear, and to learn from her where they were going. This she answered. They would go no farther East than St. Louis or Chicago. They might go South as far as Nashville until mid-May. As for the summer, it would depend on the captain and his leave of absence. It was all vague and unsettled. Mrs. Rayner was so wretched that her husband was convinced that she ought to leave for the States as soon as possible, and of course "she" must go with her. All the gladness, brightness, vivacity he had seen and heard of as her marked characteristics seemed gone; and, yet, she wanted to speak with him,—wanted to be with him. What could be wrong? he asked himself. It was not until Mrs. Waldron's step was heard returning that she nerved herself to sudden, almost desperate, effort. She startled him with her vehemence:

"Mr. Hayne, there is something I must tell you before I go. If no opportunity occur, I'll write it."

And those were the words that had been haunting him all the evening, for they were not again alone, and he had no chance to ask a question. What *could* she mean? For years he had been living a life of stern self-denial; but long before his promotion the last penny of the obligation that, justly or otherwise, had been laid upon his shoulders was paid with interest. He was a man free and self-respecting, strong, resolute, and possessed of an independence that never would have been his had his life run on in the same easy, trusting, happy-go-lucky style in which he had spent the first two years of his army career. But in his isolation he had allowed himself no thought of anything that could for a moment distract him from the stern purpose to which he had devoted every energy. He would win back, command, *compel*, the respect of his comrades,—would bring to confusion those who had sought to pull him down; and until that stood accomplished he would know no other claim. In the exile of the mountain-station he saw no women but the wives of his senior officers; and they merely bowed when they happened to meet him: some did not even do that. Now at last he had met and yielded to the first of two conquerors before whom even the bravest and the strongest go down infallibly,—Love and Death. Suddenly, but irresistibly, the sweet face and thrilling tones of that young girl had seized and filled his heart, to the utter exclusion of every other passion; and just in proportion to the emptiness and yearning of his life before their meeting was the intensity of the love and longing that possessed him now. It was useless to try and analyze the suddenness and subtilty of its approach: the power of love had overmastered him. He could only realize that it was here and he must obey. Late into the morning hours he lay there, his brain whirling with its varied and bewildering emotions. Win her he must, or the blackness and desolation of the past five years would be as nothing compared with the misery of the years to come. Woo her he would, and not without hope, if ever woman's eyes gave proof of sympathy and trust. But now at last he realized that the time had come when for her sake—not for his—he must adopt a new course. Hitherto he had scorned and repelled all overtures that were not prefaced by an expression of belief in his utter innocence in the past. Hitherto he had chosen to live the life of an anchorite, and had abjured the society of women. Hitherto he had refused the half extended proffers of comrades who had sought to continue the investigation of a chain of circumstances that, complete, might have proved him a wronged and defrauded man. The missing links were not beyond recovery in skilful hands; but in the shock and horror which he felt on realizing that it was not only possible but certain that a jury of his comrade officers could deem him guilty of a low crime, he hid his face and turned from all. *Now* the time had come to reopen the case. He well knew that a revulsion of feeling had set in which nothing but his own stubbornness held in check. He knew that he had friends and sympathizers among officers high in rank. He had only a few days before heard from Major Waldron's lips a strong intimation that it was his duty to "come out of his shell" and reassert himself. "You must remember this, Hayne," said he: "you had been only two years in service when tried by court-martial. You were an utter stranger to every member of that court. There was nothing but the evidence to go upon, and that was all against you. The court was made up of officers from other regiments, and was at least impartial. The evidence was almost all from your own, and was presumably well founded. You would call no witnesses for defence. You made your almost defiant statement; refused counsel; refused advice; and what could the court do but convict and sentence? Had I been a member of the court I would have voted just as was done by the court; and yet I believe you now an utterly innocent man."

So, apparently, did the colonel regard him. So, too, did several of the officers of the cavalry. So, too, would most of the youngsters of his own regiment if he would only give them half a chance. In any event, the score was wiped out now; he could afford to take a wife if a woman learned to love him, and what wealth of tenderness and devotion was he not ready to lavish on one who would! But he would offer no one a tarnished name. First and foremost he must now stand up and fight that calumny,—"come out of his shell," as Waldron had said, and give people a chance to see what manner of man he was. God helping him, he would, and that without delay.

XIV.

"The best-laid schemes o' mice an' men gang aft a-gley." Mrs. Rayner, ill in mind and body, had yielded to her lord's entreaties and determined to start eastward with her sister without delay. Packing was already begun. Miss Travers had promised herself that she would within thirty-six hours put Mr. Hayne in possession of certain facts or theories which in her opinion bore strongly upon the "clearing up" of the case against him; Mr. Hayne had determined that he would see Major Waldron on the coming day and begin active efforts towards the restoration of his social rights; the doctor had about decided on a new project for inducing Clancy to unbosom himself of what he knew; Captain Rayner—tired of the long struggle—was almost ready to welcome anything which should establish his subaltern's innocence, and was on the point of asking for six months' leave just as soon as he had arranged for Clancy's final discharge from service: he had reasons for staying at the post until that Hibernian household was fairly and squarely removed; and Mrs. Clancy's plan was to take Mike to the distant East, "where she had frinds." There were other schemes and projects, no doubt, but these mainly concerned our leading characters, and one and all they were put to the right-about by the events of the following day.

The colonel, with his gruff second in command, Major Stannard, had been under orders for several days to proceed on this particular date to a large town a day's journey eastward by rail. A court-martial composed mainly of field-officers was ordered there to assemble for the trial of an old captain of cavalry whose propensity it was not so much to get drunk as never to get drunk without concomitant publicity and discovery. It was a rare thing for the old war-dog to take so much as a glass of wine; he went for months without it; but the instant he began to drink he was moved to do or say something disreputable, and that was the trouble now. He was an unlucky old trooper, who had risen from the lowest grades, fought with credit, and even, at times, commanded his regiment, during the war; but war records could not save him when he wouldn't save himself, and he had to go. The court was ordered, and the result was a foregone conclusion. The colonel, his adjutant, and Major Stannard were to drive to town during the afternoon and take the east-bound train, leaving Major Waldron in command of the post; but before guard-mounting a telegram was received which was sent from department headquarters the evening before, announcing that one of the officers detailed for the court was seriously ill, and directing Major Waldron to take his place. So it resulted in the post being left to the command of the senior captain present for duty; and that man was Captain Buxton. He had never had so big a command before in all his life.

Major Waldron of course had to go home and make his preparations. Mr. Hayne, therefore, had brief opportunity to speak with him. It was seen, however, that they had a short talk together on the major's piazza, and that when they parted the major shook him warmly and cordially by the hand. Rayner, Buxton, Ross, and some juniors happened to be coming down along the walk at the moment, and, seeing them, as though with pointed meaning the major called out, so that all could hear,—

"By the way, Hayne, I wish you would drop in occasionally while I'm gone and take Mrs. Waldron out for a walk or drive: my horses are always at your service. And—a—I'll write to you about that matter the moment I've had a chance to talk with the colonel,—tomorrow, probably."

And Hayne touched his cap in parting salute, and went blithely off with brightened eye and rising color.

Buxton glowered after him a moment, and conversation suddenly ceased in their party. Finally he blurted out,—

"Strikes me your major might do a good deal better by himself and his regiment by standing up for its *morale* and discipline than by openly flaunting his favoritism for convicts in our faces. If I were in your regiment I'd cut *him*."

"You wouldn't have to," muttered one of the group to his neighbor: "the cut would have been on the other side long ago." And the speaker was Buxton's own subaltern.

Rayner said nothing. His eyes were troubled and anxious, and he looked after Hayne with an expression far more wearied than vindictive.

"The major is fond of music, captain," said Mr. Ross, with mischievous intent. "He hasn't been to the club since the night you sang 'Eileen Alanna.' That was about the time Hayne's piano came."

"Yes," put in Foster, "Mrs. Waldron says he goes and owls Hayne now night after night just to hear him play."

"It would be well for him, then, if he kept a better guard on Mr. Hayne's *other* visitors," said Buxton, with a black scowl. "I don't know how you gentlemen in the Riflers look upon such matters, but in the ___th the man who dared to introduce a woman of the town into his quarters would be kicked out in short order."

"You don't mean to say that anybody accuses Hayne of that, do you?" asked Ross, in amaze.

"I do,—*just* that. Only, I say this to you, it has but just come to light, and only one or two know it. To prove it positively he's got to be allowed more rope; for he got her out of the way last time before we could clinch the matter. If he suspects it is known he won't repeat it; if kept to ourselves he will probably try it again,—and be caught. Now I charge you all to regard this as confidential."

"But, Captain Buxton," said Ross, "this is so serious a matter that I don't like to believe it. Who can prove such a story?"

"Of course not, Mr. Ross. You are quite ready to treat a man as a thief, but can't believe he'll do another thing that is disreputable. That is characteristic of your style of reasoning," said Buxton, with biting sarcasm.

"You can't wither me with contempt, Captain Buxton. I have a right to my opinion, and I have known Mr. Hayne for years, and if I *did* believe him guilty of one crime five years ago I'm not so ready to believe him guilty of another now. This isn't—isn't like Hayne."

"No, of course not, as I said before. Now, will you tell me, Mr. Ross, just why Mr. Hayne chose that ramshackle old shanty out there on the prairie, all by himself, unless it was to be where he could have his chosen companions with him at night and no one be the wiser?"

"I don't pretend to fathom his motives, sir; but I don't believe it was for any such purpose as you seem to think."

"In other words, you think I'm circulating baseless scandal, do you?"

"I have said nothing of the kind; and I protest against your putting words into my mouth I never used."

"You intimated as much, anyhow, and you plainly don't believe it."

"Well, I don't believe—that is, I don't see how it could happen."

"Couldn't the woman drive out from town after dark, send the carriage back, and have it call for her again in the morning?" asked Buxton.

"Possibly. Still, it isn't a proved fact that a woman spent the night at Hayne's, even if a carriage was seen coming out. You've got hold of some Sudsville gossip, probably," replied Ross.

"I have, have I? By God, sir, I'll teach you better manners before we get through with this question. Do you know who saw the carriage, and who saw the woman, both at Hayne's quarters?"

"Certainly I don't! What I don't understand is how you should have been made the recipient of the story."

"Mr. Ross, just govern your tongue, sir, and remember you are speaking to your superior officer, and don't venture to treat my statements with disrespect hereafter. *I saw it myself!*"

"*You!*" gulped Ross, while amaze and incredulity shot across his startled face.

"You!" exclaimed others of the group, in evident astonishment and dismay. Rayner alone looked unchanged. It was no news to him, while to every other man in the party it was a shock. Up to that instant the prevailing belief had been, with Ross, that Buxton had found some garrison gossip and was building an edifice thereon. His positive statement, however, was too much for the most incredulous.

"Now what have you to say?" he asked, in rude triumph.

There was no answer for a moment; then Ross spoke:

"Of course, Captain Buxton, I withdraw any expression of doubt. It never occurred to me that you could have seen it. May I ask when and how?"

"The last time I was officer of the day, sir; and Captain Rayner is my witness as to the time. Others, whom I need not mention, saw it with me. There is no mistake, sir. The woman was there." And Buxton stood enjoying the effect.

Ross looked white and dazed. He turned slowly away, hesitated, looked back, then exclaimed,—

"You are sure it was—it was not someone that had a right to be there?"

"How could it be?" said Buxton, gruffly. "You know he has not an acquaintance in town, or here, who could be with him there at night."

"Does the commanding officer know of it?" asked Mr. Royce, after a moment's silence.

"*I* am the commanding officer, Mr. Royce," said Buxton, with majestic dignity,—"at least I will be after twelve o'clock; and you may depend upon it, gentlemen, this thing will not occur while I am in command without its receiving the exact treatment it deserves. Remember, now, not a word of this to anybody. You are as much interested as I am in bringing to justice a man who will disgrace his uniform and his regiment and insult every lady in the garrison by such an act. This sort of thing of course will run him out of the service for good and all. We simply have to be sure of our ground and make the evidence conclusive. Leave that to me the next time it happens. I repeat, say nothing of this to anyone."

But Rayner had already told his wife.

Just as Major Waldron was driving off to the station that bright April afternoon and his carriage was whirling through the east gate, the driver caught sight of Lieutenant Hayne running up Prairie Avenue, waving his hand and shouting to him. He reined in his spirited bays with some difficulty, and Hayne finally caught up with them.

"What is it, Hayne?" asked Waldron, with kindly interest, leaning out of his carriage.

"They will be back tonight, sir. Here is a telegram that has just reached me."

"I can't tell you how sorry I am not to be here to welcome them; but Mrs. Waldron will be delighted, and she will come to call the moment you let her know. Keep them till I get back, if you possibly can."

"Ay, ay, sir. Good-by."

"Good-by, Hayne. God bless you, and—good luck!"

A little later that afternoon Mrs. Rayner had occasion to go into her sister's room. It was almost sunset, and Nellie had been summoned down-stairs to see visitors. Both the ladies were busy with their packing,—Mrs. Rayner, as became an invalid, superintending, and Miss Travers, as became the junior, doing all the work. It was rather trying to pack all the trunks and receive visitors of both sexes at odd hours. Some of her garrison acquaintances would have been glad to come and help, but those whom she would have welcomed were not agreeable to the lady of the house, and those the lady of the house would have chosen were not agreeable to her. The relations between the sisters were somewhat strained and unnatural, and had been growing more and more so for several days past. Mrs. Rayner's desk was already packed away. She wanted to send a note, and bethought her of her sister's portfolio. Opening it, she drew out some paper and envelopes, and with the latter came an envelope sealed and directed. One glance at its superscription sent the blood to her cheek and fire to her eye. Was it possible? Was it credible? Her pet, her baby sister, her pride and delight,—until she found her stronger in will,—her proud-spirited, truthful Nell, was beyond question corresponding with Lieutenant Hayne! Here was a note addressed to him. How many more might not have been exchanged? Ruthlessly now she explored the desk, searching for something from him, but her scrutiny was vain. Oh, what could she say, what could she do, to convey to her erring sister an adequate sense of the extent of her displeasure? How could she bring her to realize the shame, the guilt, the scandal, of her course? She, Nellie Travers, the betrothed wife of Steven Van

Antwerp, corresponding secretly with this—this scoundrel, whose past, crime-laden as it had been, was as nothing compared to the present with its degradation of vice? Ah! she had it! What would ever move her as that could and must?

When the trumpets rang out their sunset call and the boom of the evening gun shook the windows in Fort Warrener and Nellie Travers came running up-stairs again to her room, she started at the sight that met her eyes. There stood Mrs. Rayner, like Juno in wrath inflexible, glaring at her from the commanding height of which she was so proud, and pointing in speechless indignation at the little note that lay upon the open portfolio.

For a moment neither spoke. Then Miss Travers, who had turned very white, but whose blue eyes never flinched and whose lips were set and whose little foot was tapping the carpet ominously, thus began:

"Kate, I do not recognize your right to overhaul my desk or supervise my correspondence."

"Understand this first, Cornelia," said Mrs. Rayner, who hated the baptismal name as much as did her sister, and used it only when she desired to be especially and desperately impressive: "I found it by accident. I never dreamed of such a possibility as this. I never, even after what I have seen and heard, could have believed you guilty of this; but, now that I have found it, I have the right to ask, what are its contents?"

"I decline to tell you."

"Do you deny my right to inquire?"

"I will not discuss that question now. The other is far graver. I will not tell you, Kate, except this: there is no word there that an engaged girl should not write."

"Of that I mean to satisfy myself, or rather—"

"You will not open it, Kate. No! Put that letter down! You have never known me to prevaricate in the faintest degree, and you have no excuse for doubting. I will furnish a copy of that for Mr. Van Antwerp at any time; but you cannot see it."

"You still persist in your wicked and unnatural intimacy with that man, even after all that I have told you. Now for the last time hear me: I have striven not to tell you this; I have striven not to sully your thoughts by such a revelation; but, since nothing else will check you, tell it I must, and what I tell you my husband told me in sacred confidence, though soon enough it will be a scandal to the whole garrison."

And when darkness settled down on Fort Warrener that starlit April evening and the first warm breeze from the south came sighing about the casements and one by one the lights appeared along officers' row, there was no light in Nellie Travers's window. The little note lay in ashes on the hearth, and she, with burning, shame-stricken cheeks, with a black, scorching, gnawing pain at her heart, was hiding her face in her pillow.

And yet it was a jolly evening, after all,—that is, for some hours and for some people. As Mrs. Rayner and her sister were so soon to go, probably by the morrow's train if their section could be secured, the garrison had decided to have an informal dance as a suitable farewell. Their announcement of impending departure had come so suddenly and unexpectedly that there was no time to prepare anything elaborate, such as a german with favors, etc.; but good music and an extemporized supper could be had without trouble. The colonel's wife and most of the cavalry ladies, on consultation, had decided that it was the very thing to do, and the young officers took hold with a will: they were always ready for a dance. Now that Mrs. Rayner was really going, the quarrel should be ignored, and the ladies would all be as pleasant to her as though nothing had happened,—provided, of course, she dropped her absurd airs of injured womanhood and behaved with courtesy. The colonel had had a brief talk with his better half before starting for the train, and suggested that it was very probable that Mrs. Rayner had seen the folly of her ways by that time,—the captain certainly had been behaving as though he regretted the estrangement,—and if encouraged by a "let's-drop-the-whole-thing" sort of manner she would be glad to reciprocate. He felt far less anxiety herein than he did in leaving the post to the command of Captain Buxton. So scrupulously had he been courteous to that intractable veteran that Buxton had no doubt in his own mind that the colonel looked upon him as the model officer of the regiment. It was singularly unfortunate that he should have to be left in command, but his one or two seniors among the captains were away on long leave, and there was no help for it. The colonel, seriously disquieted, had a few words of earnest talk with him before leaving the post, cautioning him so particularly not to interfere with any of the established details and customs that Buxton got very much annoyed, and showed it.

"If your evidence were not imperatively necessary before this court, I declare I believe I'd leave you behind," said the colonel to his adjutant. "There is no telling what mischief Captain Buxton won't do if left to himself."

It must have been near midnight, and the hop was going along beautifully, and Captain Rayner, who was officer of the day, was just escorting his wife in to supper, and Nellie, although looking a trifle tired and pale, was chatting brightly with a knot of young officers when a corporal of the guard came to the door: "The commanding officer's compliments, and he desires to see the officer of the day at once."

There was a general laugh. "Isn't that Buxton all over? The colonel would never think of sending for an officer in the dead of night, except for a fire or alarm; but old Bux. begins putting on frills the moment he gets a chance. Thank God, *I'm* not on guard tonight!" said Mr. Royce.

"What *can* he want with you?" asked Mrs. Rayner, pettishly. "The idea of one captain ordering another around like this!"

"I'll be back in five minutes," said Rayner, as he picked up his sword and disappeared.

But ten minutes—fifteen—passed, and he came not. Mrs. Rayner grew worried, and Mr. Blake led her out on the rude piazza to see what they could see, and several others strolled out at the same time. The music had ceased, and the night air was not too cold. Not a soul was in sight out on the starlit parade. Not an unusual sound was heard. There was nothing to indicate the faintest trouble; and yet Captain Buxton, the commanding officer, had been called out by his "striker" or soldier-servant before eleven o'clock, had not returned at all, and in little over half an hour had sent for the officer of the day. What did it mean? Questioning and talking thus among themselves, somebody said, "Hark!" and held up a warning hand.

Faint, far, muffled, there sounded on the night air a shot, then a woman's scream; then all was still.

"Mrs. Clancy again!" said one.

"That was not Mrs. Clancy: 'twas a far different voice," answered Blake, and tore away across the parade as fast as his long legs would carry him.

"Look! The guard are running too!" cried Mrs. Waldron. "What can it be?" And, sure enough, the gleam of the rifles could be seen as the men ran rapidly away in the direction of the east gate. Mrs. Rayner had grown ghastly, and was looking at Miss Travers, who with white lips and clinched hands stood leaning on one of the wooden posts and gazing with all her eyes across the dim level. Others came hurrying out from the hall. Other young officers ran in pursuit of the first starters. "What's the matter? What's happened?" were the questions that flew from lip to lip.

"I—I must go home," faltered Mrs. Rayner. "Come, Nellie!"

"Oh, don't go, Mrs. Rayner. It can't be anything serious."

But, even as they urged, a man came running towards them.

"Is the doctor here?" he panted.

"Yes. What's the trouble?" asked Dr. Pease, as he squeezed his burly form through the crowded doorway.

"You're wanted, sir. Loot'nant Hayne's shot; an' Captain Rayner he's hurt too, sir."

XV.

Straight as an arrow Mr. Blake had sped across the parade, darted through the east gate, and, turning, had arrived breathless at the wooden porch of Hayne's quarters. Two bewildered-looking members of the guard were at the door. Blake pushed his way through the little hall-way and into the dimly-lighted parlor, where a strange scene met his eyes: Lieutenant Hayne lay senseless and white upon the lounge across the room; a young and pretty woman, singularly like him in feature and in the color of her abundant tresses, was kneeling beside him, chafing his hands, imploring him to speak,—to look at her,—unmindful of the fact that her feet were bare and that only a loose wrapper was thrown over her white night-dress; Captain Rayner was seated in a chair, deathly white, and striving to stanch the blood that flowed from a deep gash in his temple and forehead; he seemed still stunned as by the force of the blow that had felled him; and Buxton, speechless with amaze and heaven only knows what other emotions, was glaring at a tall, athletic stranger who, in stocking-feet, undershirt, and trousers, held by three frightened-looking soldiers and covered by the carbine of a fourth, was hurling defiance and denunciation at the commanding officer. A revolver lay upon the floor at the feet of a corporal of the guard, who was groaning in pain. A thin veil of powder-smoke floated through the room. As Blake leaped in,—his cavalry shoulder-knots and helmet-cords gleaming in the light,—a flash of recognition shot into the stranger's eyes, and he curbed his fearful excitement and stopped short in his wrath.

"What devil's work is this?" demanded Blake, glaring intuitively at Buxton.

"These people resisted my guards, and had to take the consequences," said Buxton, with surly—yet shaken—dignity.

"What were the guards doing here? What, in God's name, are you doing here?" demanded Blake, forgetful of all consideration of rank and command in the face of such evident catastrophe.

"I *ordered* them here,—to enter and search."

A pause.

"Search what?—what for?"

"For—a woman I had reason to believe he had brought out here from town."

"*What?* You infernal idiot! Why, she's his own sister, and this gentleman's wife!"

The silence, broken only by the hard breathing of some of the excited men and the moaning cry of the woman, was for a moment intense.

"Isn't this Mr. Hurley?" asked Blake, suddenly, as though to make sure, and turning one instant from his furious glare at his superior officer. The stranger, still held, though no longer struggling, replied between his set teeth,—

"Certainly. I've told him so."

"By heaven, Buxton, is there no limit to your asininity? What fearful work will you do next?"

"I'll arrest *you*, sir, if you speak another disrespectful word!" thundered Buxton, recovering consciousness that as commanding officer he could defend himself against Blake's assault.

"Do it and be hanged, you know what I *would* say if a lady were not present! Do it, if you think you can stand having this thing ventilated by a court. Pah! I can't waste words on you. Who's gone for the doctor? Here, you men, let go of Mr. Hurley now. Help me, Mr. Hurley, please. Get your wife back to her room. Bring me some water, one of you." And with that he was bending over Hayne and unbuttoning the fatigue-uniform in which he was still dressed. Another moment, and the doctor had come in, and with him half the young officers of the garrison. Rayner was led away to his own quarters. Buxton, dazed and frightened now, ordered the guards back to their post, and stood pondering over the enormity of his blunder. No one spoke to him or paid the faintest attention other than to elbow him out of the way occasionally. The doctor never so much as noticed him. Blake had briefly recounted the catastrophe to those who first arrived, and as the story went from mouth to mouth it grew no better for Buxton. Once he turned short on Mr. Foster and in aggrieved and sullen tone remarked,—

"I thought you fellows in the Riflers said he had no relations."

"We weren't apt to be invited to meet them if he had; but I don't know that anybody was in position to know anything about it. What's that got to do with this affair, I'd like to hear?"

At last somebody took him home. Mrs. Waldron, meantime, had arrived and been admitted to Mrs. Hurley's room. The doctor refused to go to Captain Rayner's, even when a messenger came from Mrs. Rayner herself. He referred her to his assistant, Dr. Grimes. Hayne had regained consciousness, but was sorely shaken. He had been floored by a blow from the butt of a musket; but the report that he was shot proved happily untrue. His right hand still lay near the hilt of his light sword: there was little question that he had raised his weapon against a superior officer and would have used it with telling effect.

Few people slept that night along officers' row. Never had Warrener heard of such excitement. Buxton knew not what to do. He paced the floor in agony of mind, for he well understood that there was no shirking the responsibility. From beginning to end he was the cause of the whole catastrophe. He had gone so far as to order his corporal to fire, and he knew it could be proved against him. Thank God, the perplexed corporal had shot high, and the other men, barring the one who had saved Rayner from a furious lunge of the lieutenant's sword, had used their weapons as gingerly and reluctantly as possible. At the very least, he knew, an investigation and fearful scandal must come of it. Night though it was, he sent for the acting adjutant and several of his brother captains, and, setting refreshments before them, besought their advice. He was still commanding officer *de jure*, but he had lost all stomach for its functions. He would have been glad to send for Blake and beg his pardon for submitting to his insubordinate and abusive language, if that course could have stopped inquiry; but he well knew that the whole thing would be noised abroad in less than no time. At first he thought to give orders against the telegraph-operator's sending any messages concerning the matter; but that would have been only a temporary hinderance: he could not control the instruments and operators in town, only three miles away. He almost wished he had been knocked down, shot, or stabbed in the *mêlée*; but he had kept in the rear when the skirmish began, and Rayner and the corporal were the sufferers. They had been knocked "endwise" by Mr. Hurley's practised fists after Hayne was struck down by the corporal's musket. It was the universal sentiment among the officers of the ___th as they scattered to their homes that Buxton had "wound himself up this time, anyhow;" and no one had any sympathy for him,—not one. The very best light in which he could tell the story only showed the affair as a flagrant and inexcusable outrage.

Captain Rayner, too, was in fearful plight. He had simply obeyed orders; but all the old story of his persecution of Hayne would now be revived; all men would see in his participation in the affair only additional reason to adjudge him cruelly persistent in his hatred of the young officer, and, in view of the utter ruthlessness and wrong of this assault, would be more than ever confident of the falsity of his position in the original case. As he was slowly led up-stairs to his room and his tearful wife and silent sister-in-law bathed and cleansed his wound, he saw with frightful clearness how the crush of circumstances was now upon him and his good name. Great heaven! how those words of Hayne's five years before rang, throbbed, burned, beat like trip-hammers through his whirling brain! It seemed as though they followed him and his fortunes like a curse. He sat silent, stunned, awe-stricken at the force of the calamity that had befallen him. How could he ever induce an officer and a gentleman to believe that he was no instigator in this matter?—that it was all Buxton's doing, Buxton's low imagination that had conceived the possibility of such a crime on the part of Mr. Hayne, and Buxton's blundering, bull-headed abuse of authority that had capped the fatal climax? It was some time before his wife could get him to speak at all. She was hysterically bemoaning the fate that had brought them into contact with such people, and from time to time giving vent to the comforting assertion that never had there been a cloud on their domestic or regimental sky until that wretch had been assigned to the Riflers. She knew from the hurried and guarded explanations of Dr. Grimes and one or two young officers who helped Rayner home that the fracas had occurred at Mr. Hayne's,—that there had been a mistake for which her husband was not responsible, but that Captain Buxton was entirely to blame. But her husband's ashen face told her a story of something far deeper: she knew that now he was involved in fearful trouble, and, whatever may have been her innermost thoughts, it was the first and irresistible impulse to throw all the blame upon her scapegoat. Miss Travers, almost as pale and quite as silent as the captain, was busying herself in helping her sister; but she could with difficulty restrain her longing to bid her be silent. She, too, had endeavored to learn from her escort on their hurried homeward rush across the parade what the nature of the disturbance had been. She, too, had suggested Clancy, but the officer by her side set his teeth as he replied that he wished it had been Clancy. She had heard, too, the message brought by a cavalry trumpeter from Mr. Blake: he wanted Captain Ray to come to Mr. Hayne's as soon as he had seen Mrs. Ray safely home, and would he please ask Mrs. Stannard to come with him at the same time? Why should Mr. Blake want Mrs. Stannard at Mr. Hayne's? She saw Mr. Foster run up and speak a few words to Mrs. Waldron, and heard that lady reply, "Certainly. I will go with you now." What could it mean? At last, as she was returning to her sister's room after a moment's absence, she heard a question at which her heart stood still. It was Mrs. Rayner who asked,—

"But the creature was there, was she not?"

The answer sounded more like a moan of anguish:

"The creature was his sister. It was her husband who—"

But, as Captain Rayner buried his battered face in his hands at this juncture, the rest of the sentence was inaudible. Miss Travers had heard quite enough, however. She stood there one moment, appalled, dropped upon the floor the bandage she had been making, turned and sought her room, and was seen no more that night.

Over the day or two that followed this affair the veil of silence may best be drawn, in order to give time for the sediment of truth to settle through the whirlpool of stories in violent circulation. The colonel came back on the first train after the adjournment of the court, and could hardly wait for that formality. Contrary to his custom of "sleeping on" a question, he was in his office within half an hour after his return to the post, and from that time until near tattoo was busily occupied taking the statements of the active participants in the affair. This was three days after its occurrence; and Captain Rayner, though up and able to be about, had not left his quarters. Mrs. Rayner had abandoned her trip to the East, for the present at least. Mr. Hayne still lay weak and prostrate in his darkened room, attended hourly by Dr. Pease, who feared brain-fever, and nursed assiduously by Mrs. Hurley, for whom Mrs. Waldron, Mrs. Stannard, and many other ladies in the garrison could not do enough to content themselves. Mr. Hurley's wrist was badly sprained and in a sling; but the colonel went purposely to call upon him and to shake his other hand, and he begged to be permitted to see Mrs. Hurley, who came in pale and soft-eyed and with a gentle demeanor that touched the colonel more than he could tell. Her cheek flushed for a moment as he bent low over her hand and told her how bitterly he regretted that his absence from the post had resulted in so grievous an experience: it was not the welcome he and his regiment would have given her had they known of her intended visit. To Mr. Hurley he briefly said that he need not fear but that full justice would be meted out to the instigator or instigators of the assault; but, as a something to make partial amends for their suffering, he said that nothing now could check the turn of the tide in their brother's favor. All the cavalry officers except Buxton, all the infantry officers except Rayner, had already been to call upon him since the night of the occurrence, and had striven to show how distressed they were over the outrageous blunders of their temporary commander. Buxton had written a note expressive of a desire to see him and "explain," but was informed that explanations from him simply aggravated the injury; and Rayner, crushed and humiliated, was fairly in hiding in his room, too sick at heart to want to see anybody, and waiting for the action of the authorities in the confident expectation that nothing less than court-martial and disgrace would be his share of the outcome. He would gladly have resigned and gone at once, but that would have been resigning under virtual charges: he *had* to stay, and his wife had to stay with him, and Nellie with her. By this time Nellie Travers did not want to go. She had but one thought now,—to make amends to Mr. Hayne for the wrong her thoughts had done him. It was time for Mr. Van Antwerp to come to the wide West and look after his interests; but Mrs. Rayner had ceased to urge, while he continued to implore her to bring Nellie East at once. Almost any man as rich and independent as Steven Van Antwerp would have gone to the scene and settled matters for himself. Singularly enough, this one solution of the problem seemed never to occur to him as feasible.

Meantime, the colonel had patiently unravelled the threads and had brought to light the whole truth and nothing but the truth. It made a singularly simple story, after all but that was so much the worse for Buxton. The only near relation Mr. Hayne had in the world was this one younger sister, who six years before had married a manly, energetic fellow, a civil engineer in the employ of an Eastern railway. During Hayne's "mountain-station" exile Hurley had brought his wife to Denver, where far better prospects awaited him. He won promotion in his profession, and was now one of the principal engineers employed by a road running new lines through the Colorado Rockies. Journeying to Salt Lake, he came around by way of Warrener, so that his wife and he might have a look at the brother she had not seen in years. Their train was due there early in the afternoon, but was blocked by drifts and did not reach the station until late at night. There they found a note from him begging them to take a carriage they would find waiting for them and come right out and spend the night at his quarters: he would send them back in abundant time to catch the westward train in the morning. He could not come in, because that involved the necessity of asking his captain's permission, and they knew his relations with that captain. It was her shadow Buxton had seen on the window-screen; and as none of Buxton's acquaintances had ever mentioned that Hayne had any relations, and as Hayne, in fact, had had no one for years to talk to about his personal affairs, nobody but himself and the telegraph-operator at the post really knew of their sudden visit. Buxton, being an unmitigated cad, had put the worst interpretation on his discovery, and, in his eagerness to clinch the evidence of conduct unbecoming an officer and a gentleman upon Mr. Hayne, had taken no wise head into his confidence. Never dreaming that the shadow could be that of a blood-relation, never doubting that a fair, frail companion from the frontier town was the explanation of Mr. Hayne's preference for that out-of-the way house and late hours, he stated his discovery to Rayner as a positive fact, going so far as to say that his sentries had recognized her as she drove away in the carriage. If he had not been an ass as well as a cad, he would have interviewed the driver of the carriage; but he had jumped at his theory, and his sudden elevation to the command of the post gave him opportunity to carry out his virtuous determination that no such goings-on should disgrace his administration. He gave instructions to certain soldier clerks and "daily-duty" men employed in the quartermaster, commissary, and ordnance offices along Prairie Avenue to keep their eyes open and let him know of any visitors coming out to Hayne's by night, and if a lady came in a carriage he was to be called at once. Mr. Hurley promised that on their return from Salt Lake they would come back by way of Warrener and spend two days with Hayne, since only an hour or two had they enjoyed of his company on their way West; and the very day that the officers went off to the court came the telegram saying the Hurleys would arrive that evening. Hayne had already talked over their prospective visit with Major Waldron, and the latter had told his wife; but all intercourse of a friendly character was at an end between them and the Rayners and Buxtons; there were no more gossipy chats among the ladies. Indeed, it so happened that only to one or two people had Mrs. Waldron had time to mention that Mr. Hayne's sister was coming, and neither the Rayners nor Buxtons had heard of it; neither had Nellie Travers, for it was after the evening of her last visit that Mrs. Waldron was told.

Hayne ran with his telegram to the major, and the latter had introduced himself and Major Stannard to Mrs. Hurley when, after a weary wait of some hours, the train arrived. Blake, too, was there, on the lookout for some friends, and he was presented to Mrs. Hurley while her husband was attending to some matters about the baggage. The train went on eastward, carrying the field-officers with it. Blake had to go with his friends back to the post, and Mr. and Mrs. Hurley, after the former had attended to some business and seen some railway associates of his at the hotel, took the carriage they had had before and drove out to the garrison, where Private Schweinkopf saw the lady rapturously welcomed by Lieutenant Hayne and escorted into the house, while Mr. Hurley remained settling with the driver out in the darkness. It was not long before the commanding officer *pro tem*, was called from the hop-room, where the dance was going on delightfully, and notified that the mysterious visitor had again appeared, with evident intention of spending the night, as the carriage had returned to town. "Why, certainly," reasoned Buxton. "It's the very night he would choose, since everybody will be at the hop: no one will be apt to interfere, and everybody will be unusually drowsy and less inclined to take notice in the morning." Here was ample opportunity for a brilliant stroke of work. He would first satisfy himself she was there, then surround the house with sentries so that she could not escape, while he, with the officer of the day and the corporal of the guard, entered the house and confronted him and her. *That* would wind up Mr. Hayne's career beyond question: nothing short of dismissal could result. Over he went, full of his project, listened at Hayne's like the eaves-dropping sneak he was, saw again the sha- dow of the graceful form and heard the silvery, happy laugh, and then it was he sent for Rayner. It was near midnight when he led his forces to the attack. A light was now burning in the second story, which he thought must be Sam's; but the lights had been turned low in the parlor, and the occupants had disappeared from sight and hearing. By inquiry he had ascertained that Hayne's bedroom was just back of the parlor. A man was stationed at the back door, others at the sides, with orders to arrest any one who attempted to escape; then softly he stepped to the front door, telling Rayner to follow him, and the corporal of the guard to follow both. To his surprise, the door was unlocked, and a light was burning in the hall. Never knocking, he stepped in, marched through the hall into the parlor, which was empty, and, signalling "Come on" to his fol- lowers, crossed the parlor and seized the knob of the bedroom door. It was locked. Rayner, looking white and worried, stood just behind him, and the corporal but a step farther back. Before Buxton could knock and demand admission, which was his inten- tion, quick footsteps came flying down the stairs from the second story, and the trio wheeled about in surprise, to find Mr. Hayne, dressed in his fatigue uniform, standing at the threshold and star- ing at them with mingled astonishment, incredulity, and indigna- tion. A sudden light seemed to dawn upon him as he glanced from one to the other. With a leap like a cat he threw himself upon Buxton, hurled him back, and stood at the closed door confronting them with blazing eyes and clinching fists.

"Open that door, sir!" cried Buxton. "You have a woman hidden there. Open, or stand aside."

"You hounds! I'll kill the first man who dares enter!" was the furious answer; and Hayne had snatched from the wall his long infantry sword and flashed the blade in the lamplight. Rayner made a step forward, half irresolute. Hayne leaped at him like a tiger. "Fire! Quick!" shouted Buxton, in wild excitement. Bang! went the carbine, and the bullet crashed through the plaster overhead, and, seeing the gleaming steel at his superior's throat, the corporal had sent the heavy butt crashing upon the lieutenant's skull only just in time: there would have been murder in another second. The next instant he was standing on his own head in the corner, seeing a multitude of twinkling, whirling stars, from the midst of which Captain Rayner was reeling backward over a chair and a number of soldiers were rushing upon a powerful picture of furious manhood,—a stranger in shirt-sleeves, who had leaped from the bedroom.

Told as it was—as it had to be—all over the department, there seemed but one thing to say, and that referred to Buxton: "Well! *isn't* he a phenomenal ass?"

XVI.

Mr. Hayne was up and around again. The springtime was coming, and the prairie roads were good and dry, and the doctor had told him he must live in the open air awhile and ride and walk and drive. He stood in no want of "mounts," for three or four of his cavalry friends were ready to lend him a saddle-horse any day. Mr. and Mrs. Hurley, after making many pleasant acquaintances, had gone on to Denver, and Captain Buxton was congratulating himself that he, at least, had not run foul of the engineer's powerful fists. Buxton was not in arrest, for the case had proved a singular "poser." It occurred during the temporary absence of the colonel: *he* could not well place the captain under arrest for things he had done when acting as post commander. In obedience to his orders from department headquarters, he made his report of the affair, and indicated that Captain Buxton's conduct had been inexcusable. Rayner had done nothing but, as was proved, reluctantly obey the captain's orders, so he could not be tried. Hayne, who had committed one of the most serious crimes in the military catalogue,—that of drawing and raising a weapon against an officer who was in discharge of his duty (Rayner),—had the sympathy of the whole command, and nobody would prefer charges against him. The general decided to have the report go up to division headquarters, and thence it went with its varied comments and endorsements to Washington: and now a court of inquiry was talked of. Meantime, poor bewildered Buxton was let severely alone. What made him utterly miserable was the fact that in his own regiment, the ___th, nobody spoke of it except as something that everybody knew was sure to happen the moment he got in command. If it hadn't been that 'twould have been something else. The only certainty was that Buxton would never lose a chance of making an ass of himself. Instead of being furious with him, the whole regiment—officers and men—simply ridiculed and laughed at him. He had talked of preferring charges against Blake for insubordination, and asked the adjutant what he thought of it. It was the first time he had spoken to the adjutant for weeks, and the adjutant rushed out of the office to tell the crowd to come in and "hear Buxton's latest." It began to look as though nothing serious would ever come of the affair, until Rayner reappeared and people saw how very ill he was. Dr. Pease had been consulted; and it was settled that he as well as his wife must go away for several months and have complete rest and change. It was decided that they would leave by the 1st of May. All this Mr. Hayne heard through his kind friend Mrs. Waldron.

One day when he first began to sit up, and before he had been out at all, she came and sat with him in his sunshiny parlor. There had been a silence for a moment as she looked around upon the few pictures and upon that bareness and coldness which, do what he will, no man can eradicate from his abiding-place until he calls in the deft and dainty hand of woman.

"I shall be so glad when you have a wife, Mr. Hayne!" was her quiet comment.

"So shall I, Mrs. Waldron," was the response.

"And isn't it high time we were beginning to hear of a choice? Forgive my intrusiveness, but that was the very matter of which the major and I were talking as he brought me over."

"There is something to be done first, Mrs. Waldron," he answered. "I cannot offer any woman a clouded name. It is not enough that people should begin to believe that I was innocent and my persecutors utterly in error, if not perjured. I must be able to show who was the real culprit, and that is not easy. The doctor and I thought we saw a way not long ago; but it proved delusive." And he sighed deeply. "I had expected to see the major about it the very day he got back from the court; but we have had no chance to talk."

"Mr. Hayne," she said, impulsively, "a woman's intuition is not always at fault. Tell me if you believe that anyone on the post has any inkling of the truth. I have a reason for asking."

"I *did* think it possible, Mrs. Waldron. I cannot be certain now; and it's too late, anyway."

"How, too late? What's too late?"

He paused a moment, a deeper shadow than usual on his face; then he lifted his head and looked fairly at her:

"I should not have said that, Mrs. Waldron. It can never be too late. But what I mean is that—just now I spoke of offering no woman a clouded name. Even if it were unclouded, I could not offer it where I would."

"Because you have heard of the engagement?" was the quick, eager question. There was no instant of doubt in the woman as to where the offering would be made, if it only could.

"I knew of the engagement only a day ago," he answered, with stern effort at self-control. "Blake was speaking of her, and it came out all of a sudden."

He turned his head away again. It was more than Mrs. Waldron could stand. She leaned impetuously towards him, and put her hand on his:

"Mr. Hayne, that is no engagement of heart to heart. It is entirely a thing of Mrs. Rayner's doing; and I *know* it. She is poor,—dependent,—and has been simply sold into bondage."

"And you think she cares nothing for the position, the wealth and social advantages, this would give her? Ah, Mrs. Waldron, consider."

"I *have* considered. Mr. Hayne, if I were a man, like you, that child should never go back to him. And they are going next week. You *must* get well."

It was remarked that Mr. Hayne was out surprisingly quick for a fellow who had been so recently threatened with brain-fever. The Rayners were to go East at once, so it was said, though the captain's leave of absence had not yet been ordered. The colonel could grant him seven days at any time, and he had telegraphic notification that there would be no objection when the formal application reached the War Department. Rayner called at the colonel's office and asked that he might be permitted to start with his wife and sister. His second lieutenant would move in and occupy his quarters and take care of all his personal effects during their absence; and Lieutenant Hayne was a most thorough officer, and he felt that in turning over his company to him he left it in excellent hands. The colonel saw the misery in the captain's face, and he was touched by both looks and words:

"You must not take this last affair too much to heart, Captain Rayner. We in the ___th have known Captain Buxton so many years that with us there is no question as to where all the blame lies. It seems, too, to be clearly understood by Mr. Hayne. As for your previous ideas of that officer, I consider it too delicate a matter to speak of. You must see, however, how entirely beyond reproach his general character appears to have been. But here's another matter: Clancy's discharge has arrived. Does the old fellow know you had requested it?"

"No, sir," answered Rayner, with hesitation and embarrassment. "We wanted to keep him straight, as I told you we would, and he would probably get on a big tear if he knew his service-days were numbered. I didn't look for its being granted for forty-eight hours yet."

"Well, he will know it before night; and no doubt he will be badly cut up. Clancy was a fine soldier before he married that harridan of a woman."

"She has made him a good wife since they came into the Riflers, colonel, and has taken mighty good care of the old fellow."

"It is more than she did in the ___th, sir. She was a handsome, showy woman when I first saw her,—before my promotion to the regiment,—and Clancy was one of the finest soldiers in the brigade the last year of the war. She ran through all his money, though, and in the ___th we looked upon her as the real cause of his break-down,—especially after her affair with that sergeant who deserted. You've heard of him, probably. He disappeared after the Battle Butte campaign, and we hoped he'd run off with Mrs. Clancy; but he hadn't. She was there when we got back, big as ever, and growing ugly."

"Do you mean that Mrs. Clancy had a lover when she was in the ___th?"

"Certainly, Captain Rayner. We supposed it was commonly known. He was a fine-looking, black-eyed, dark-haired, dashing fellow, of good education, a great swell among the men the short time he was with us, and Mrs. Clancy made a dead set at him from the start. He never seemed to care for *her* very much."

"This is something I never heard of," said Rayner, with grave face, "and it will be a good deal of a shock to my wife, for she had arranged to take her East with Clancy and Kate, and they were to invest their money in some little business at her old home."

"Yes: it was mainly on the woman's account we wouldn't re-enlist Clancy in the ___th. We could stand him, but she was too much for us,—and for the other sergeant, too. He avoided her before we started on the campaign, I fancy. Odd! I can't think of his name.—Billings, what was the name of that howling swell of a ser-geant who was in Hull's troop at Battle Butte,—time Hull was killed? I mean the man that Mrs. Clancy was said to have eloped with."

"Sergeant Gower, sir," said the adjutant, without looking up from his work. He did look up, however, when a moment after the captain hurriedly left the office, and he saw that Rayner's face was deathly white: it was ghastly.

"What took Rayner off so suddenly?" said the colonel, wheel-ing around in his chair.

"I don't know, sir, unless there was something to startle him in the name."

"Why should there be?"

"There are those who think that Gower got away with more than his horse and arms, colonel: he was not at Battle Butte, though, and that is what made it a mystery."

"Where was he then?"

"Back with the wagon-train, sir; and he never got in sight of the Buttes or Rayner's battalion. You know Rayner had four companies there."

"I don't see how Gower could have taken the money, if that's what you mean, if he never came up to the Buttes: Rayner swore it was there in Hull's original package. Then, too, how could Gower's name affect him if he had never seen him?"

"Possibly he has heard something. Clancy has been talking."

"I have looked into that," said the colonel. "Clancy denies knowing anything,—says he was drunk and didn't know what he was talking about."

All the same it was queer, thought the adjutant, and he greatly wanted to see the doctor and talk with him; but by the time his office-work was done the doctor had gone to town, and when he came back he was sent for to the laundress's quarters, where Mrs. Clancy was in hysterics and Michael had again been very bad.

Soon after the captain's return to his quarters, it seems, a messenger was sent from Mrs. Rayner requesting Mrs. Clancy to come and see her at once. She was ushered up-stairs to madame's own apartment, much to Miss Travers's surprise, and that young lady was further astonished, when Mrs. Clancy reappeared, nearly an hour later, to see that she had been weeping violently. The house was in some disorder, most of the trunks being packed and in readiness for the start, and Miss Travers was entertaining two or three young officers and waiting for her sister to come down to luncheon. "The boys" were lachrymose over her prospective departure,—at least they affected to be,—and were variously sprawled about the parlor when Mrs. Clancy descended, and the inflamed condition of her eyes and nose became apparent to all. There was much chaff and fun, therefore, when Mrs. Rayner finally appeared, over the supposed affliction of the big Irishwoman at the prospect of parting with her patroness. Miss Travers saw with singular sensations that both the captain and her usually self-reliant sister were annoyed and embarrassed by the topic and strove to change it; but Foster's propensity for mimicry and his ability to imitate Mrs. Clancy's combined brogue and sniffle proved too much for their efforts. Kate was in a royally bad temper by the time the youngsters left the house, and when Nellie would have made some laughing allusion to the fun the young fellows had been having over her morning caller, she was suddenly and tartly checked with—

"We've had too much of that already. Just understand now that you have no time to waste, if your packing is unfinished. We start tomorrow afternoon."

"Why, Kate! I had no idea we were to go for two days yet! Of course I can be ready; but why did you not tell me before?"

"I did not know it—at least it was not decided—until this morning, after the captain came back from the office. There is nothing to prevent our going, now that he has seen the colonel."

"There was not before, Kate; for Mr. Billings told me yesterday morning, and I told you, that the colonel had said you could start at once, and you replied that the captain could not be ready for several days,—three at least."

"Well, now he *is*; and that ends it. Never mind what changed his mind."

It was unsafe to trifle with Nellie Travers, as Mrs. Rayner might have known. She saw that something had occurred to make the captain eager to start at once; and then there was that immediate sending for Mrs. Clancy, the long, secret talk up in Kate's room, the evident mental disturbance of both feminines on their respective reappearances, and the sudden announcement to her. While there could be no time to make formal parting calls, there were still some two or three ladies in the garrison whom she longed to see before saying adieu; and then there was Mr. Hayne, whom she had wronged quite as bitterly as anyone else had wronged him. He was out that day for the first time, and she longed to see him and longed to fulfil the neglected promise. *That* she must do at the very least. If she could not see him, she must write, that he might have the note before they went away. All these thoughts were rushing through her brain as she busied herself about her little room, stowing away dresses and dropping everything from time to time to dart into her sister's room in answer to some querulous call. Yet never did she leave without a quick glance from her window up and down the row. For whom was she looking?

It was just about dusk when she heard crying down-stairs,—a child, and apparently in the kitchen. Mrs. Rayner was with the baby, and Miss Travers started for the stairs, calling that she would go and see what it meant. She was down in the hall before Mrs. Rayner's imperative and repeated calls brought her to a full stop.

"What is it?" she inquired.

"You come back here and hold baby. I know perfectly what it is. It is Kate Clancy; and she wants me. You can do nothing."

Too late, madame! The intervening doors were opened, and in marched cook, leading the poor little Irish girl, who was sobbing piteously. Mrs. Rayner came down the stairs with all speed, bringing her burly son and heir in her arms. She would have ordered Nell aloft, but what excuse could she give? and Miss Travers was already bending over the child and striving to still her heart-breaking cries.

"What is it? Where's your father?" demanded Mrs. Rayner.

"Oh, ma'am, I don't know. I came here to tell the captain. Shure he's discharged, ma'am, an' his heart's broke entirely, an' mother says we're all to go with the captain tomorrow, an' he swears he'll kill himself before he'll go, an' I can't find him, ma'am. It's almost dark now."

"Go back and tell your mother I want her instantly. We'll find your father. Go!" she repeated, as the child shrank and hesitated. "Here,—the front way!" And little Kate sped away into the shadows across the dim level of the parade.

Then the sisters faced each other. There was a fire in the younger's eye that Mrs. Rayner would have escaped if she could.

"Kate, it is to get Clancy away from the possibility of revealing what he knows that you have planned this sudden move, and I *know* it," said Miss Travers. "You need not answer."

She seized a wrap from the hat-rack and stepped to the doorway. Mrs. Rayner threw herself after her.

"Nellie, where are you going? What will you do?"

"To Mrs. Waldron's, Kate; if need be, to Mr. Hayne's."

A bright fire was burning in Major Waldron's cosey parlor, where he and his good wife were seated in earnest talk. It was just after sunset when Mr. Hayne dropped in to pay his first visit after the few days in which he had been confined to his quarters. He was looking thin, paler than usual, and far more restless and eager in manner than of old. The Waldrons welcomed him with more than usual warmth, and the major speedily led the conversation up to the topic which was so near to his heart.

"You and I must see the doctor and have a triangular council over this thing, Hayne. Three heads are better than none; and if, as he suspects, old Clancy really knows anything when he's drunk that he cannot tell when he's sober, I shall depart from Mrs. Waldron's principles and join the doctor in his pet scheme of getting him drunk again. '*In vino veritas*,' you know. And we ought to be about it, too, for it won't be long before his discharge comes, and, once away, we should be in the lurch."

"There seems so little hope there, major. Even the colonel has called him up and questioned him."

"Ay, very true, but always when the old sergeant was sober. It is when drunk that Clancy's conscience pricks him to tell what he either knows or suspects."

A light, quick footstep was heard on the piazza, the hall door opened, and without knock or ring, bursting impetuously in upon them, there suddenly appeared Miss Travers, her eyes dilated with excitement. At sight of the group she stopped short, and colored to the very roots of her shining hair.

"How glad I am to see you, Nellie!" exclaimed Mrs. Waldron, as all rose to greet her. An embarrassed, half distraught reply was her only answer. She had extended both hands to the elder lady; but now, startled, almost stunned, at finding herself in the presence of the very man she most wanted to see, she stood with downcast eyes, irresolute. He, too, had not stepped forward,—had not offered his hand. She raised her blue eyes for one quick glance, and saw his pale, pain-thinned face, read anew the story of his patience, his suffering, his heroism, and realized how she too had wronged him and that her very awkwardness and silence might tell him that shameful fact. It was more than she could stand.

"I came—purposely. I hoped to find you, Mr. Hayne. You—you remember that I had something to tell you. It was about Clancy. You ought to see him. I'm sure you ought, for he *must* know—he or Mrs. Clancy—something about your—your trouble; and I've just this minute heard that they—that he's going away tomorrow; and you must find him tonight, Mr. Hayne: indeed you must."

Who can paint her as she stood there, blushing, pleading, eager, frightened, yet determined? Who can picture the wild emotion in his heart, reflected in his face? He stepped quickly to her side with the light leaping to his eyes, his hands extended as though to grasp hers; but it was Waldron that spoke first:

"Where is he going?—how?"

"Oh, with us, major. We go tomorrow, and they go with us. My sister has some reason—I cannot fathom it. She wants them away from here, and Clancy's discharge came today. He *must* see him first," she said, indicating Mr. Hayne by the nod of her pretty head. "They say Clancy has run off and got away from his wife. He doesn't want to be discharged. They cannot find him now; but perhaps Mr. Hayne can.—Mr. Hayne, try to. You—you must."

"Indeed we must, Hayne, and quick about it," said the major. "Now is our chance, I verily believe. Let us get the doctor first; then little Kate will best know where to look for Clancy. Come, man, get your overcoat." And he hastened to the hall.

Hayne followed as though in a dream, reached the threshold, turned, looked back, made one quick step toward Miss Travers with outstretched hand, then checked himself as suddenly. His yearning eyes seemed fastened on her burning face, his lips quivered with the intensity of his emotion. She raised her eyes and gave him one quick look, half entreaty, half command; he seemed ineffectually struggling to speak,—to thank her. One moment of irresolution, then, without a word of any kind, he sprang to the door. She carried his parting glance in her heart of hearts all night long. There was no mistaking what it told.

XVII.

The morning report of the following day showed some items under the head of "Alterations" that involved several of the soldier characters of this story. Ex-Sergeant Clancy had been dropped from the column of present "on daily duty" and taken up on that of absent without leave. Lieutenant Hayne was also reported absent. Dr. Pease and Lieutenant Billings drove into the garrison from town just before the cavalry trumpets were sounding first call for guard-mounting, and the adjutant sent one of the musicians to give his compliments to Mr. Royce and ask him to mount the guard for him, as he had just returned and had important business with the colonel. The doctor and the adjutant together went into the colonel's quarters, and for the first time on record the commanding officer was not at the desk in his office when the shoulder-straps began to gather for the *matinée*.

Ten minutes after the usual time the adjutant darted in and plunged with his characteristic impetuosity into the pile of passes and other papers stacked up by the sergeant-major at his table. To all questions as to where he had been and what was the matter with the colonel he replied, with more than usual asperity of manner,—the asperity engendered of some years of having to answer the host of questions propounded by vacant minds at his own busiest hour of the day,—that the colonel would tell them all about it himself; *he* had no time for a word. The evident manner of suppressed excitement, however, was something few failed to note; and every man in the room felt certain that when the colonel came there would be a revelation. It was with something bordering on indignation, therefore, that the assemblage heard the words that intimated to them that all might retire. The colonel had come in very quietly, received the report of the officer of the day, relieved him, and dismissed the new officer of the day with the brief formula, "Usual orders, sir," then glanced quickly around the silent circle of grave, bearded or boyish faces. His eyes rested for an instant with something like shock and trouble upon one face, pale, haggard, with almost bloodless lips, and yet full of fierce determination,—a face that haunted him long afterwards, it was so full of agony, of suspense, almost of pleading,—the face of Captain Rayner.

Then, dispensing with the customary talk, he quietly spoke the disappointing words,—

"I am somewhat late this morning, gentlemen, and several

matters will occupy my attention: so I will not detain you further."

The crowd seemed to find their feet very slowly. There was visible disinclination to go. Every man in some inexplicable way appeared to know that there was a new mystery hanging over the garrison, and that the colonel held the key. Every man felt that Billings had given him the right to expect to be told all about it when the colonel came. Some looked reproachfully at Billings, as though to remind him of their expectations: Stannard, his old stand-by, passed him with a gruff "Thought you said the colonel had something to tell us," and went out with an air of injured and defrauded dignity. Rayner arose, and seemed to be making preparations to depart with the others, and some of the number, connecting him unerringly with the prevailing sensation, appeared to hold back and wait for him to precede them and so secure to themselves the satisfaction of knowing that, if it was a matter connected with Rayner, they "had him along" and nothing could take place without their hearing it. These men were very few, however; but Buxton was one of them. Rayner's eyes were fixed upon the colonel and searching for a sign, and it came,—a little motion of the hand and a nod of the head that signified "Stay." Then, as Buxton and one or two of his stamp still dallied irresolute, the colonel turned somewhat sharply to them: "Was there any matter on which you wished to see me, gentlemen?" and, as there was none, they *had* to go. Then Rayner was alone with the colonel; for Mr. Billings quickly arose, and, with a significant glance at his commander, left the room and closed the door.

Mrs. Rayner, gazing from her parlor windows, saw that all the officers had come out except one,—her husband,—and with a moan of misery she covered her face with her hands and sank upon the sofa. With cheeks as white as her sister's, with eyes full of trouble and perplexity, but tearless, Nellie Travers stepped quickly into the room and put a trembling white hand upon the other's shoulder:

"Kate, it is no time for so bitter an estrangement as this. I have done simply what our soldier father would have done had he been here. I am fully aware of what it must cost me. I knew when I did it that you would never again welcome me to your home. Once East again, you and I can go our ways; I won't burden you longer; but is it not better that you should tell me in what way your husband or you can have been injured by what I have done?"

Mrs. Rayner impatiently shook away the hand.

"I don't want to talk to you," was the blunt answer. "You have carried out your threat and—ruined *us*: that's all."

"What *can* you mean? Do you want me to think that because Mr. Hayne's innocence may be established your husband was the guilty man? Certainly your manner leads to that inference; though his does not, by any means."

"I don't want to talk, I tell you. You've had your way,—done your work. You'll see soon enough the hideous web of trouble you've entangled about my husband. Don't you dare say—don't you dare think"—and now she rose with sudden fury—"that he was the—that he lost the money! But that's what all others will think."

"If that were true, Kate, there would be this difference between his trouble and Mr. Hayne's: Captain Rayner would have wife, wealth, and friends to help him bear the cross; Mr. Hayne has borne it five long years unaided. I pray God the truth *has* been brought to light."

What fierce reply Mrs. Rayner might have given, who knows? but at that instant a quick step was heard on the piazza, the door opened suddenly, and Captain Rayner entered with a rush. The pallor had gone; a light of eager, half incredulous joy beamed from his eyes, he threw his cap upon the floor, and his wife had risen and thrown her arms about his neck.

"Have they found him?" was her breathless question. "*What* has happened? You look so different."

"Found him? Yes; and he has told everything?"

"Told—what?"

"Told that he and Gower were the men. They took it all."

"*Clancy!*—and Gower! The thieves, do you mean? Is that—is *that* what he confessed?" she asked, in wild wonderment, in almost stupefied amaze, releasing him from her arms and stepping back, her eyes searching his face.

"Nothing else in the world, Kate. I don't understand it at all. I'm all a-tremble yet. It clears Hayne utterly. It at least explains how I was mistaken. But what—what could she have meant?"

Mrs. Rayner stood like one in a dream, her eyes staring, her lips quivering; and Nellie, with throbbing pulses and clasping hands, looked eagerly from husband to wife, as though beseeching some explanation.

"What did she mean? What *did* she mean? I say again," asked Rayner, pressing his hand to his forehead and gazing fixedly at his wife.

A moment longer she stood there, as though a light—a long-hidden truth—were slowly forcing itself upon her mind. Then, with impulsive movement, she hurried through the dining-room, threw open the kitchen door, and startled the domestics at their late breakfast.

"Ryan," she called to the soldier-servant who rose hastily from the table, "go and tell Mrs. Clancy I want her instantly. Do you understand? Instantly!" And Ryan seized his forage-cap and vanished.

It was perhaps ten minutes before he returned. When he did so it was apparent that Mrs. Rayner had been crying copiously, and that Miss Travers, too, was much affected. The captain was pacing the room with nervous strides in mingled relief and agitation. All looked up expectant as the soldier re-entered. He had the air of a man who knew he bore tidings of vivid and mysterious interest, but he curbed the excitement of his manner until it shone only through his snapping eyes, saluted, and reported with professional gravity:

"Mrs. Clancy's clean gone, sir."

"Gone where?"

"Nobody knows, sir. She's just lit out with her trunk and best clothes some time last night."

"Gone to her husband in town, maybe?"

"No, sir. Clancy's all right: he was caught last evening, and hadn't time to get more'n half drunk before they lodged him. Lootenant Hayne got him, sir. They had him afore a justice of the peace early this morning—"

"Yes, I know all that. What I want is *Mrs.* Clancy. What has become of her?"

"Faith, I don't know, sir, but the women in Sudsville they all say she's run away, sir,—taken her money and gone. She's afraid of Clancy's peaching on her."

"By heavens! the thing is clearing itself!" exclaimed Rayner to his gasping and wild-eyed wife. "I must go to the colonel at once with his news." And away he went.

And then again, as the orderly retired, and the sisters were left alone, Nellie Travers with trembling lips asked the question,—

"Have I done so much harm, after all, Kate?"

"Oh, Nellie! Nellie! forgive me, for I have been nearly mad with misery!" was Mrs. Rayner's answer, as she burst into a fresh paroxysm of tears. "That—that woman has—has told me fearful lies."

There was a strange scene that day at Warrener when, towards noon, two carriages drove out from town and, entering the east gate, rolled over towards the guard-house. The soldiers clustered about the barrack porches and stared at the occupants. In the first—a livery hack from town—were two sheriff's officers, while cowering on the back seat, his hat pulled down over his eyes, was poor old Clancy, to whom clung faithful little Kate. In the rear carriage—Major Waldron's—were Mr. Hayne, the major, and a civilian whom some of the men had no difficulty in recognizing as the official charged with the administration of justice towards offenders against the peace. Many of the soldiers strolled slowly up the road, in hopes of hearing all about the arrest, and what it meant, from straggling members of the guard. All knew it meant something more than a mere "break" on the part of Clancy; all felt that it had some connection with the long-continued mystery that hung about the name of Lieutenant Hayne. Then, too, it was being noised abroad that Mrs. Clancy had "skipped" and between two suns had fled for parts unknown. *She* could be overhauled by telegraph if she had left on either of the night freights or gone down towards Denver by the early morning passenger-train; it would be easy enough to capture her if she were "wanted," said the garrison; but what did it mean that Clancy was pursued by officers of the post and brought back under charge of officers of the law? He had had trouble enough, poor fellow!

The officer of the guard looked wonderingly at the carriages and their occupants. He saluted Major Waldron as the latter stepped briskly down.

"You will take charge of Clancy, Mr. Graham," said the major. "His discharge will be recalled: at least it will not take effect today. You will be interested in knowing that his voluntary confession fully establishes Mr. Hayne's innocence of the charges on which he was tried."

Mr. Graham's face turned all manner of colors. He glanced at Hayne, who, still seated in the carriage, was as calmly indifferent to him as ever: he was gazing across the wide parade at the windows in officers' row. Little Kate's sobs as the soldiers were helping her father from the carriage suddenly recalled his wandering thoughts. He sprang to the ground, stepped quickly to the child, and put his arms about her.

"Clancy, tell her to come with us. Mrs. Waldron will take loving care of her, and she shall come to see you every day. The guard-house is no place for her to follow you. Tell her so, man, and she will go with us.—Come, Katie, child!" And he bent tenderly over the sobbing little waif.

"Thank ye, sir. I know ye'll be good to her. Go with the lootenant, Kate darlin'; go. Shure I'll be happier then."

And, trembling, he bent and kissed her wet cheeks. She threw her arms around his neck and clung to him in an agony of grief. Gently they strove to disengage her clasping arms, but she shrieked and struggled, and poor old Clancy broke down. There were sturdy soldiers standing by who turned their heads away to hide the unbidden tears, and with a quiver in his kind voice the major interposed:

"Let her stay awhile: it will be better for both. Don't put him in the prison-room, Graham. Keep them by themselves for a while. We will come for her by and by." And then, before them all, he held forth his hand and gave Clancy's a cordial grasp:

"Cheer up, man. You've taken the right step at last. You are a free man today, even if you are a prisoner for the time being. Better this a thousand times than what you were."

Hayne, too, spoke a few kind words in a low tone, and gave the old soldier his hand at parting. Then the guard closed the door, and father and daughter were left alone. As the groups around the guard-house began to break up and move away, and the officers, re-entering the carriages, drove over to headquarters, a rollicking Irishman called to the sergeant of the guard,—

"Does he know the ould woman's skipped, sargent? Shure you'd better tell him. 'Twill cheer him, like."

But when, a few moments after, the news was imparted to Clancy, the effect was electric and startling. With one bound and a savage cry he sprang to the door. The sergeant threw himself upon him and strove to hold him back, but was no match for the frenzied man. Deaf to Kate's entreaties and the sergeant's commands, he hurled him aside, leaped through the doorway, shot like a deer past the lolling guardsmen on the porch, and, turning sharply, went at the top of his speed down the hill towards Sudsville before man could lay hand on him. The sentry on Number One cocked his rifle and looked inquiringly at the officer of the guard, who came running out. With a wild shriek little Kate threw herself upon the sentry, clasping his knees and imploring him not to shoot. The lieutenant and the sergeant both shouted, "Never mind! Don't fire!" and with others of the guard rushed in pursuit. But, old and feeble as he was, poor Clancy kept the lead, never swerving, never flagging, until he reached the doorway of his abandoned cot; this he burst in, threw himself upon his knees by the bedside, and dragged to light a little wooden chest that stood by an open trap in the floor. One look sufficed: the mere fact that the trap was open and the box exposed was enough. With a wild cry of rage, despair, and baffled hatred, he clinched his hands above his head, rose to his full height, and with a curse upon his white lips, with glaring eyes and gasping breath, turned upon his pursuers as they came running in, and hurled his fists at the foremost. "Let me follow her,

I say! She's gone with it all,—his money! Let me go!" he shrieked; and then his eyes turned stony, a gasp, a clutch at his throat, and, plunging headlong, he fell upon his face at their feet.

Poor little Kate! The old man was, indeed, free at last.

XVIII.

There had been a scene of somewhat dramatic nature at the colonel's office but a short time before, and one that had fewer witnesses. Agitated, nervous, and eventually astonished as Captain Rayner had been when the colonel had revealed to him the nature of Clancy's confession, he was far more excited and tremulous when he returned a second time. The commanding officer had been sitting deep in thought. It was but natural that a man should show great emotion on learning that the evidence he had given, which had condemned a brother officer to years of solitary punishment, was now disproved. It was to be expected that Rayner should be tremulous and excited. He had been looking worse and worse for a long time past; and now that it was established that he must have been mistaken in what he thought he saw and heard at Battle Butte, it was to be expected that he should show the utmost consternation and an immediate desire to make amends. He *had* shown great emotion; he was white and rigid as the colonel told him Clancy had made a full confession; but the expression on his face when informed that the man had admitted that he and Sergeant Gower were the only ones guilty of the crime—that Clancy and Gower divided the guilt as they had the money—was a puzzle to the colonel. Captain Rayner seemed daft: it was a look of wild relief, half unbelief, half delight, that shot across his haggard features. It was evident that *he had not heard at all what he expected*. This was what puzzled the colonel. He had been pondering over it ever since the captain's hurried departure "to tell his wife."

"We—we had expected—made all preparations to take this afternoon's train for the East," he stammered. "We are all torn up, all ready to start, and the ladies ought to go; but I cannot feel like going in the face of this."

"There is no reason why you should not go, captain. I am told Mrs. Rayner should leave at once. If need be, you can return from Chicago. Everything will be attended to properly. Of course you will know what to do towards Mr. Hayne. Indeed, I think it might be best for you to go."

But Rayner seemed hardly listening; and the colonel was not a man to throw his words away.

"You might see Mrs. Rayner at once, and return by and by," he said; and Rayner gladly escaped, and went home with the wonderful news he had to tell his wife.

And now a second time he was back, and was urging upon the

commanding officer the necessity of telegraphing and capturing Mrs. Clancy. In plain words he told the colonel he believed that she had escaped with the greater part of the money. The colonel smiled:

"That was attended to early this morning, captain. Hayne and the major asked that she be secured, and the moment we found her fled it confirmed their suspicions, and Billings sent despatches in every direction. She can't get away! She was his temptress, and I mean to make her share all the punishment."

"Colonel," exclaimed Rayner, while beads of sweat stood out on his forehead, "she is worse,—a thousand times worse! The woman is a fiend. She is the devil in petticoats—and ingenuity. My God! sir, I have been in torment for weeks past,—my poor wife and I. I have been criminally, cowardly weak; but I did not know what to do,—where to turn,—how to take it,—how to meet it. Let me tell you." And now great tears were standing in his eyes and beginning to trickle down his cheeks. He dashed them away. His lips were quivering, and he strode nervously up and down the matted floor. "When you refused to left Clancy reenlist in the ___th, two years after Battle Butte, he came to me and told me a story. He, too, had declared, as I did, that he had seen the money-packages in Hayne's hands; and he said the real reason he was kicked out of the ___th was because the officers and men took sides with Hayne and thought he had sworn his reputation away. He begged me not to 'go back on him' as his own regiment had, and I thought he was being persecuted because he told the truth. God knows I fully believed Hayne guilty for more than three years,—it is only within the last year or so I began to have doubts; and so I took Clancy into B Company and soon made Mrs. Clancy a laundress. But she made trouble for us all, and there was something uncanny about them. She kept throwing out mysterious hints I could not understand when rumors of them reached me; and at last came the fire that burned them out, and then the stories of what Clancy had said in his delirium; and then she came to my wife and told her a yarn that—she swore to its truth, and nearly drove Mrs. Rayner wild with anxiety. She swore that when Clancy got to drinking he imagined he had seen *me* take that money from Captain Hull's saddle-bags and replace the sealed package: she said he was ready to swear that he and Gower—the deserter—and two of our men, honorably discharged now and living on ranches down in Nebraska, could all swear—would all swear—to the same thing,—that I was the thief. 'Sure you know it couldn't be so, ma'am; and yet he wants to go and tell Mr. Hayne,' she would say: 'there's the four of 'em would swear to it, though Gower's evidence would be no good; but the two men could hurt the captain.' Her ingenuity was devilish; for one of the men I had severely punished once in the Black Hills, and both hated me and had sworn they would get even with me yet. God help me, colonel! seeing every day the growing conviction that Hayne was innocent, that somebody else *must* be guilty, I thought, what if this man *should*, in drunken gratitude to Hayne for saving his life, go to him and tell him this story, then back it up before the officials and call in these two others? I was weak, but it appalled me. I determined to get him out of the way of such a possibility. I got his discharge, and meantime strove to prevent his drinking or going near Hayne. *She* knew the real story he *would* tell. This was her devilish plan to keep me on watch against him. I never dreamed the real truth. She swore to me that three hundred dollars was all the money they had. I believed that when he confessed it would be what she declared. I never dreamed that Clancy and his confederate were the thieves: I never believed the money was taken until after Hayne received it. I saw how Hayne's guilt was believed in even in the face of contradictory evidence before the court. What would be the tendency if three men together were to swear against me, now that everybody thought him wronged? I know very well what you will think of my cowardice. I know you and your officers will say I should have given him every chance,—should have courted investigation; and I meant to do so, but first I wanted to hear from those discharged men in Nebraska. The whole scheme would have been exploded two months ago had I not been a coward; but night after night something kept whispering to me, 'You have wrecked and ruined a friendless young soldier's life. You shall be brought as low.'"

The colonel was, as he afterwards remarked, hardly equal to the occasion. He had as much contempt for moral weakness in a soldier as he had for physical cowardice; but Rayner's almost abject recital of his months of misery really left him nothing to say. Had the captain sought to defend or justify any detail of his conduct, he would have pounced on him like a panther. Twice the adjutant, sitting an absorbed and silent listener, thought the chief on the verge of an outbreak; but it never came. For some minutes after Rayner ceased the colonel sat steadily regarding him. At last he spoke:

"You have been so frank in your statement, captain, that I feel you fully appreciate how such deplorable weakness must be regarded in an officer. It is unnecessary for me to speak of that. The full particulars of Clancy's confession are not yet with me. Major

Waldron has it all in writing, and Mr. Billings has merely told me the general features. Of course you shall have a copy of it in good time. As you go East today and have your wife and household to think for, it may be as well that you do not attempt to see Mr. Hayne before starting. And this matter will not be discussed."

And so it happened that when the Rayners drove to the station that bright afternoon, and a throng of ladies and officers gathered to see them off, some of the youngsters going with them into town to await the coming of the train, Nellie Travers had been surrounded by chattering friends of both sexes, constantly occupied, and yet constantly looking for the face of one who came not. For an hour before their departure every tongue in garrison that wagged at all—and few there were that wagged not—was discoursing on the exciting events of the morning,—Hayne's emancipation from the last vestige of suspicion, Clancy's capture, confession, and tragic death, Mrs. Clancy's flight and probable future. At Rayner's, people spoke of these things very guardedly, because everyone saw that the captain was moved to the depths of his nature. He was solemnity itself, and Mrs. Rayner watched him with deep anxiety, fearful that he might be exposed to some thoughtless or malicious questioning. Her surveillance was needless, however: even Ross made no allusion to the events of the morning, though he communicated to his fellows in the subsequent confidences of the club-room that Midas looked as though he'd been pulled through a series of knotholes. "Looks more's though he were going to his own funeral than on leave," he added.

As for Hayne, he had been closeted with the colonel and Major Waldron for some time after his return,—a conference that was broken in upon by the startling news of Clancy's death. Then he had joined his friend the doctor at the hospital, and was still there, striving to comfort little Kate, who could not be induced to leave her father's rapidly stiffening form, when Mrs. Waldron reentered the room. Drawing the child to her side and folding her motherly arms about her, she looked up in Hayne's pale face:

"They are going in five minutes. Don't you mean to see her?"

"Not there,—not under his roof or in that crowd. I will go to the station."

"I must run over and say good-by in a moment,—when the carriage goes around. Shall—shall I say you will come?"

There was a light in his blue eyes she was just beginning to notice now as she studied his face. A smile flickered one instant about the corners of his mouth, and then he held out his hand:

"She knows by this time, Mrs. Waldron."

An hour later Mrs. Rayner was standing on the platform at the station, Ross and others of her satellites hanging about her; Captain Rayner was talking in subdued tones with one or two of the senior officers; Miss Travers, looking feverishly pretty, was chatting busily with Royce and Foster, though a close observer could have noted that her dark eyes often sought the westward prairie over which wound the road to the distant post. It was nearly train-time, and three or four horsemen could be seen at various distances, while, far out towards the fort, long skirmish-lines and fluttering guidons were sweeping over the slopes in mimic war-array.

"I have missed all this," she said, pointing to the scene; "and I do love it so that it seems hard to go just as all the real soldier life is beginning."

"Goodness knows you've had offers enough to keep you here," said Foster, with not the blithest laugh in the world. "Any girl who will go East and marry a 'cit' and leave six or seven penniless subs sighing behind her, I have my opinion of: she's eminently level-headed," he added, with rueful and unexpected candor.

"I have hopes of Miss Travers yet," boomed Royce, in his ponderous basso,—"not personal hopes, Foster; you needn't feel for your pistol,—but I believe that her heart is with the army, like the soldier's daughter she is." And, audacious as was the speech and deserving of instant rebuke, Mr. Royce was startled to see her reddening vividly. He would have plunged into hasty apology, but Foster plucked his sleeve:

"Look who's coming, you galoot! She hasn't heard a word either of us has said."

And though Nellie Travers, noting the sudden silence, burst into an immediate and utterly irrelevant lament over the loss of the Maltese kitten,—which had not been seen all that day and was not to be found when they came away,—it was useless. The effort was gallant, but the flame in her cheeks betrayed her as, throwing his reins to the orderly who followed him, Mr. Hayne dismounted at the platform and came directly towards her. To Mrs. Rayner's unspeakable dismay, he walked up to the trio, bowed low over the little gloved hand that was extended in answer to the proffer of his own, and next she saw that Royce and Foster had, as though by tacit consent, fallen back, and, *coram publico*, Mr. Hayne was sole claimant of the regards of her baby sister. There was but one comfort in the situation: the train was in sight. Forgetful, reckless for the moment, of what was going on around her, she stood gazing at the pair. No woman could fail to read the story; no woman could see his face, his eyes, his whole attitude and expression, and not read therein that old, old story that grows sweeter with every century of its life. That he should be inspired with sudden, vehement love for her exquisite Nell was something she could readily understand; but what—what meant *her* downcast eyes, the flutter of color on her soft and rounded cheek, the shy uplifting of the fringed lids from time to time as though in response to eager question or appeal? Heavens! would that train *never* come? The whistle was sounding in the distance, but it would take ages to drag those heavy Pullmans up the grade from the bridge where they had yet to stop. She could almost have darted forward, seized her sister by the wrist, and whispered again the baleful reminder that of late had had no mention between them,—"Thou art another's;" but in her distress her weak blue eyes sought her husband's face. He saw it all, and shook his head. Then there was nothing to be done.

As the train came rumbling finally into the station, she saw him once more clasp her sister's hand; then, with one long look into the sweet face that was hidden from her jealous eyes, he raised his forage-cap and stepped quickly back to where his horse was held. Her husband hastened to her side:

"Kate, I must speak to him. I don't care how he may take it; I cannot go without it."

They all watched the tall captain as he strode across the platform. Every man in uniform seemed to know instinctively that Rayner at last was seeking to make open reparation for the bitter wrong he had done. One or two strove to begin a general chat and affect an interest in something else, for Mrs. Rayner's benefit, but she, with trembling lips, stood gazing after her husband and seemed to beg for silence. Then all abandoned other occupation, and every man stood still and watched them. Hayne had quickly swung into saddle, and had turned for one more look, when he saw his captain with ashen face striding towards him, and heard him call his name.

"By Jove!" muttered Ross, "what command that fellow has over himself!" for, scrupulously observant of military etiquette, Mr. Hayne on being addressed by his superior officer had instantly dismounted, and now stood silently facing him. Even at the distance, there were some who thought they could see his features twitching; but his blue eyes were calm and steady,—far clearer than they had been but a moment agone when gazing good-by into the sweet face they worshipped. None could hear what passed between them. The talk was very brief; but Ross almost gasped with amaze, other officers looked at one another in utter astonishment, and Mrs. Rayner fairly sobbed with excitement and emotion, when Mr. Hayne was seen to hold forth his hand, and Rayner, grasping it eagerly in both his own, shook it once, then strode hastily away towards the rear of the train. His eyes were filled with tears he could not repress and could not bear to show.

That evening, as the train wound steadily eastward into the shadows of the night, and they looked out in farewell upon the slopes they had last seen when a wintry gale swept fiercely over the frozen surface and the shallow ravines were streaked with snow, Kate Rayner, after a long talk with her husband, and abandoning her boy to the sole guardianship of his nurse, settled herself by Nellie's side, and Nellie knew that she either sought confidences or had them to impart. Something of the old, quizzical look was playing about the corner of her pretty mouth as her elder sister, with feminine indirectness, began her verbal skirmishing with the subject. It was some time before the question was reached which led to her real objective:

"Did he—did Mr. Hayne tell you much about Clancy?"

"Not much. There was no time."

"You had fully ten minutes, I'm sure. It seemed even longer."

"Four by the clock, Kate."

"Well, four, then. He must have had something of greater interest."

No answer. Cheeks reddening, though.

"Didn't he?"—persistently.

"I will tell you what he told me of Clancy, Kate. Mrs. Clancy had utterly deceived you as to what he had to tell, had she not?"

"Utterly." And now it was Mrs. Rayner's turn to color painfully.

"Mr. Hayne tells me that Clancy's confession really explained how Captain Rayner was mistaken. It was not so much the captain's fault, after all."

"So Mr. Hayne told him. You knew they—you saw Mr. Hayne offer him his hand, didn't you?"

"I did not see: I knew he would." More vivid color, and much hesitation now.

"*Knew* he would! Why, Nellie, what do you mean? He didn't tell you that he was to see Captain Rayner. He couldn't have known."

"But I knew, Kate; and I told him how the captain had suffered."

"But how could you know that he would shake hands with him?"

"He promised me."

The silence was unbroken for a moment. Nellie Travers could hear the beating of her own heart as she nestled closer to her sister and stole a hand into hers. Mrs. Rayner was trying hard to be dutiful, stern, unbending, to keep *her* faith with the distant lover in the East, whether Nell was true or no; but she had been so humbled, so changed, so shaken, by the events of the past few weeks, that she felt all her old spirit of guardianship ebbing away. "Must I give you up, Nell? and must he, too?—Mr. Van Antwerp?"

"He has not answered my last letter, Kate. It is nearly a week since I have heard from him."

"What did you write, Nellie?"

"What I had done twice before,—that he ought to release me."

"And—is Clancy's the only confession you have heard today?"

"The only one." A pause: then, "I know what you mean, Kate; but he is not the man to—to offer his love to a girl he knows is pledged to another."

"But if you were free, Nellie? Tell me."

"I have no right to say, Kate; but"—and two big tears were welling up into her brave eyes, as she clasped her hands and stretched them yearningly before her—"shall I tell you what I think a girl would say if she were free and had won his love?"

"What, Nellie?"

"She would say, 'Ay.' No woman with a heart could leave a man who has borne so much and come through it all so bravely."

Poor Mrs. Rayner! Humbled and chastened as she was, what refuge had she but tears, and then—prayer?

XIX.

Within the week succeeding the departure of the Rayners and Miss Travers, Lieutenant Hayne's brother-in-law and his remarkably attractive sister were with him in garrison and helping him fit up the new quarters which the colonel had rather insisted on his moving into and occupying, even though two unmarried subalterns had to move out and make way for him. This they seemed rather delighted to do. There was a prevailing sentiment at Warrener that nothing was too good for Hayne nowadays; and he took all this adulation so quietly and modestly that there was difficulty in telling just how it affected him. Towards those who had known him well in the days of his early service he still maintained a dignity and reserve of manner that kept them at some distance. To others, especially to the youngsters in the ___th as well as to those in the Riflers, he unbent entirely, and was frank, unaffected, and warm-hearted. He seemed to bask in the sunshine of the respect and consideration accorded him on every side. Yet no one could say he seemed happy. Courteous, grave far beyond his years, silent and thoughtful, he impressed them all as a man who had suffered too much ever again to be light-hearted. Then it was more than believed he had fallen deeply in love with Nellie Travers; and that explained the rarity and sadness of his smile. To the women he was a centre of intense and romantic interest. Mrs. Waldron was an object of jealousy because of the priority of her claims to his regard. Mrs. Hurley—the sweet sister who so strongly resembled him—was the recipient of universal attention from both sexes. Hayne and the Hurleys, indeed, would have been invited to several places an evening could they have accepted. And yet, with it all, Mr. Hayne seemed at times greatly preoccupied. He had a great deal to think of.

To begin with, the widow Clancy had been captured in one of the mining towns, where she had sought refuge, and brought back by the civil authorities, nearly three thousand dollars in greenbacks having been found in her possession. She had fought like a fury and proved too much for the sheriff's posse when first arrested, and not until three days after her incarceration was the entire amount brought to light. There was no question what ought to be done with it. Clancy's confession established the fact that almost the entire amount was stolen from Captain Hull nearly six years before, the night previous to his tragic death at Battle Butte. Mrs. Clancy at first had furiously declared it all a lie; but Waldron's and Billings's precaution in having Clancy's entire story taken down by a notary public and sworn to before him eventually broke her down. She made her miserable, whining admissions to the sheriff's officers in town,—the colonel would not have her on the post even as a prisoner,—and there she was still held, awaiting further disclosures, while little Kate was lovingly cared for at Mrs. Waldron's. Poor old Clancy was buried and on the way to be forgotten.

What proved the hardest problem for the garrison to solve was the fact that, while Mr. Hayne kept several of his old associates at a distance, he had openly offered his hand to Rayner. This was something the Riflers could not account for. The intensity of his feeling at the time of the court-martial none could forget: the vehemence of his denunciation of the captain was still fresh in the memory of those who heard it. Then there were all those years in which Rayner had continued to crowd him to the wall; and finally there was the almost tragic episode of Buxton's midnight visitation, in which Rayner, willingly or not, had been in attendance. Was it not odd that in the face of all these considerations the first man to whom Mr. Hayne should have offered his hand was Captain Rayner? Odd indeed! But then only one or two were made acquainted with the full particulars of Clancy's confession, and none had heard Nellie Travers's request. Touched as he was by the sight of Rayner's haggard and trouble-worn face, relieved as he was by Clancy's revelation of the web that had been woven to cover the tracks of the thieves and ensnare the feet of the pursuers, Hayne could not have found it possible to offer his hand; but when he bent over the tiny glove and looked into her soft and brimming eyes at the moment of their parting he could not say no to the one thing she asked of him: it was that if Rayner came to say, "Forgive me," before they left, he would not repel him.

There was one man in garrison whom Hayne cut entirely, and for whom no one felt the faintest sympathy; and that, of course, was Buxton. With Rayner gone, he hardly had an associate, though the *esprit de corps* of the ___th prompted the cavalry officers to be civil to him when he appeared at the billiard-room. As Mr. Hurley was fond of the game, an element of awkwardness was manifest the first time the young officers appeared with their engineer friend. Hayne had not set foot in such a place for five years, and quietly declined all invitations to take a cue again. It was remembered of him that he played the prettiest game of French caroms of all the officers at the station when he joined the Riflers as a boy. Hurley could only stay a very short time, and the subalterns were doing their best to make it lively for him. Some, indeed, showed strong inclination to devote themselves to Mrs. Hurley; but she was too busy with her brother's household affairs to detect their projects. Hurley had turned very red and glared at Buxton the first time the two met at the club-room, but the bulky captain speedily found cover under which to retire, and never again showed himself in general society until the engineer with the scientific attainments as a boxer as well as road-builder was safely out of the post.

And yet there came a day very soon when Mr. Hayne wished that he could go to Buxton's quarters. He had in no wise changed his opinion of the man himself, but the Rayners had not been gone a fortnight before Mrs. Buxton began to tell the ladies of the charming letters she was receiving from Mrs. Rayner,—all about their travels. There were many things he longed to know, yet could not ask.

There came to him a long and sorrowful letter from the captain himself, but, beyond a few matters relating to the company and the transfer of its property, it was all given up to a recapitulation of the troubles of the past few years and to renewed expressions of his deep regret. Of the ladies he made but casual mention. They were journeying down the Mississippi on one of its big steamers when he wrote, and Mrs. Rayner was able to enjoy the novelties of the trip, and was getting better, but still required careful nursing. Miss Travers was devoted to her. They would go to New Orleans, then possibly by sea around to New York, arriving there about the 5th of June: that, however, was undecided. He closed by asking Hayne to remind Major Waldron that his copy of Clancy's confession had not yet reached him, and he was anxious to see it in full.

"The one thing lacking to complete the chain is Gower," said the major, as he looked up over his spectacles. "It would be difficult to tell what became of him. We get tidings of most of the deserters who were as prominent among the men as he appears to have been; but I have made inquiry, and so has the colonel, and not a word has ever been heard of him since the night he appeared before Mrs. Clancy and handed over the money to her. He was a strange character, from all accounts, and must have had some conscience, after all. Do you remember him at all, Hayne?"

"I remember him well. We made the march from the Big Horn over to Battle Butte together, and he was a soldier one could not help remarking. Of course I never had anything to say to him; but we heard he was an expert gambler when the troop was over there at Miners' Delight."

"Of course his testimony isn't necessary. Clancy and his wife between them have cleared you, after burying you alive five years. But nothing but his story could explain his singular conduct,—planning the whole robbery, executing it with all the skill of a professional jailbird, deserting and covering several hundred miles with his plunder, then daring to go to the old fort, find Mrs. Clancy, and surrender every cent, the moment he heard of your trial. What a fiend that woman was! No wonder she drove Clancy to drink!"

"Will you send copies of her admission with Clancy's affidavits?" asked Hayne.

"Here they are in full," answered the major. "The colonel talks of having them printed and strewn broadcast as warnings against 'snap judgment' and too confident testimony in future."

Divested of the legal encumbrances with which such documents are usually weighted, Clancy's story ran substantially as follows:

"I was sergeant in K troop, and Gower was in F. We had been stationed together six months or so when ordered out on the Indian campaign that summer. I was dead broke. All my money was gone, and my wife kept bothering me for more. I owed a lot of money around headquarters, too, and Gower knew it, and sometimes asked me what I was going to do when we got back from the campaign. We were not good friends, him and I. There was money dealings between us, and then there was talk about Mrs. Clancy fancying him too much. The paymaster came up with a strong escort and paid off the boys late in October, just as the expedition was breaking up and going for home, and all the officers and men got four months' pay. There was Lieutenant Crane and twenty men of F troop out on a scout, but the lieutenant had left his payrolls with Captain Hull, and the men had all signed before they started, and so the captain he drew it all for them and put each man's money in an envelope marked with his name, and the lieutenant's too, and then crowded it all into some bigger envelopes. I was there where I could see it all, and Gower was watching him close. 'It's a big pile the captain's got,' says he. 'I'd like to be a road-agent and nab him.' When I told him it couldn't be over eleven hundred dollars, he says, 'That's only part. He has his own pay, and six hundred dollars company fund, and a wad of greenbacks he's been carryin' around all summer. It's nigh on to four thousand dollars he's got in his saddlebags this day.'

"And that night, instead of Lieutenant Crane's coming back, he sent word he had found the trail of a big band of Indians, and the whole crowd went in pursuit. There was four companies of infantry, under Captain Rayner, and F and K troops,—what was left of them,—that were ordered to stay by the wagons and bring them safely down; and we started with them over towards Battle Butte, keeping south of the way the regiment had gone to follow Mr. Crane. And the very next day Captain Rayner got orders to bring his battalion to the river and get on the boat, while the wagons kept on down the bank with us to guard them. And Mr. Hayne was acting quartermaster, and he stayed with us; and him and Captain Hull was together a good deal. There was some trouble, we heard, because Captain Rayner thought another officer should have been made quartermaster and Mr. Hayne should have stayed with his company, and they had some words; but Captain Hull gave Mr. Hayne a horse and seemed to keep him with him; and that night, in sight of Battle Butte, the steamboat was out of sight ahead when we went into camp, and I was sergeant of the guard and had my fire near the captain's tent, and twice in the evening Gower came to me and said now was the time to lay hands on the money and skip. At last he says to me, 'You are flat-broke, and they'll all be down on you when you get back to the post. No man in America wants five hundred dollars more than you do. I'll give you five hundred in one hour from now if you'll get the captain out of his tent for half an hour.' Almost everybody was asleep then; the captain was, and so was Mr. Hayne, and he went on to tell me how he could do it. He'd been watching the captain. It made such a big bundle, did the money, in all the separate envelopes that he had done it all up different,—made a memorandum of the amount due each man, and packed the greenbacks all together in one solid pile,—his own money, the lieutenant's, and the men's,—done it up in paper and tied it firmly and put big blotches of green sealing-wax on it and sealed them with the seal on his watch-chain. Says Gower, 'You get the captain out, as I tell you, and I'll slip right in, get the money, stuff some other paper with a few ones and twos in the package; his seal, his watch, and everything is there in the saddlebags under his head, and I can reseal and replace it in five minutes, and he'll never suspect the loss until the command all gets together again next week. By that time I'll be three hundred miles away. Everybody will say 'twas Gower that robbed him, and you with your five hundred will never be suspected.' I asked him how could he expect the captain to go and leave so much money in his bags with no one to guard it; and he said he'd bet on it if I did it right. The captain had had no luck tracking Indians that summer, and the regiment was laughing at him. He knew they were scattering every which way now, and was eager to strike them. All I had to do was to creep in excited-like, wake him up sudden, and tell him I was sure I had heard an Indian drum and their scalp-dance song out beyond the pickets,—that they were over towards Battle Butte, and he could hear them if he would come out on the riverbank. 'He'd go quick,' says Gower, 'and think of nothing.'

"And—I wouldn't believe it, but he did. He sprang up and went right out with me, just flinging his overcoat round him; and he never seemed to want to come in. The wind was blowing soft-like from the southeast, and he stood there straining his ears trying to hear the sounds I told him of; but at last he gave it up, and we went back to camp, and he took his lantern and looked in his saddlebags, and I shook for fear; but he seemed to find everything all right, and in the next ten minutes he was asleep, and Gower came and whispered to me, and I went with him, and he gave me five hundred dollars, in twenties. 'Now you're bound,' says he; 'keep the sentries off while I get my horse.' And that's the last I ever saw of him. Then a strange thing happened. 'Twas hardly daylight when a courier came galloping up, and I called the captain, and he read the despatch, and says he, 'By heaven, Clancy, you were right after all. There *are* Indians over there. Why didn't I trust your ears? Call up the whole command. The Riflers have treed them at Battle Butte, and Captain Rayner has gone with his battalion. We are to escort the wagons to where the boat lies beyond the bend, and then push over with all the horsemen we can take.' It was after daylight when we got started, but we almost ran the wagons 'cross country to the boat, and there Captain Hull took F troop and what there was of his own, leaving only ten men back with the wagons; and not till then was Gower missed; but all were in such a hurry to get to the Indians that no one paid attention. Mr. Hayne he begged the captain to let him go too: so the train was left with the wagon-master and the captain of the boat, and away we went. You know all about the fight, and how 'twas Mr. Hayne the captain called to and gave his watch and the two packages of money when he was ordered to charge. I was right by his side; and I swore—God for-give me!—that through the crack and tear in the paper I could see the layers of greenbacks, when I knew 'twas only some ones and twos Gower had slipped in to make it look right; and Captain Rayner stood there and saw the packet, too, and Sergeant Walshe and Bugler White; but them two were killed with him: so that 'twas only Captain Rayner and I was left as witnesses, and never till we got to Laramie after the campaign did the trouble come. I never dreamed of anything ever coming of it but that everyone would say

Gower stole the money and deserted; but when the captain turned the packages over to Mr. Hayne, and then got killed, and Mr. Hayne carried the packages, with the watch, seal, saddlebags, and all, in to Cheyenne, and never opened them till he got there,—two weeks after, when we were all scattered,—then they turned on him, his own officers did, and said he stole it and gambled or sent it away in Cheyenne.

"I had lost much of my money then, and Mrs. Clancy got the rest, and it made me crazy to think of that poor young gentleman accused of it all; but I was in for it, and knew it meant prison for years for me, and perhaps they couldn't prove it on him. I got to drinking then, and told Captain Rayner that the ___th was down on me for swearing away the young officer's character; and then he took me to Company B when the colonel wouldn't have me any more in the ___th; and one night when Mrs. Clancy had been raising my hair and I wanted money to drink and she'd give me none, little Kate told me her mother had lots of money in a box, and that Sergeant Gower had come and given it to her while they were getting settled in the new post after the Battle Butte campaign, and he had made her promise to give it to me the moment I got back,—that somebody was in trouble, and that I must save him; and I believed Kate, and charged Mrs. Clancy with it, and she beat me and Kate, and swore it was all a lie; and I never could get the money. And at last came the fire; and it was the lieutenant that saved my life and Kate's, and brought back to her all that pile of money through the flames. It broke my heart then, and I vowed I'd go and tell him the truth; but they wouldn't let me. She told me the captain said he would kill me if I blabbed, and she would kill Kate. I didn't dare, until they told me my discharge had come; and then I was glad when the lieutenant and the major caught me in town. When they promised to take care of little Kate I didn't care what happened to me. The money Mrs. Clancy has—except perhaps two hundred dollars—all belongs to Lieutenant Hayne, since he paid off every cent that was stolen from Captain Hull."

Supplemented by Mrs. Clancy's rueful and incoherent admissions, Clancy's story did its work. Mrs. Clancy could not long persist in her various denials after her husband's confession was brought to her ears, and she was totally unable to account satisfactorily for the possession of so much money. Little Kate had been too young to grasp the full meaning of what Gower said to her mother in that hurried interview; but her reiterated statements that he came late at night, before the regiment got home, and knocked at the door until he waked them up, and her mother cried when he came in, he looked so different, and had spectacles, and a patch on his cheek, and ranch clothes, and he only stayed a little while, and told her mother he must go back to the mountains, the police were on his track,—she knew now he spoke of having deserted,—and he gave her mother lots of money, for she opened and counted it afterwards and told her it must all go to papa to get someone out of trouble,—all were so clear and circumstantial that at last the hardened woman began to break down and make reluctant admissions. When an astute sheriff's officer finally told her that he knew where he could lay hands on Sergeant Gower, she surrendered utterly. So long as he was out of the way,—could not be found,—she held out; but the prospect of dragging into prison with her the man who had spurned her in years gone by and was proof against her fascinations was too alluring. She told all she could at his expense. He had ridden eastward after his desertion, and, making his way down the Missouri, had stopped at Yankton and gone thence to Kansas City, spending much of his money. He had reached Denver with the rest, and there—she knew not how—had made or received more, when he heard of the fact that Captain Hull had turned over his property to Lieutenant Hayne just before he was killed, and that the lieutenant was now to be tried for failing to account for it. He brought her enough to cover all he had taken, but—here she lied—strove to persuade her to go to San Francisco with him. She promised to think of it if he would leave the money,—which he did, swearing he would come for her and it. That was why she dared not tell Mike when he got home. He was so jealous of her.

To this part of her statement Mrs. Clancy stoutly adhered; but the officers believed Kate.

One other thing she told. Kate had declared he wore a heavy patch on his right cheek and temple. Yes, Mrs. Clancy remembered it. Some scoundrels had sought to rob him in Denver. He had to fight for life and money both, and his share of the honors of the fray was a deep and clean cut extending across the cheek-bone and up above the right ear.

As these family revelations were told throughout the garrison and comment of every kind was made thereon, there is reason for the belief that Mrs. Buxton found no difficulty in filling her letters with particulars of deep interest to her readers, who by this time had carried out the programme indicated by Captain Rayner. Mid-June had come; the ladies, apparently benefited by the sea-voyage, had landed in New York and were speedily driven to their old quarters at the Westminster; and while the captain went to headquarters of the department to report his arrival on leave and get his letters, a card was sent up to Miss Travers which she read with cheeks that slightly paled:

"He is here, Kate."

"Nellie, you—you won't throw him over, after all he has done and borne for you?"

"I shall keep my promise," was the answer.

XX.

"And so she's really going to marry Mr. Van Antwerp", said Mrs. Buxton to Mrs. Waldron a few days later in the month of sunshine and roses.

"I did not think it possible when she left," was the reply. "Why do you say so now?"

"Oh, Mrs. Rayner writes that the captain had to go to Washington on some important family matters, and that she and Nellie were at the seashore again, and Mr. Van Antwerp was with them from morning till night. He looked so worn and haggard, she said, that Nellie could not but take pity on him. Heavens! think of having five hundred thousand dollars sighing its life away for you!—especially when he's handsome. Mrs. Rayner made me promise to send it right back, because he would never give her one before, but she sent his picture. It's splendid. Wait, and I'll show you." And Mrs. Buxton darted into the house.

When she reappeared, three or four young cavalrymen were at the gate, chatting with Mrs. Waldron, and the picture was passed from hand to hand, exciting varied comment. It was a simple *carte de visite*, of the style once spoken of as vignette,—only the head and shoulders being visible,—but it was the picture of a strong, clear-cut face, with thick, wavy black hair just tingeing with gray, a drooping moustache, and long English whiskers. The eyes were heavy-browed, and, though partially shaded by the gold-rimmed *pince-nez*, were piercing and fine. Mr. Van Antwerp was unquestionably a fine-looking man.

"Here comes Hayne," said Royce. "Show it to him. He likes pictures; though I wouldn't like this one if I were in his place."

Mr. Hayne stopped in some surprise when hailed, greeted Mrs. Waldron warmly, and bowed courteously to Mrs. Buxton, who was watching him narrowly.

"Want to see a picture of the man you ought to go and perforate?" asked Webster, with that lofty indifference which youngsters have to the ravages of the tender passion on subjects other than themselves.

"To whom do you refer?" asked Hayne, smiling gravely, and little imagining what was in store for him.

"This," said Webster, holding out the card. Hayne took it, gave one glance, started, seized it with both hands, studied it eagerly, while his own face rapidly paled, then looked up with quick, searching eyes.

"Who is this?" he asked.

"The man who's engaged to Miss Travers,—Mr. Van Antwerp."

"This—*this*—Mr. Van Antwerp!" exclaimed Hayne, his face white as a sheet. "Here, take it, Royce!" And in an instant he had turned and gone.

"Well, I'll be hanged if I knew he was *that* hard hit," drawled Webster. "Did you, Royce?"

But Royce did not answer.

A gorgeous moonlight is bathing the Jersey coast in sparkling silver. The tumbling billows come thundering in to the shining strand, and sending their hissing, seething, whirling waters, all shimmer and radiance, to the very feet of the groups of spectators. There are hundreds of people scattered here and there along the shingle, and among the groups a pale-faced young man in tweed travelling-suit has made his way to a point where he can command a view of all the passers-by. It is nearly eleven o'clock before they begin to break up and seek the broad corridors of the brilliantly-lighted hotel. A great military band of nearly forty pieces is playing superbly at intervals, and every now and then, as some stirring martial strains come thrilling through the air, a young girl in a group near at hand beats time with her pretty foot and seems to quiver with the influence of the soldier melodies. A tall, dark-eyed, dark-haired man bends devotedly over her, but he, too, seems to rise to his full height at times, and there is something in the carriage and mien that tells that soldier songs have thrilled his veins ere now. And this man the young traveller in gray watches as though his eyes were fascinated. Standing in the shade of a little summer-house, he never ceases his scrutiny of the group.

At last the musicians go, and the people follow. The sands are soon deserted; the great piazzas are emptied of their promenaders; the halls and corridors are still patronized by the few belated chaperons and their giddy charges. The music-loving girl has gone aloft to her room, and her aunt, the third member of the group that so chained the attention of the young map in gray, lingers for a moment to exchange a few words with their cavalier. He seems in need of consolation.

"Don't be, so down-hearted, Mr. Van Antwerp. It is very early in the summer, and you have the whole season before you."

"No, Mrs. Rayner: it is very different from last year. I cannot explain it, but I know there has been a change. I feel as—as I used to in my old, wild days when a change of luck was coming. It's like the gambler's superstition; but I cannot shake it off. Something told me she was lost to me when, you boarded that Pacific Express last February. I was a fool ever to have let her go."

"Is she still so determined?"

"I cannot shake her resolution. She says that at the end of the year's time originally agreed upon she will keep her promise; but she will listen to no earlier marriage. I have about given up all hope. Something again—that fearful something I cannot shake off—tells me that my only chance lay in getting her to go with me this month. Once abroad with her, I could make her happy; but—"

He breaks off irresolutely, looking about him in the strange, hunted manner she has noted once or twice already.

"You are all unstrung, Mr. Van Antwerp. Why not go to bed and try and sleep? You will be so much brighter tomorrow."

"I cannot sleep. But don't let me keep you. I'll go out and smoke a cigar. Good-night, Mrs. Rayner. Whatever comes of it all, I shall not forget your kindness."

So he turns away, and she still stands at the foot of the staircase, watching him uneasily. He has aged greatly in the past few months. She is shocked to see how gray, how fitful, nervous, irritable, he has become. As he moves towards the doorway, she notes how thin his cheek has grown, and wonders at the irresolution in his movements when he reaches the broad piazza. He stands there an instant, the massive doorway forming a frame for a picture *en silhouette*, his tall spare figure thrown black upon the silver sea beyond. He looks up and down the now-deserted galleries, fumbles in his pockets for his cigar-case, bites off with nervous clip the end of a huge "Regalia," strikes a light, and before the flame is half applied to his weed throws it away, then turns sharply and strides out of sight towards the office.

Another instant, and, as though in pursuit, a second figure, erect, soldierly, with quick and bounding step strides across the glittering moon-streak, and Mrs. Rayner's heart stands still.

Only for an instant, though. She has seen and recognized Lawrence Hayne. Concealed from them he is following Mr. Van Antwerp, and there can be but one purpose in his coming here,—Nellie. But what can he want with her—her rightful lover? She springs from the lower step on which she has been standing, runs across the tessellated floor, and stops short in the doorway, gazing after the two figures. She is startled to find them close at hand,—one, Van Antwerp, close to the railing, facing towards her, his features ghastly in the moonlight, his left hand resting, and supporting him, on one of the tall wooden pillars; the other, Hayne, with white clinching fists, advancing upon him. Above the low boom and roar of the surf she distinctly hears the clear tenor ring of his voice in the tone of command she last heard under the shadow of the Rockies, two thousand miles away:

"Halt!"

No wonder a gentleman in civil life looks amazed at so peremptory a summons from a total stranger. In his high indignation will he not strike the impertinent subaltern to earth? As a well-bred woman, it occurs to her that she ought to rush out and avert hostilities by introducing them, or something; but she has no time to act. The next words simply take her breath away:

"Sergeant Gower, I arrest you as a deserter and thief! You deserted from F troop, ___th Cavalry, at Battle Butte!"

She sees the fearful gleam on the dark man's face; there is a sudden spring, a clinch, a straining to and fro of two forms,—one tall, black, snaky, the other light, lithe, agile, and trained; muttered curse, panting breath, and then, sure as fate, the taller man is being borne backward against the rail. She sees the dark arm suddenly relax its grasp of the gray form and disappear an instant. Then, there it comes again, and with it a gleam of steel. With one shriek of warning and terror she springs towards them,—just in time. Hayne glances up, catches the lifted wrist, hurls his whole weight upon the tottering figure, and over goes the Knickerbocker prone upon the floor. Hayne turns one instant: "Go in-doors, Mrs. Rayner. This is no place for you. Leave him to me."

And in that instant, before either can prevent, Steven Van Antwerp, *alias* Gower, springs to his feet, leaps over the balcony rail, and disappears in the depths below. It is a descent of not more than ten feet to the sands beyond the dark passage that underlies the piazza, but he has gone down into the passage itself. When Mr. Hayne, running down the steps, gains his way to the space beneath the piazza, no trace of the fugitive can he find.

Nor does Mr. Van Antwerp appear at breakfast on the following morning, nor again to any person known to this story. An officer of the ___th Cavalry, spending a portion of the following winter in Paris, writes that he met him face to face one day in the galleries of the Louvre. Being in civilian costume, of course, and much changed in appearance since he was a youth in the straps of a second lieutenant, it was possible for him to take a good long look at the man he had not seen since he wore the chevrons of a dashing sergeant in the Battle Butte campaign. "He has grown almost white," wrote the lieutenant, "and I'm told he has abandoned his business in New York and never will return to the United States."

Rayner, too, has grown gray. A telegram from his wife summoned him to the seaside from Washington the day after this strange adventure of hers. He found her somewhat prostrate, his sister-in-law very pale and quiet, and the clerks of the hotel unable to account for the disappearance of Mr. Van Antwerp. Lieutenant Hayne, they said, had told them he received news which compelled him to go back to New York at once; but the gentleman's traps were all in his room. Mr. Hayne, too, had gone to New York; and thither the captain followed. A letter came to him at the Westminster which he read and handed in silence to Hayne. It was as follows:

"By the time this reaches you I shall be beyond reach of the law and on my way to Europe to spend what may be left of my days. I hope they may be few; for the punishment that has fallen upon me is more than I can bear, though no more than I deserve. You have heard that my college days were wild, and that after repeated warnings my father drove me from home, sending me to Wyoming to embark in the cattle-business. I preferred gambling, and lost what he gave me. There was nothing then left but to enlist; and I joined the __th. Mother still believed me in or near Denver, and wrote regularly there. The life was horrible to me after the luxury and lack of restraint I had enjoyed, and I meant to desert. Chance threw in my way that temptation. I robbed poor Hull the night before he was killed, repacked the paper so that even the torn edges would show the greenbacks, resealed it,—all just as I have had to hear through her pure and sacred lips it was finally told and her lover saved.

"God knows I was shocked when I heard in Denver he was to be tried for the crime. I hastened to Cheyenne, not daring to show myself to him or anyone, and restored every cent of the money, placing it in Mrs. Clancy's hands, as I dared not stay; but I had hoped to give it to Clancy, who had not arrived. The police knew me, and I *had* to go. I gave every cent I had, and *walked* back to Denver, then got word to mother of my fearful danger; and, though she never knew I was a deserter, she sent me money, and I came East and went abroad. Then my whole life changed. I was appalled to think how low I had fallen. I shunned companionship, studied, did well at Heidelberg; father forgave me, and died; but God has not forgiven, and at the moment when I thought my life redeemed this retribution overtakes me.

"If I may ask anything, it is that mother may never know the truth. I will tell her that Nellie could not love me, and I could not bear to stay."

Some few weeks later that summer Miss Travers stood by the same balcony rail, with an open letter in her hand. There was a soft flush on her pretty, peachy cheek, and a far-away look in her sweet blue eyes.

"What news from Warrener, Nellie?" asked Mrs. Rayner.

"Fluffy has reappeared."

"Indeed! Where?"

"At Mr. Hayne's. He writes that as he returned, the moment he entered the hall she came running up to him, arching her back and purring her delight and welcoming him just as though she belonged there now; and—"

"And what, Nellie?"

"He says he means to keep her until I come to claim her."

THE END